Her nostril flared. Oh, she wanted to punch him! She wanted to punch him so bad! He was talking to her as if she were an idiot and, worse, she couldn't think of a way to come back at him.

"Now come on, Keisha. We both know why you're *really* angry." His voice and his face softened as he took another step closer to her. "And it has nothing to do with me deceiving you. You're frustrated . . . just like I am." He raised his hand to her face and lightly trailed his fingers along her cheek, sending tingles down her spine. "You feel the tension, too, don't you?" His eyelids and voice lowered. "You want me . . . and I want you."

Keisha's eyes widened. A rush of blood began to sing in her ears. The world around her seemed to disappear and all she could hear were the words Will was whispering to her.

"You don't have to be afraid. I won't bite. I swear," he said with a wicked smile as he cupped her face and began to lower his mouth to hers. "Unless . . . you want me to."

THE RIGHT MANEUVER

L.S. CHILDERS

Genesis Press, Inc.

INDIGO LOVE STORIES

An imprint of Genesis Press, Inc.
Publishing Company

Genesis Press, Inc.
P.O. Box 101
Columbus, MS 39703

All characters in this book have no existence outside the imagination of the author and have no relation whatsoever to anyone bearing the same name or names. They are not even distantly inspired by any individual known or unknown to the author and all incidents are pure invention.

ISBN: 13 DIGIT : 978-1-58571-394-3
ISBN: 10 DIGIT : 1-58571-394-5
Manufactured in the United States of America

First Edition

Visit us at www.genesis-press.com
or call at 1-888-Indigo-1-4-0

DEDICATION

To Andrew. Thank you for loving me, becoming part of my family, and believing in me when I did not. I am blessed (yes, *blessed*) to call you my husband and best friend.

CHAPTER 1

I've got to get out of here, Keisha Reynolds thought desperately as she made her way toward the conference room's "Exit" sign. She gulped what little water remained in her lime-colored Dixie cup, then crushed it in the palm of her hand—as she had so many times that night. In fact, in an effort to calm her nerves; she had consumed so much liquid that it had pushed her bladder to the brink at least four times in the past three hours. While everyone else was huddled around the widescreen televisions set up along the back wall, waiting for the votes from each precinct to appear on screen, Keisha had been trapped in the Hilton's posh bathrooms.

"Keisha! Where are you going?" someone yelled over the '60s soul music blaring through nearby speakers. Keisha vaguely registered the voice in her panicked state.

"I need *air*," she murmured absently. She licked her full lips, which were already licked clean of any of the pink lipstick she had started with that evening. Keisha took several deep breaths, fighting the urge to rip her navy blue suit from her curvy five-foot, seven-inch frame.

Why did I decide to wear wool today, she silently lamented as she felt her body temperature rise. *What in the world was I thinkin'?*

Beads of sweat were forming along her brow. She wiped her clammy hands against the front of her skirt and sighed.

Keisha continued to walk toward the double doors, keeping her gaze fixed on the four neon letters that hovered above them. The word EXIT was like a lighthouse beacon in the distance. But focusing on anything was nearly impossible. Around her was a thundering sea of people. Some were holding hands and praying aloud, others jumping up and down, shouting with jubilation as each total came in. A few were even raising their glasses, boldly saluting victory as if it were inevitable.

Many of them, like Keisha, wore a blue and red "Vote for Parker" button on their lapels. Many, like Keisha, had been confined in the almost suffocating conference room since the polls had closed. But unlike Keisha, the success of this congressional campaign didn't seem to rest squarely on their shoulders. If Sydney Parker won the Democratic primary, his twenty-nine-year-old deputy campaign manager would feel vindicated. No one could whisper anymore that Parker had made a foolish decision by entrusting so much responsibility to Keisha, a woman thought by many to be too young and too green for the job. But if he lost . . . well . . . that would mean the end of Keisha's exciting yet short-lived political career. She would also have to live with the knowledge that she had ruined a great man's chances to make a difference in Congress.

It'll be all my fault, she thought mournfully.

"Keisha!" the voice shouted again. Keisha stopped only when she felt someone grab her forearm. She turned and was greeted by the warm smile of the campaign's field director, Tanya Starks. "Girl, I've been callin' you and callin' you," Tanya said, placing her hands on her round hips. "You didn't hear me?"

Tanya had bettered many in the room in showing her support for her boss. She had changed out of her ivory blouse into a "Vote for Parker" T-shirt. The shirt, paired with the purple pencil skirt and the black three-and-a-half-inch heels she wore, made for an interesting ensemble.

Keisha blinked her large, doe eyes, loudly swallowed, and shrugged. "No, sorry, Tanya. I-I guess I didn't," she muttered in response. Keisha watched as the late thirty-something woman eyed her with concern and narrowed her dark eyes, scanning Keisha's stricken face.

"Are you all right?" she asked, her smile now replaced with an intense frown. She tilted her head, causing her bob to swing like a brown velvet curtain over her eyes. "You look like you need a drink, girl. And I mean a big one!"

"I'm fine . . . really," Keisha said, far from convincingly. "I-I-I . . ." She paused and took another deep breath to stop herself from stuttering. "I just need some . . . air." She then forced a wide smile. Despite her efforts, it came out more as a pained, lopsided grimace.

Tanya's face softened as she sighed. "You don't have to worry, Keisha," she assured her, rubbing the younger woman's shoulder. "I've been through this many times before. Believe me, girl, Parker is going to win. Hell, we busted our hind parts to get him here. He better win!"

She laughed. "Besides, the exit polls had him ahead by more than four points. So grab a drink, loosen up, and celebrate like everyone else!"

But sometimes the polls are wrong, Keisha thought as her gaze drifted to the paisley carpeted floor. The Republican race had been called hours ago. The incumbent, Vincent Dupré, had won by a landslide. But the Democratic race was still dragging on. That couldn't be a good sign.

"Oh, I'm not worried, Tanya," she bluffed as she fiddled with one of her suit buttons. She then pulled back her jacket and glanced at the BlackBerry slung on her hip, pretending to feel it vibrate. "Who could be calling me now?" Keisha murmured as she gazed at the BlackBerry's blank screen. "I guess I should take this, Tanya. Look, I'll catch up with you in a little bit."

Tanya raised an eyebrow. She opened her mouth as if to speak again, but then suddenly closed it and slowly nodded. "Okay, I'll call you if you're not back by the time the results are in."

With that, Keisha abruptly turned and almost sprinted the remaining few yards to the double doors. She hated to lie, especially to Tanya, who, in the past few months, had become less like a fellow campaign director and more like a friend—a big sister even. Tanya had reassured her and made her laugh or smile during some of the rougher patches in the course of the campaign. But Keisha couldn't pour her heart out to Tanya, not today, not now—no matter how much she wanted to. If Keisha started, the flood gates would open and she knew she would tell Tanya everything: how she had felt since the beginning that she was in over her head and how she feared she had let everyone down. It would be an emotional scene. In fact, she could feel the tears welling in her eyes now.

"Get it together, Keisha," she whispered, fanning her reddened face as her high heels clicked against the hotel's travertine floor. She dodged the suitcases that were strewn around the foyer near the check-in desk and finally approached the revolving doors that led to the parking lot. Keisha pushed her way through, fighting back the tears as she did so. When she arrived outside, she felt a blast of cold air from the crisp February evening and heard the steady chug of the hotel shuttle bus as it pulled up to the curb. A second later, she landed *hard* on the concrete walkway.

In the midst of her distraction she had run into something massive, something solid. She slowly shook her head and looked up—dazed, expecting to find a brick wall. Instead she discovered the frowning face of one of the most handsome men she had ever seen—outside of a soap opera. Even a woman like her who wasn't easily distracted by an attractive face could see that this guy was definitely gorgeous, downright delectable.

"Are you okay?" he asked worriedly, grabbing her hands and tugging her to her feet. "I'm really sorry. I should have paid attention to where I was going."

She stared up into his warm, dark brown eyes and was suddenly at a loss for words. Heat seemed to radiate from his hands, up her arms, and across her entire body, making her pulse quicken. A nest of butterflies started to flutter in her stomach. Keisha croaked helplessly, willing herself to speak. Instead her mouth hung open like that of a dead fish.

She watched as he tilted his head and cocked an eyebrow. His frown deepened. "Are . . . *you* . . . okay?" he repeated once again, enunciating the words slowly this time as if she were lip reading or English wasn't her first language.

He was several inches taller than she was with a soft, cinnamon brown complexion that was accented by his jet black brows, heavy lashes, goatee, and the fine curls on his closely cropped head. He smelled nice, too, so nice that part of Keisha wanted to bury her face in his chest again so that she could inhale the rest of his scent, which was a mixture of aftershave and soap, and all man.

Keisha, what are you doing, a voice inside her head asked. *You're salivating over some stranger when the biggest night of your life is going on right now! Snap out of it!*

Keisha blinked, regaining her senses. She loudly cleared her throat before politely pulling her hands out of his grasp.

"I'm . . . I'm fine," she finally mumbled, tucking behind her ear a lock of hair that had escaped from her chignon. She adjusted her suit jacket and wiped at her skirt. "Sorry for running into you. I can be clumsy sometimes."

"No, my apologies," he said. He finally smiled, revealing a deep dimple in his left cheek. "I think I was the one that ran into you."

For some reason she couldn't meet his eyes, so she stared at the lapels of a fairly expensive, tailored charcoal suit that showed off his broad shoulders and solid, Olympic swimmer-like build. Keisha took a deep breath as she scanned his no-nonsense white shirt and baby-blue tie. She could tell this guy was headed somewhere important, and, from the way he looked, he obviously meant business. If a woman waited on the other end of his mission . . .

"She's one lucky girl," Keisha absently muttered.

He frowned again. "Excuse me?"

Keisha blinked. "Sorry," she murmured. "I was . . . I mean it was . . . never mind." She gave a half smile and slowly walked around him with eyes downcast.

"Is it that bad?" he asked.

Keisha turned and suddenly looked up. When her eyes met that handsome face again, her heartbeat began to race. "What? Oh!" She smiled with embarrassment. "No, the fall wasn't that bad. I have a lot of . . . umm . . . cushion," she murmured, as she momentarily touched her posterior.

His smile widened. "That's good to hear. Actually, I meant whatever is putting that worried look on your face . . . in your eyes," he said quietly. "I hope it isn't that bad."

She tilted her head, finding it odd that someone would show this much concern for a total stranger. She shrugged. "It's just that it's . . . it's an important night," Keisha explained, having no idea why she was telling him this. "There's a lot of pressure . . . on me."

He slowly nodded. "I see," he said softly.

"I just don't . . . I just don't want to mess up," she blurted out, despite herself. Keisha stood awkwardly in front of him, shifting from one foot to the other. "I feel like I'm just not prepared for all . . . that's . . . happening. Everyone's expectations are so high and . . . and . . ."

He gazed at her with bemusement.

Oh, God, she thought. *Here I am babbling and he has absolutely no idea what I'm talking about. Why* couldn't he just let her slink away?

His face suddenly softened and he fixed her with a warm gaze. "Well," he began, "all you can do is try your best and hope for the best, right? No one can fault you for that."

Keisha nodded. "You're right. Th-that's true," she mumbled. "You . . . have a good night," she said over her shoulder with a halfhearted wave after she abruptly turned on her heel. She began to quickly walk away from the revolving doors, now thoroughly embarrassed by her ineptness.

"You have a good night, too," he called after her. "I hope things get better."

Keisha thought she could still feel his eyes boring into her back, but when she was about ten yards away she turned—only to find that he was no longer there. She let out a deflated sigh.

Real smooth, Keisha, she thought, rolling her eyes. *Real smooth.*

CHAPTER 2

Ah, well, I've got bigger things to focus on, Keisha thought as she crossed the parking lot, trying to push the vision of the mystery man out of her head. She absently rubbed her wrists, still feeling the heat of his hands there. Her lashes lowered as she sighed.

"Okay, stop it," she said aloud. "Focus, Keisha. Focus!" But focus on what? Something she could no longer control? The election was out of their hands now—and firmly in the hands of the voters.

Keisha glanced down at her BlackBerry, willing it to buzz. Tanya should be calling her by now with news about the race, but she wasn't. Keisha sighed deeply and grabbed the locket around her neck that her mother had given her when she was eleven years old. She often rubbed the silver piece when she got nervous. Just feeling it in her hands reassured her.

"God, this is torture," she murmured, pacing back and forth on the sidewalk. She wondered if Sydney Parker was going through the same anxiety right now, though she doubted it. Parker had said from the beginning that if it was meant to happen, it would happen. That had been his attitude even before he decided to take the plunge and make his first run for elected office four years ago.

Back then, he had been a well-liked political science professor who had often joked about running for mayor of their college town so that he could "make some badly needed changes around here." She had been one of his many grad students who had been in awe of him. One minute, Parker was a fumbling, scruffy, bearded professor with wrinkled clothes and salt and pepper hair that looked badly in need of a comb. The next minute he was a commanding presence in front of the class, talking passionately in his heavy baritone about the U.S. Constitution and the Bill of Rights, bouncing between references to Thomas Payne and Martin Luther King Jr. He could be downright inspiring.

Keisha remembered the day as if it were yesterday when she had walked up to him after class and issued her challenge. She had waited until most of the other students had left to go to their next class and watched as he packed up his laptop and a pile of books near the lectern. "Dr. Parker," she had ventured hesitantly. He quickly looked up at her over the top of his horn-rimmed glasses and smiled.

"Yes, Keisha. How can I help you?" he asked. Despite having more than five hundred students, he was always quickly able to identify his star pupils by name.

"Dr. Parker," she paused and cleared her throat, "why do you always talk about what you'd do as mayor of College Park . . . if you aren't going to run?"

At that, he chuckled. "The joke's getting old, huh?" Parker closed his leather satchel and pulled the strap over his shoulder. "So you're saying I should think up a new one? Come up with fresher material?"

She emphatically shook her head. "No, Dr. Parker, I'm saying that I think you should run!"

She watched as his brown eyes widened behind the lenses of his glasses. He then started to laugh, hearty and loud, making her frown.

"What's so funny?" she asked.

"I'm sorry," he said, waving his hands. "I didn't mean to laugh like that, Keisha, but I have neither the time, the money, nor the experience needed to run for mayor. I appreciate your vote of confidence, though." He glanced down at his watch. "Shouldn't you be getting to your next class?"

"But why not?" she persisted as she followed him toward the lecture hall doors. "You say all the time that even a monkey could do a better job than the mayor we have now! I could help you, you know." She had to walk quickly to keep up with his long strides as they made their way down the echoing corridor. Students milled about the hallway. One drank from a nearby water fountain. "I could help organize stuff for you," she insisted. "I could build your web site. And I know plenty of students here that would be willing to volunteer for your campaign. I could—"

"Keisha . . ." Dr. Parker sighed as he rolled his eyes.

"No, really," she persisted. "Look, Dr. Parker, you always say that politics is more than just speeches, dinners, and handshaking. It means using the system to actually *do* something! It's about believing in an objective and working towards that goal. Why can't this be one of *your* goals? What do you have to lose?"

His pace slowed as he considered her words. He then turned to face her, narrowing his eyes. "You sure this isn't an elaborate way to get extra credit points?"

She laughed and shook her head. "No, I'm serious, Dr. Parker!"

He took a deep breath and sighed. "Okay, I'll think about it," he said, making her grin and clap her hands.

"For real?" she exclaimed.

"I didn't say yes, Keisha. I'm just going to think about it," he repeated sternly, though his face softened as he gave her a wry smile. "I'll let you know in a week or two."

But it didn't take Parker that long to decide. The next time she came to class he told her that he would run for mayor and, if she wanted, she could be his campaign manager. Keisha jumped at the opportunity. Initially, he hadn't taken the mayoral run all that seriously, but she had. Keisha built a web site for him, as she had promised, and she recruited more than two dozen of his other students to become campaign volunteers. They got enough signatures to put Parker on the ballot and made signs, pins, and bumper stickers that were plastered with his name. They tagged along with Parker as he went door to door, talking to constituents, telling them what he would do if he became mayor. They posted flyers everywhere and camped out at the polls.

Their low-budget grassroots campaign drew scorn from the standing mayor, who had lots of powerful business people and money behind him. But it also drew lots of press. The newspapers loved Parker, a firebrand who seemed to inspire hope in the residents of their small town as he had in his students. In a surprising upset, Parker won the election. Keisha graduated from college that year, knowing that she left with more than just a master's degree and a job offer as a high school U.S. government teacher in Baltimore. Thanks to Parker, she had gained experiences that she would treasure for the rest of her life and that she assumed she would never have again.

So Keisha was more than just a little surprised when four years later Parker called her again, this time with his own challenge. By then, Keisha was getting frustrated with teaching, discouraged by the state of inner city schools. She wasn't sure what she wanted to do with her life. Should she strike out on a new career path? Go back to school for her Ph.D.?

"Why don't you come to work for me?" Parker had asked her over the phone.

She frowned. "You mean work at the mayor's office in College Park, sir? You have an opening?"

"No." She heard him sigh on the other end of the line. "I'm running for office again, Keisha, and I'd like to have you on my campaign."

She laughed. "Well, thank you, Dr. Parker, but I don't know if I'm up to that again. That took a lot of time and energy out of me the first time and—"

"I'm not running for mayor again, Keisha," he said. "Look, you'll be well compensated if you worked for me. It's just running for Congress isn't something that should be taken lightly. It's definitely a more precarious playing field and if I'm going to do this, I have to do it right. I want people around me that I can trust."

Keisha paused, wondering if she had heard him correctly. "You're running for *Congress*?"

"I know. It seems far-fetched, doesn't it? Especially considering that I've only been mayor for one term, but the Democrats are desperate to put someone out there they think can finally knock out Vincent Dupré."

"That makes sense," Keisha murmured.

Dupré was a conservative Republican for Maryland's Fifth Congressional District. He was admired by many of the white citizens (and despised by about half of the black citizens) in the state. His ties in Maryland both professionally and socially, thanks to his many businesses and the wealth of his family, were widespread and deeply entrenched. Gregarious and good-looking, Dupré would be a hard man to beat come November. In the past eighteen years the nine opponents that had bothered to challenge him lost to him.

Parker sighed. "The Democrats are rounding up every Tom, Dick, and Harry to do this. I guess my name got thrown into the hat because of my popularity and the positive press we got a few years ago."

"Maybe the Democrats feel if there's a time to take out Dupré, it's probably now," she said.

"Maybe," he murmured. "But regardless, I got suckered into this and I told them I would give it a shot. So what do you say? Are you up to it, Keisha? Will you join my campaign? We're going to start up soon so I need an answer pretty quickly."

She should have told him she needed at least a day to think about it. It was a big decision that should require some reflection. But Keisha didn't do that. She heard herself impulsively say, "Yes," and the deal was done. Within two weeks she had quit her job, packed up her bags, and had begun her new position as Parker's deputy campaign manager.

Now as she paced the hotel parking lot, Keisha wondered if she had made the right decision all those months ago. The campaign this time around had been nothing like the one when he ran for mayor. It was no longer just a bunch of well-intentioned, twenty-something college students. Now it was lots of highly-paid strategists who talked about focus groups and straw polls. Though they still went from door to door to campaign every now and then, they were more likely to attend $200-a-plate fundraisers and sit in meeting after meeting with unions, associations, and business leaders. Keisha still found her new job exciting, but there were moments when she felt as if she had been cast in the wrong movie that was turning out to be her life. Was she really prepared for all this? Was she really meant for the big leagues?

She stopped pacing when she heard a buzzing noise coming from her hip. Her eyes widened. That was probably Tanya giving her the news about the election results. Keisha took a deep breath before unclipping her BlackBerry from her hip. She slowly pressed the button to answer, raised the device to her ear, and closed her eyes.

"Hello?" she said shakily.

"Girl, get back in here!" Tanya shouted over the clamor in the background. "*He won!* He won, Keisha!"

Keisha's eyes suddenly opened as she gasped, "Are you kidding?"

"No, I'm not kidding, girl! Come on and celebrate!"

Keisha hung up the phone. "Oh, my God! Oh, my God, we did it!" she yelped. She then broke into an end zone dance, ignoring the stares of the few people walking by her. In seconds she was back in the conference room, where the party was in full swing. Someone had released at least a hundred red, white, and blue balloons and handed out party horns, which several people blew loudly. It was hard to hear Tanya shouting over the loud noise, but Keisha did.

"I told you he'd win!" Tanya said as she flew into Keisha's arms and gave the younger woman a bear hug. Keisha laughed.

"Indeed, you did."

"So you know what this means," Tanya said as she handed her a champagne glass. "We have to celebrate, girl."

Keisha raised her eyebrows as she took a sip. "What do you call this?" she said, pointing around the room at Parker's jubilant supporters.

"Oh, *no*, my dear!" Tanya exclaimed, waving her hands dismissively. "I mean *really* celebrate. We are getting out of this hotel, going to the city, finding us some fine-ass men, and dropping it real low on the dance floor, Keisha." Tanya raised her eyebrows. "Don't let the clothes and the age fool you, girl. I can shake it like the best of them."

Keisha slowly shook her head, dying from laughter. "Tanya, there is no way I'm going into the city tonight!"

"Why not?"

"*Why not?* For one, I don't even have clothes to go out dancing! Secondly, I am completely exhausted. It's almost midnight and I've been on my feet since 4 a.m. As soon as Parker makes his speech, I'm going upstairs, putting on my pajamas, and crashing."

Tanya narrowed her eyes and smiled mischievously. "No, you're not."

Keisha fervently nodded her head as she finished the last of her champagne. "Yes, I am."

"No, you're not."

"Yes, *I am,* Tanya!"

CHAPTER 3

An hour later Keisha stepped off the hotel elevator, sighing as she did so. She had expected to find Tanya waiting for her in the lobby but instead discovered it to be deserted. The only people who seemed to be lingering were the few who were milling near the hotel bar.

Keisha reached into her purse to pull out her BlackBerry to see if a message from Tanya waited for her. There was one.

"Runnin late," the text message read. "Meet U at bar"

Keisha rolled her eyes and chuckled before tucking the BlackBerry back into her purse. She then shrugged out of her wool jacket and tossed it over her forearm. *Might as well get comfortable*, Keisha thought while walking across the lobby. She had rushed to get ready, looking for anything that looked remotely "clubbish" that she could wear tonight. After checking and rechecking her suitcase, she had finally settled on a pair of hip-hugger jeans she had planned to wear on her way back home tomorrow and a tight, white tank top she had planned to sleep in that night. She accented the outfit by wrapping around her waist a gold threaded scarf her mother had given her last Christmas. Instead of the simple chignon she usually wore, Keisha let her thick, glossy mane fall around her shoulders to the center of her back. After touching up her makeup, she had given herself one final examination in the bathroom mirror.

Not bad, she had thought.

The look was somewhat Bohemian. In fact, with her honey-colored skin, flowing, thick, dark hair, and dark eyes, she kind of looked like a modern-day gypsy.

Keisha had managed to do her transformation from drab to fab in less than thirty minutes, but it seemed that Tanya was still working on her transformation.

"Hopefully, she won't be too late," Keisha thought as she glanced down at her wristwatch and headed toward the bar. A basketball game replay blared on the flat screen TV overhead, putting several of the men who leaned against the bar's granite counter top into a near trance that was broken periodically when they raised their beer bottles to their lips. But when Keisha walked into the room, something in the atmosphere changed. Many of the men who turned to casually glance at her over their shoulders did a double take. She tried her best to ignore their admiring stares, not having anticipated that she would draw this much attention. One man in particular—a freckled redhead with a handlebar mustache—even leapt up from his bar stool. He pointed to the stool, motioning for her to sit down. Keisha scanned the bar. She would have to accept his offer. It was the only stool open.

"Thank you," she murmured.

"No problem." He licked his lips and smiled as she sat down. He then openly leered as he let his gaze wander over her. His eyes rested for several seconds on her chest. "Can I buy you a drink?"

"No thanks," she said dismissively as he leaned toward her. She didn't want to be rude, but she was really in no mood to talk. She raised her hand to get the bartender's attention. "Can I have an apple martini, please?"

The bartender nodded.

"You're very exotic looking," the redhead muttered.

Keisha fought the urge to roll her eyes. *Like I haven't heard that one before,* she thought.

"I would guess Puerto Rican, right? Dominican, maybe?" a Hispanic guy with ruddy brown skin asked, obviously seeing the other man striking out as an opportunity to step up to the plate. "I'm from out of town— Colorado," he said as he tipped his Budweiser to his lips. "I'm here on business."

"Both of us are from Colorado," the redhead interjected. "Where're you from?"

Keisha sighed. *Great. I'm surrounded,* she thought. Where the hell was Tanya? She should be suffering through this with her.

"I'm local," Keisha answered succinctly, feeling the space around her become even more constricted as the men drew closer.

"Really?" the Latino guy continued, his gaze getting warmer. "You know, I'm here for another day or two. And I've been looking for someone to show me the sights." His voice dropped several octaves. "Maybe you could."

Keisha smiled tightly, knowing instinctively what "sights" this guy wanted to see. Chances were that they weren't tourist attractions. "Oh, I doubt I'd be much of a tour guide," she mumbled.

"I bet you'd do just *fine*," he said, now almost on top of her.

"Sorry I'm late," a baritone voice suddenly boomed from over her shoulder. "I hope you didn't have to wait too long."

Keisha frowned and turned. Her eyes widened in surprise as the mystery man from earlier that evening smiled down at her. He gave her a barely discernable wink.

"Uh, no," she said, finally catching on that he was trying to save her from the clutches of bad come-ons. "No, I-I just . . . got here."

Keisha fought the urge to giggle as the shoulders of the two men standing beside her slumped simultaneously.

"That's good," mystery man said. He pointed over her shoulder. "Is that your drink? I'll take care of that for you. Excuse me, fellas," he said as he pushed passed the redhead, who was narrowing his eyes angrily. Keisha watched as mystery man reached into his leather wallet before tossing $15 onto the bar. He then took her coat and wrapped his arm around her shoulders, making her pulse quicken again. "You want to sit at the table in the corner, honey?"

"Uh, sure," she said breathlessly as she retrieved her drink and purse and slowly climbed off the bar stool. *Anywhere you want*, she thought dreamily.

When they drew closer to the small bistro table in the dimly lit corner, he removed his arm from around her shoulders and she regained her ability to breathe.

"Sorry, I couldn't help myself," he said with a chuckle as he held out a chair for her. "You looked like you needed some rescuing."

She watched as he unbuttoned his suit jacket and sat in the seat across from her. Everything about him, from his look to his movements, seemed so smooth, so striking. Who was this guy and how did he have the uncanny ability to pop up at the best possible moment?

"Your name isn't Gabriel, is it?" she asked with a slight smile, gazing at him wide-eyed.

He leaned back in his chair and frowned. "No, it's Will. Why? Do I look like someone you know named Gabriel?"

She quickly shook her head. "No, I was just . . . wondering." She took a quick sip from her martini, too embarrassed to explain that she was referring to the Angel Gabriel. Too many years of inner city Catholic school messing with her brain, she supposed.

"What's your name, by the way?" he asked. "We haven't had proper introductions."

She smiled and out of habit held out her hand for a shake. "It's Keisha Reynolds."

"Pleased to meet you, Keisha." He tilted his head and took her hand in his own. *Big mistake!* Keisha suddenly felt goose bumps shoot up her arm. It was hard to believe that one guy could make her feel so much from a simple touch.

"Well, I'm glad I ran into you again," he said as he shook her hand firmly. "I'm also glad to see that you seem a lot better than you did a few hours ago. I guess everything worked out, then?"

She breathed deeply, taking a few seconds to recover from his touch. "You're right. I am a lot better. Everything worked out the way I hoped it would."

"Good to hear," he murmured, fixing her with an intense gaze.

After that, they sat in silence for so long that she began to fidget. "So . . . so," Keisha said, trying desperately to think of something to say or to ask him. "So what brings you here today, W—"

"Will Blake!" Tanya suddenly exclaimed. "What are *you* doing here?"

Keisha watched as Tanya strode over to their table with narrowed eyes and hands on hips. Tanya was dressed to the nines in a short black slip dress and stiletto heels. But her dazzling appearance contrasted sharply with the ugly look of suspicion on her face.

Keisha frowned, now more than just a little confused. "You guys . . . know each other?"

Will stood and smiled. "Yes, we do." He extended his hand. "It's nice to see you again, Tanya. It's been awhile."

Oh, God, Keisha thought. *Had Tanya once dated Will?* If she had, this was going to be awkward.

Tanya gazed down at Will's large, open palm for several seconds before she grudgingly shook it. "I'd think you'd be back at your own celebration tonight, Will," she said with curled lips before crossing her arms over her chest. "Or did they already shut it down? I heard the Republicans do like to get to bed early. I guess destroying the world can take a lot out of you."

He smirked at her jab. "No, I'm pretty sure the party's still going on over there. But I was sent on a mission."

Tanya's eyes narrowed even further. "A mission to do what?"

"To learn more about the competition." He shrugged. "Quite frankly, Parker wasn't someone that we had pegged as a contender, let alone the primary winner, so we're playing a game of catch-up."

Keisha blinked. "You . . . you're with Vincent Dupré's campaign, Will?"

He opened his mouth to speak but Tanya cut him off.

"Not only is he 'with' the campaign but he was just appointed *deputy campaign manager*, the same as you, Keisha." She returned her attention to Will. "I'm surprised you didn't tell her who you were, Will."

At that, Will narrowed his eyes. His thick brows lowered and knitted together. He gritted his teeth, causing a slight muscle tick along his chin. "I didn't tell her because I didn't think I needed to tell her, Tanya," he said with an eerie calm. "I didn't know that she worked for Parker, either. I'm just as surprised as she."

Tanya nodded her head impatiently. "Yeah, well, now you know. We should get going, Keisha," she said as she quickly patted her friend's shoulder. "Sorry, Will, but I'm going to have to pull her away from you. We have places to be, things to do."

Keisha wanted to ask Tanya why she was being so rude, but she could tell from the look of warning in Tanya's eyes that she should probably save that question for a later time. Keisha uneasily rose from the table and gathered her purse and coat. "It was nice meeting you again, Will. Thank you for the drink . . . and the rescue," she said quietly with a laugh.

"Don't mention it," he replied warmly. "It was my pleasure."

They shook hands again and locked gazes. Several awkward seconds passed in silence with neither breaking their grasp. Keisha didn't want to let go and she suspected he didn't, either. A current that was almost electric seemed to pass between them, the voltage intensifying with each passing second. Her heart rate was speeding up again. She could feel her face flush.

"Come on, Keisha," Tanya huffed, tugging the younger woman away, abruptly breaking the magic spell. Keisha blinked as if someone had just shaken her awake.

She caught a last glimpse of Will as she and Tanya quickly walked out of the bar and into the lobby. Keisha waved goodbye to him one last time as Tanya loudly sucked her teeth.

"I swear, that man could have been in the CIA with how damn sneaky he is!" Tanya spat. "I don't believe for one damn second that he didn't know you were on Parker's staff!" She flashed her eyes toward Keisha. "He didn't ask you anything about Parker or the campaign, did he? You didn't tell him anything, did you, Keisha?"

She fired her questions as they pushed their way through the hotel's revolving doors to the outside.

Keisha quickly shook her head as she shrugged into her coat. "No, he didn't ask me anything. We didn't talk about the election at all." She shivered as they were hit by a sudden blast of air from the chilly February night. Funny, in Will's presence everything felt a lot warmer. "Actually, I ran into him two times tonight, and each time he was very nice, Tanya. In fact, I thought he was . . ."

Amazing, handsome, riveting, Keisha thought.

She cleared her throat. "I thought he was . . ."

Debonair and downright the most beautiful man I have ever seen, her mind exclaimed.

"Umm . . . charming," she finally uttered.

"Uh-huh, I bet you did," Tanya said flatly, giving her a side glance as they walked across the parking lot.

Keisha sighed as they approached Tanya's blue Saab. She paused near the passenger door and looked at Tanya over the roof of the car. She shook her head again. "I don't think he's as bad as you think he is, Tanya. Really, he seemed like a nice guy."

"Girl," Tanya said with a roll of her eyes, "don't—and I mean *don't*—let Will's smooth talk and his fine ass fool you! He's no Prince Valiant, that's for sure!" she spat before swinging open the driver's side door. Keisha quickly climbed in after her. "Will Blake has a reputation for playin' rough when it comes to politics, and I wouldn't be surprised if he'd do just about anything to help Vincent Dupré get a leg up over the competition. That includes makin' goo-goo eyes at gullible women just to pump them for information."

Keisha slumped into her seat and cringed. *Gullible?* Tanya thought she was gullible?

Tanya noticed the stricken look on Keisha's face and sighed. She slowly shook her head. "I'm sorry, Keisha. That came out wrong. You know me: chronic foot-in-the-mouth disease."

Keisha waved her hand dismissively. "Don't worry about it, Tanya."

"No, I really didn't mean it that way, girl." She sighed again. "Look, what I meant to say was that you're beautiful, but I know Will is up to no good because you're not his type. I heard Will doesn't take his coffee with cream, if you know what I mean." She shifted into reverse. "In fact, he prefers to skip the coffee and just stick with the cream. It's typical for them—the black conservatives. Uncle Toms," Tanya spat. "You can't get anywhere over there without some white wife or girlfriend on your arm. So, no offense, but if he seemed like he was into you, I'd still keep my guard up on that one. Will knows the game, girl, and he *knows* how to play it! This is one of many maneuvers that you'll have to deal with now that Parker won the primary, so be prepared."

Keisha listened to Tanya's venomous words, trying to reconcile the man Tanya was describing now with the same man that Keisha had sat with minutes earlier. She hadn't seen any cunning in Will. He hadn't asked her anything about herself that wasn't outside of basic interest in her as a human being. And she thought she had felt a palpable attraction between them.

But maybe that was how he operated. Maybe he made you think that he cared. He made you think that he was interested only to weasel his way inside your confidence and find out what he wanted.

The thought that anyone could be that cold, calculating and deceitful sickened her. Her image of Will as the Angel Gabriel suddenly shifted to the fallen angel Lucifer.

"What is *wrong* with people?" Keisha murmured aloud, slowly shaking her head in bewilderment. "How can he live with himself?"

"Humph," Tanya breathed through her nose. "You'd be surprised, girl."

"I could never do anything like that!"

Tanya cocked an eyebrow as she pulled out of the parking space. "Well, now you're playin' with the big boys, and they do! So wear a cup!"

CHAPTER 4

Will cruised down I-95 in his Audi Roadster and shifted gears, trying his best to focus on the highway in front of him, though it was a challenge. Every time that his mind drifted to the events of that night he cursed aloud to himself. *How the hell did that happen?* Out of all the women he could have run into, why did it have to be Parker's deputy campaign manager?

For a man known in his industry to be methodical, to strategize like a chess player who expertly shifted pawns, rooks, and knights around a board, Will Blake definitely had not anticipated this opening move.

He had told Tanya the truth. That night, he *had* come to the Hilton in Greenbelt to learn more about Parker. The instant that the Dupré campaign saw that it looked like the relative unknown was going to win the Democratic primary, Will had set aside his canapé and champagne glass and pulled out the dossier that his assistant had compiled on all of the candidates. The file on Parker was a little on the thin side and filled only with the essential details, like Parker's twenty years as a college professor; a mention of his wife, Suzanne Parker, who was also a teacher; a printout of his mission statement from his web site; and several glowing articles about his mayoral campaign five years ago. Will knew this slight information wasn't going to cut it. He'd have to see this man in person. He wanted to see how Parker worked a room and how people reacted to him. Will believed in order to defeat an adversary you had to understand his strengths and weaknesses.

It had taken almost a half an hour to get to the hotel from Dupré's campaign headquarters in Annapolis. He'd planned to remain low key, fade into the background of the room, and just observe. He had tried to concentrate, telling himself to make mental notes of everything. But the instant he and Keisha had run into each other at the hotel door, all concentration faded.

Seeing her pretty young face marred with sadness had tugged at his heart strings. He had been enchanted by those watery, doe-like eyes and that pink, down-turned mouth set against skin the color of honey. Despite the fact that he didn't know her, he had wanted to pick her up and comfort her, reassure her that everything was going to be fine. When she tried to walk away something told him to back off, to leave her alone so that she could quietly cry in a corner if she wanted to, but he couldn't help himself. Will kept talking to her despite her obvious efforts to get out of their awkward encounter. Not one to harass a woman to get her attention, Will let her go, but his mind stayed focused on her the rest of the night, destroying his concentration and frustrating him.

When Will saw her again a couple hours later as he entered the hotel bar, he knew it was Providence. He had planned to head straight home to Annapolis after Parker's huge celebration ended, but, at the last minute, decided to stop at the bar to grab a quick glass of wine before he started his drive. And there she was, looking more stunning and alluring than he remembered. She had literally let her hair down and had changed out of her constricting suit. But this time she was also surrounded by a group of guys who panted at her like slobbery, starving dogs and hovered over her like black ops helicopters.

Will had lied. He hadn't come to her side just to rescue her. Some of it had been fueled by jealousy. *Oh, hell no,* he thought angrily as he watched the trio. There was no way he was going to let some chumps try anything on her. Will had restrained himself earlier, but if anyone was going to take her home tonight, it would be him!

And she seemed to be responding to him. Keisha kept licking her full lips as she spoke and nervously ran her hands along her flushed neckline. Her eyelashes fluttered as she pushed her hair back over her shoulders and she kept crossing and uncrossing those seductive legs. A student of human behavior after years in politics, Will knew the signs. Keisha was definitely attracted to him. He was playing it cool, but inside he felt the same way about her. Though he knew he wouldn't and probably couldn't bed her tonight, he certainly expected a soulful kiss based on the heavy undercurrent of lust that seemed to be flowing between them. He'd get her number and call her in a day or two. They'd go out on a few dates. Then he would have her.

But Tanya Starks had put the brakes on all that when she came barging in, stomping over to their table. Tanya was just as loud and belligerent as Will remembered her back in the 1990s when they were in their early twenties and both legislative aides on Capitol Hill. Back then, he had been able to ignore her "bull in a china shop" persona, but tonight he couldn't. She had particularly pissed him off when she insinuated that he had tried to fool Keisha by not telling her about his job. Will could have probably defended himself better, but he wasn't about to explain to Tanya that when you're mentally undressing a person, exchanging résumés isn't really what comes to mind. Besides, how was he supposed to know that Keisha was Parker's deputy campaign manager? Keisha was barely . . . what . . . thirty, if that? How the hell did she get a position like that? When Will was her age, which was eight to ten years ago, he was a recent law school grad begging to be given some real responsibility on a congressional campaign. Was she some kind of wunderkind, a political genius? Why had he never heard of her before?

He shook his head. "Let it go, Will," he said aloud as he pulled onto the side street that led to his cul-de-sac. "Forget about her," he said. He yawned and glanced down at the digital clock on his dashboard.

It was well past 3 a.m. and most of his neighbors— young families and retirees—had turned in for the night hours ago. With the exception of the corner street lamps and one stray dog, the neighborhood was dark and completely deserted.

Will was used to seeing his neighborhood this way. In his line of work, especially during election years, he would often arrive home late after spending hours at some event or at a remote meeting that ran long. Will was grateful for his job and was happy to get a leading position in the campaign of an old family friend like Vincent Dupré, but he missed the quiet evening hours when he could just lie on the couch and watch a basketball game. He missed his home. He rarely got the chance to enjoy the two-story Tudor with its charming wrought iron gate and draping ivy.

Will had purchased it almost a year ago, despite his realtor's warnings that it didn't fit him. A single guy with a busy career like his would be much better off in a condo in some trendy neighborhood in D.C., she had argued. A house like this needed to be filled with people—not left vacant all the time. It was meant for a family. But he had stubbornly ignored her, thinking that if he met the right woman one day, he could fill the house with a family of his own.

As he drove, Will let himself imagine that right woman. She'd have to understand his drive and maybe be just as driven herself. She'd have to complement him; she'd be the "yin" to his "yang." He'd want a partner that he felt just as comfortable lying in bed with at night as he would taking her to an important fundraiser luncheon during the day. Suddenly, an image of Keisha came to mind again. Keisha was in his field and holding so much power at a young age that she had to be driven. She was beautiful and intriguing and . . .

Will quickly shook his head. *Enough*, he thought.

Now that he knew Keisha worked for the opposition, all thoughts about her should be pushed aside. Forgetting about her was the only logical course. Usually Will was good at clicking some internal switch that allowed him to operate with reason, not emotion. But he was having a hard time doing that this time around. Whenever he closed his eyes, he saw her face, that luscious mouth, and the full curve of her breasts. Hell, he could even smell her—a pungent scent of jasmine that had only whetted his appetite.

"Sleep it off," he mumbled sternly to himself. He shifted uncomfortably on the leather seat, feeling himself harden at the thought of her. There were bound to be serious repercussions if he tried to pursue Keisha. *Sex and politics mix like oil and water*, Will thought as he turned the wheel of his Audi, preparing to pull into his driveway.

That was the last thought he had before he abruptly slammed on the brakes, making his car squeal to a halt. His seatbelt tightened as he jerked forward. Will gritted his teeth. He had barely missed hitting the black sports car that was parked in front of him. Will narrowed his eyes as he watched one of the car doors swing open.

CHAPTER 5

"Will!" Gretchen exclaimed. "Where have you been? I've been waiting for you for over an hour!"

Will took a deep breath and sighed as he leaned back against the headrest. He watched as the perky redhead scampered over to his car. *Case in point for why politics and sex don't mix*, he thought sardonically.

He and Gretchen, who was also Dupré's press secretary, had slept together *once* three months ago after going out one night after work and having one drink too many. The instant Will woke up the next morning with a throbbing headache and Gretchen in his bed, he knew he had made a mistake. Gretchen was a cute girl, but she wasn't his type. She was way too clingy. And her eagerness, which was great for PR, was more than just a little annoying when he had to deal with it day after day after day.

She had hinted and then outright asked Will to go out with her again, but he had made up excuses. Gretchen obviously wasn't a woman who could be easily deterred. He slowly shook his head as she tapped on his car window and gave him her 100-watt smile. He couldn't believe it. Now she was waiting for him at his house! *What the hell have I gotten myself into?*

Will pressed the electronic button to lower his driver's side window. "What are you doing here, Gretchen?" he asked, getting straight to the point.

Gretchen tilted her head, batted her big blue eyes, and licked her lips seductively. She tightened the belt of her red wool coat and smiled as she leaned down to speak to him. "Well," she said, sending a gust of steam into the cold night air, "I had an important question to ask you but I didn't get the chance to ask because you left so early."

"If you had a question, why didn't you call my cell?" he asked as he unbuckled his seatbelt. "I would have answered. You didn't have to come all the way here, Gretchen."

She smirked. "Because it's one I prefer to ask in person, silly."

Will watched as she pulled his car door handle. When the door wouldn't budge, Gretchen pouted and wrinkled her pert, freckled nose.

"Do you plan to stay in that car all night, Will, or are you going to climb out of there and invite me inside?" she cooed, looking over her shoulder toward his house.

I'd rather stay in the car, he thought.

When he didn't answer her, Gretchen's pout deepened. "It's really cold out here, Will."

He sighed, rolled his eyes, and motioned for her to step away from the car as he raised his car window. Will backed out onto the street and parallel parked along the curb near his front lawn, not wanting to give Gretchen an excuse to stay any longer than she needed because she was blocked in his driveway. He was leaving the path completely open for her to pull out and go home.

After he exited his Audi, she met him halfway up the driveway and followed closely at his heels. They walked to his front door and he opened it. *Ten minutes*, Will thought. *I'll let her stay ten minutes and then I'll politely ask her to leave.*

His mother had taught him well. No matter how downright crazy a woman seemed, he couldn't be rude to her.

"Got anything to drink?" Gretchen piped as she pushed her way around him and walked across the hardwood foyer into his kitchen. "Ooooh, this looks yummy," she murmured as she spotted an already uncorked bottle of Merlot on his marble kitchen counter. Will's eyes widened as he watched her through a cut-out between his living room and kitchen wall. Gretchen quickly opened cabinets, presumably in search of a wine glass.

"Make yourself at home," he muttered sarcastically as he tossed his coat onto a wrought iron stand near his front door.

"Want some?" she asked after finally retrieving a wine glass and filling it.

"No, thanks," he said. "I've already had enough tonight." And Will had no desire to repeat the same incident as three months ago.

"It's up to you." She shrugged as she took a gulp of Merlot. "So why'd you disappear from the party, anyway? You left so early."

"I had to go to Greenbelt for Parker's primary win. He was throwing a party at the Hilton."

She frowned, tilted her head, and took another gulp. She then cleared her throat. "Why on earth would you go to *his* party?"

"I wanted to see what he was like in person and get a better idea of who was working on his campaign." Will slowly walked into his kitchen, removed his suit jacket, and tossed it over the back of one of his dinette chairs. "We don't know too much about him. Now that Dupré's running against him, I figured we should."

She slowly smiled as she clicked her pink talons against the side of her wine glass. "So you were spying?"

Will quickly shook his head. "I wasn't spying. I was doing research."

"I see," she said, pouring herself another glass. "So what did you find out during your 'research'?" she asked, slowly making air quotes.

Will leaned back against the kitchen wall and crossed his arms over his broad chest. "Parker's a phenomenal speaker and pretty charismatic. He knows how to command a room, which could be a problem down the road since Dupré admits that speeches have never been his strong point. Dupré's much better one-on-one with voters or with smaller groups."

Gretchen raised an eyebrow. "That's all you discovered?"

That . . . and the fact that I wouldn't mind taking Parker's deputy campaign manager to bed, Will thought, but he wasn't about to tell Gretchen that.

He shrugged. "That's all for now," he said.

Gretchen rolled her eyes as she propped her elbow against the kitchen counter. "Well, I personally don't see what the big deal is about this guy." She waved her hand dismissively. "He's good at making speeches. So *what!* Dupré has more experience and a much better record. This guy was . . . what? The mayor of some podunk town for one term?"

Will rolled his eyes. "Correction: Parker was a popular mayor of a town in a county that has the highest concentration of the richest, most educated African-Americans in Maryland . . . in the entire country, for that matter." He sighed. "And we all know how well Dupré plays in the black community."

She shrugged again. "We don't *need* the black community."

At that statement, Will seethed quietly. In his line of work, he had heard lots of statements like this. And each time he did the same thing: took a deep breath and counted to ten. Logic, not emotion, was the best way to handle these situations.

"Maybe that's the case where you come from, Gretchen," he said, careful of his tone. "But I wouldn't count on that in Maryland. The black people here can swing elections if enough of them turn out. Besides, praying that African-Americans won't show up at the polls should not be the tactic we take with this campaign. I keep saying that we should try to woo them to our side. There are a lot of black Independents out there. We shouldn't assume they're all tied to the Democratic Party when the general election rolls around."

"Well, Dupré keeps managing to win without them," Gretchen said as she tossed her red tresses over her shoulder and poured herself another drink. "Why fix what isn't broken?"

Will frowned as he watched Gretchen sip from her glass. *Three glasses of wine in twenty minutes?* he thought. *Was she* trying *to get herself drunk?*

"Don't you think you should slow down, Gretchen?" he asked with narrowed eyes. "Remember . . . you still have to drive home."

At that she defiantly gulped the rest of her wine and began to giggle.

Will took the glass out of her hand, his patience now pushed to the brink. "All right, maybe you should ask the question now that you wanted to ask me. It's getting pretty late and we both have to get up soon."

"Ooookaaaay," she sang before twirling her belt and loosening the knot. "Well," she said slowly as she took several steps toward him. "I'd really like your opinion on something."

"I'm listening," he said with a nod. "My opinion on what?"

"On . . . this," she said before she dramatically threw opened her coat. *"Taa-daa!"*

Will's eyes widened. She wasn't wearing a stitch of clothing, save for a black lace bra and panties that were so thin and tiny she could have gone without wearing them. He watched as she pushed her coat off her shoulders to give him a better look. Will wanted to kick himself.

Why didn't I see this coming?

"Well," she said before doing a 360-degree turn, wiggling her butt and cocking her hip. She flashed another 100-watt smile. "What do you think?"

He sighed again. "It's nice."

"Nice?" she repeated in disbelief. She closed the divide between them and snaked her hands around his neck. "That's all you have to say, that it's 'nice'?" She clucked her tongue. "You didn't say that the last time you saw me in my underwear."

Will gritted his teeth. He didn't want to be nasty, but there was no polite way to get out of this, especially now that Gretchen had begun to unbutton his collar and he could feel her hot breath panting against his neck. He felt even more unease as she stood on her toes and began to nibble on his ear lobe, pressing her breasts against his chest as she did so.

Sorry, Mom, he thought. Despite his mother's warnings to always remain a gentleman, he'd definitely have to be more firm with Gretchen.

Will eased her back, tore her hands from around his neck, and held them in front of her.

"Gretchen, I think you should go home."

"But why, Will? Trust me. You won't have to do *anything*."

He watched, completely shocked, as she slowly dropped to her knees. "Just lay back, relax, and I'll handle everything. Trust me. You'll enjoy it."

Don't let her do this, Will, he thought as she lowered his pants zipper. But another part of him replied, "Why the hell not?" As soon as Gretchen left, his thoughts would inevitably return to Keisha: those eyes, that mouth, those legs. Gretchen could be an excellent distraction, or at least an outlet for his fettered lust.

"Well, it looks like at least one part of you doesn't want me to go," she whispered huskily.

He felt Gretchen's warm hand reach inside his pants and his manhood jerked instinctively. *No, this isn't right*, he thought, despite the quickening of his pulse and the thudding in his ears. Doing this would just lead Gretchen on, and her weird stalking would never end.

"Stop. Stop!" he shouted. He grabbed her shoulders, dragging her back to her feet. "Put on your coat. It's time to go."

Gretchen pouted, completely crestfallen. "But—"

"No buts," he said as he returned his zipper to its rightful place and firmly wrapped his hand around her wrist. He had to practically drag her out of the kitchen to his front door. "You have to leave."

"Wait! Wait!" she shouted.

Will ignored her.

"Why do I have to leave, Will?" she whined as he urged back into her coat, holding it up so that she could shove her arms into the sleeves. "I thought . . . I thought we had a good time together. Didn't you have a good time that night?"

He sighed gruffly. "Yes, I did, but—"

"But *what?*" Her eyebrows furrowed as she pouted.

"Gretchen, this just isn't going to work. Trust me."

"Why not, Will? I like you. You like me," she murmured before snaking her hands around his waist. She abruptly paused. "Or . . . have you . . . have you met someone else?"

His eyes widened. Maybe that was a way out of this. Will emphatically nodded his head as he tore her arms from around him and opened his front door. "Yes," he lied. "Yes, I have. That relationship could have a lot of potential and I don't want to mess it up."

She sighed. "Well . . . you could have just told me that," she murmured sadly as she stood in his doorway.

"I'm sorry," he said. "It's just that it's . . . it's still very new, Gretchen."

She tightened the belt of her coat. "Well," she said with a shrug, "don't hesitate to give me a call if, you know, it doesn't work out."

"I'll keep that in mind," he said with as much solemnity as he could muster, though in his heart of hearts he knew it would be a cold day in hell before he would ever be insane or desperate enough to sleep with this woman again.

"Good night, Will."

"Good night, Gretchen." He closed his front door behind her, slumping back against it in sheer exhaustion. "Never again," Will murmured.

CHAPTER 6

Keisha pulled up to the two-story townhouse on Eighteenth Street in D.C., admiring the cherry blossoms that lined the sidewalk. Now that the weather was warmer, all the trees were in bloom and bushes and lawns were starting to sprout a few flowers.

Keisha always loved D.C. in the spring. It was an ideal time of year before the temperatures were sweltering and all the tourists arrived. Today would have been a nice day for a leisurely walk along the waterfront or maybe even to read a book on the Mall, but, unfortunately, she had been stuck over the border in Maryland between four walls for the past nine hours, forced to sit through meeting after meeting. There had been many more meetings lately, mostly to get endorsements and raise money for the Parker campaign. He would need them now that he was up against Big Bad Vincent Dupré.

Keisha sighed, trying to put thoughts about work aside as she closed the door to her Ford Focus and slowly climbed the concrete steps of her mother's front stoop. She rang the doorbell and examined the colorful wicker wreath that adorned the brass knocker. Keisha waited for several seconds. She rang the doorbell again but there was no answer. She pulled out a key from her purse. She was absolutely exhausted.

In addition to the seemingly endless meetings, Keisha had stayed late at campaign headquarters to catch up on missed emails and last minute work. She could have told her mother that she wasn't coming this evening and curled up in her pajamas with a good book at home, but she didn't. The two women always had dinner together on Thursdays. It had been their weekly ritual since Lena Reynolds had moved from Philly back to the city of her roots more than a year ago to be closer to her daughter. And besides, Keisha liked Thursday nights with her mother. Whenever they cooked dinner together it brought back twenty-year-old memories of the two of them in a dingy apartment in West Philly. Lena would be chopping vegetables, singing loudly to some '70s funk tune, while Keisha stood on her tiptoes, stirring whatever was in the pot on the stove. She would always chime in with the chorus.

"Just the Reynolds girls doin' their thang," her mother would say with a laugh before she threw her vegetables into the brewing stew.

Keisha yawned as she inserted her key and unlocked the door. The instant she stepped inside, she was met with the smell of incense and a blast of music. She rolled her eyes and chuckled. *Some things never change*, she thought.

"Ma!" Keisha shouted over the noise as she shrugged out of her trench coat. She hung it in a hallway closet and paused to listen to her mother sing off-key with Stevie Wonder. "Ma!" she repeated. There was no response.

Keisha slowly trudged up the steps to the second floor, shaking her head and laughing at the pictures that adorned the wall. They were all of herself at various ages: some as a drooling baby, others as a crooked-toothed toddler with pompom-sized braids on the sides of her head, and some as an awkward teenager with braces. The photos ended with a picture of Keisha at her grad school graduation.

In some of her photos her mother stood proudly at her side or held Keisha in her lap. In all of them Keisha's father was conspicuously absent.

Keisha's dad had died tragically in a car accident, only months before she was born. She always felt robbed in some way that she hadn't at least met him. She'd have liked to have some memories of him, even tenuous ones.

The only thing she knew about her father was based on what her mother had told her. He had been tall like Keisha, had a similar complexion, and loved to dance, something her mom adored since she had been a dancer all her life. Lena had also told Keisha that she acted a lot like him: ambitious, but kind at heart. Besides that, Lena had never really revealed much else about the man. He had no real family as far as Lena knew. His whole life he had been a transient, never staying long enough in one place to grow roots, her mother explained.

Keisha had tried when she was nineteen to find out more about him. She had even visited one of the neighborhoods where her mother said he once lived, but no one there remembered him. Keisha tried to press her mother for more details so she could attempt to find some of her father's friends or family. He wasn't born in a cabbage patch, Keisha had argued. He had to have some surviving relatives. Maybe she could locate a long-lost grandparent or cousin. But Keisha stopped her pursuit when Lena suddenly burst into tears one day, crying that she couldn't answer any more questions. The memories of him were sweet but painful, she lamented. It was like digging up his grave, Lena had said.

From that point on Keisha stopped asking questions. She didn't want to torture her mother with memories and make her cry again. Keisha figured she'd have to be happy with it being just the Reynolds girls and leave it at that.

Keisha tapped one of the pictures with her index finger and continued her slow climb up the steps. She laughed again when she caught a glimpse of her mother dancing in front of a canvas in her bedroom. Lena Reynolds did a leap worthy of someone thirty years younger as she flicked the canvas with blue paint from her brush, still belting out Stevie Wonder off-key.

"Are you selling tickets or do I get to watch this for free?" Keisha exclaimed with a smile.

Her mother suddenly turned in shock, causing her long dreads to swing over her shoulders. But the older woman didn't miss a beat. She tossed her paintbrush aside and held out her hands to Keisha. Despite her tiredness, Keisha obliged her. She giggled as they began to dance in the center of the bedroom, shimmying back and forth and twirling in a circle. All the while the two women sang their duet, just like the old days. Within minutes, the song drew to an end and the two laughed hysterically before collapsing into an embrace.

They were a study in contrasts. At five feet, one inch tall, the top of Lena's head barely reached her daughter's shoulder. Lena was in her late 40s, but her luminous dark skin and bright dark eyes made her look several years younger. Having been a dancer since the age of seven, she still retained her taut, slim, ballet-worthy body, even after Keisha was born.

In comparison, Keisha was many shades lighter and much curvier. Instead of dreads, she preferred to keep her long, curly hair in a tight chignon.

Lena smiled as she stood on the tips of her toes to kiss her daughter's cheek. "Honey, you surprised me. I didn't know you were standing there," she murmured, fighting to catch her breath. "How long have you been here?"

Keisha removed her suit jacket, kicked off her heels, and lay spread-eagled across her mother's four-poster bed, inhaling the fragrant scent of black currant and vanilla wafting from the mattress. *Ahhh, that feels better*, she thought.

"Not long," Keisha finally said, "but I did ring the doorbell *twice*."

"Ah, well," Lena conceded with a laugh and a shrug as she sat on the edge of the bed. "You know how I am when I get into music or my art." She ran her hand over her daughter's head and frowned. "You okay? You look tired, KeKe."

"I *am* tired," Keisha said, her voice now muffled by her mother's blue comforter.

"Is work that bad?"

Keisha propped her head up on her palm. She gazed at her mother's comely face and smiled. "Not bad, it's just busy. We have a lot of things we have to do before the general election. Things are pretty hectic right now," she muttered, pulling at a loose thread in the comforter, a habit that had persisted from her younger days.

Lena slumped back against one of the cherry wood posts. "You know, everything you tell me about your work, Keisha, keeps making me think you shouldn't have left that teaching job."

Keisha pursed her lips. *So we're going to revisit this old discussion?*

When Keisha told her mother last year that Parker had chosen her as his deputy campaign manager for the race against Vincent Dupré, she had thought her mother would be happy for her. She had thought Lena would be encouraging, as in the past when something good happened in Keisha's life. But for some reason her mother had become instantly pessimistic, telling Keisha that she was too sensitive for politics and would probably miss working with children. Now Lena voiced those concerns at every opportunity.

"You were *so* good at teaching, KeKe," her mother lamented, frowning as she gazed at her daughter. "And the kids loved you. They really did. This new job sounds so stressful. Maybe it's too much for you, baby." Her mother tilted her head and nudged Keisha's shoulder. "You know, it's not even summer yet. I'm sure some of the schools around here are still looking for teachers for the next school year, and with your experience—"

Keisha held up her hand to silence her mother. "Ma, I told you before, I'm *not* quitting this job, okay?" She sighed. "Sure, it's stressful and yes, I do occasionally question myself, but I like what I'm doing and I believe in Parker. I want to help him. He's up against some stiff competition. It's even worse now than it was in the primary. He needs as much help as he can get. We have to be prepared, and I'm really trying to stay focused."

"Well," Lena gave a weak smile, "you know what I always say. It's easier to focus when you give yourself a break every now and then. Sounds like you're in desperate need of some distraction, baby."

"I know. I've tried to take up a hobby I could do on the road. Maybe I could—"

"I was talking about distraction of the *male* kind, KeKe," her mother said quietly.

Keisha crossed her arms under breasts. Distraction of the male kind was exactly what she *didn't* need. In fact she had been trying to avoid it for the past two months, and hearing it from her mom was the last thing she needed. It was now early April, but she was still finding it hard to forget Will Blake, especially when he kept popping up everywhere.

It seemed that the schedulers for both camps had a knack for setting up speeches and meetings that always put the Parker and Dupré campaigns in proximity to one another. At least once a week Keisha would find herself climbing out of her car, scrambling to make it on time to some gathering, just as Will, Dupré, and their campaign manager, George, were walking across the parking lot with cell phones in hand. Keisha would try her best to ignore them, keeping her eyes focused ahead even though she could feel Will's gaze boring into her back. Once he had even tried to get her attention by calling her name, but she'd pointed to her watch in a gesture to show that she was already late for her appointment and politely waved before hurrying away.

Keisha had decided the night Tanya gave her the low-down on Will that it was best to avoid him, and the more she found out about him, the more she resolved that this was the right decision. It angered her that somehow he had pinpointed her as the sucker of their group. Yes, she was young and new to politics but she wasn't gullible, so if Will Blake thought he could play head games with her, he had another think coming!

"You need a date, KeKe," her mother persisted, wagging her index finger. "It's been how long since you've gone out with a guy? Six months? *Eight* months?"

Keisha's eyes widened. "Well, how long has it been since *you've* been on a date?" she asked, turning the tables on her mother.

Lena sighed, gazing down at her lap. "That's not important. I'm an old woman who has other things to worry about," she muttered.

"Old woman?" Keisha repeated. She then snorted. "Come on, Ma. You're only forty-eight!"

Her mother nodded. "That's right, I'm forty-eight. I'm a forty-eight-year-old woman who's already had and lost the love of my life and given birth to and raised a child who's now grown. You haven't," she said, making

Keisha grumble. "I've had many wonderful experiences, Keisha, that didn't involve work. I just want the same for you. I'd like to see you get married. I'd like to have grand-children before I'm old and gray and too decrepit to enjoy them! And none of that's going to happen if you don't stop every now and then and smell the roses!"

"Yeah," Keisha said, rolling her eyes. "So you keep telling me."

"I keep telling you but you don't listen!" Lena exclaimed. "Now given your level of experience—"

"Ma!" Keisha yelled, her face now coloring with embarrassment.

"I'm just saying, baby, that it's a good idea for you to get your feet wet. There are a lot of *experiences* that you haven't had that many other women your age have."

"How do you know what I've had?" Keisha exclaimed with outrage.

"None," Lena continued, undaunted by her daughter's outburst, "of that's going to change, KeKe, if the only time you go out to dinner is when you're eating with your mama."

"I've had 'experiences,' okay?" Keisha said impatiently. "So can we please change the subject?"

Her mother cocked an eyebrow before crossing her arms over her chest. "No, we cannot change the subject because I'm not finished," she said testily.

"Ma, I don't have time to go out to dinner with some man. I don't have time to talk about what movies I like over pasta!" she exclaimed angrily as she pushed herself to a sitting position. "I work fourteen-hour days and I take work home! I'm still answering phone calls at 10 o'clock at night! The only time I'm not doing something related to the campaign is when I'm *sleeping,* and, even then, I'm only getting four hours of sleep a night! And why am I doing all this? Because I know what we're up against! I've got to stay focused!"

Lena pursed her lips. "And you think going out on one date will make you lose focus?"

Keisha vehemently nodded her head. "Oh, I don't think. I know!" She sighed. "Look, Ma, for the past two decades Vincent Dupré has beaten every single opponent that has run against him. One year he even had thyroid surgery and couldn't campaign and he *still* won. He's already raised over a half a million dollars more than us. He's already collected over a dozen endorsements more than us, too. He has people working for him that used to work for George H.W. Bush! Some of those guys are old timers who have pulled just about every dirty trick in the book. We have to be on our guard. We've got to be ready for when Dupré finally turns the dogs on us!"

"Turns the dogs on you?" Lena gazed at her daughter intently. "KeKe, you don't think you're taking all this a little bit too seriously, baby?"

Keisha rolled her eyes in exasperation.

"All this talk," Lena continued, "about being on your guard and—"

"Ma, it is impossible to be too serious when it comes to that evil bigot. Believe me!"

Lena froze. She frowned and gazed at her daughter with a pained expression. She opened her mouth and then closed it. "Keisha," she began softly, shaking her head. "Keisha, I can't believe that . . . how you could you call that man a bigot when you don't even know—"

"Look, Ma, I know it's in your nature to defend people, but, believe me, Dupré is not worth it. I know him and the people who work for him!" she vehemently insisted. "His deputy campaign manager, Will Blake, is the worst of them. He consults for the America's Bright Future Foundation. The same foundation that released some quack study last year that said premarital sex could cause cancer! Before that, Blake was chief of staff for Congressman Taylor, the same guy that refused to vote for a bill that would have given free health care to the elderly and children. He turned around and submitted a bill that would prevent tobacco companies from getting sued." Keisha shook her head. "Will's played dirty tricks. He's planted stories about opponents in the press. And the worst part is, Ma, you wouldn't even know how wicked they are just by looking at them. Will Blake, in particular, would definitely fool you. He's really handsome and charming, but, underneath it all, he's pure evil."

Lena tilted her head and narrowed her eyes. "Pure evil, huh? Then I guess it's good you know so much about them, especially that Will Blake guy."

Keisha could be wrong, but she could swear her mother was fighting back a smile.

Keisha shrugged. "Yeah, well, it helps to do your research."

"I bet it does," Lena murmured.

CHAPTER 7

Will walked up the driveway, listening to the steady crunch of gravel beneath his feet. He shoved his hands into the pockets of his khakis and slowly looked around him, noting that little had changed on Vincent Dupré's property over the past twenty and some odd years. The weeping willow was still at the end of the driveway. The stone birdbath still sat in front of the house, surrounded by a ring of yellow tulips. The family's fishing boat still bobbed listlessly at the edge of a creaky dock nearly a football field away.

Will could remember visiting this place, this vacation home on the Eastern Shore of Maryland, back when he was still in high school and Dupré and his father were still partners in their law firm. In fact, the Blake family's summer home wasn't far from here, less than a mile up the road.

Back then, Will would walk up Dupré's pristine white, wooden front steps the way he was doing now, but his father, Theodore Blake, would be at his side with a fishing pole in hand. The three of them would disappear for hours on the Chesapeake Bay in search of gray trout, and he would listen to his dad and Dupré tell stories about their youth.

Will loved those days out on the water, listening to the two men he admired most. He had always respected his "Uncle Vincent"; though he rarely, if ever, called him that anymore, especially not in front of the campaign staff. In front of others, their relationship was more formal. Now he was "sir" or simply "Dupré."

Dupré wasn't a self-made man like Will's father, who had grown up poor and acquired wealth over time. Dupré had been born into a well-off Louisiana family who moved to D.C. back in the 1960s and had become even richer when they bought businesses and real estate in the region. But despite the money, Dupré never carried a sense of entitlement about him. He was open-minded, open-hearted, and color-blind. He believed in hard work and expected the same out of those around him. In fact, he had told Will just that when he offered him his first job as an office assistant many years ago.

He had made the job offer during one of their boating trips out on the Chesapeake Bay. Will was nineteen then, had just finished his sophomore year at Georgetown, and Dupré had just won his first congressional race. "You think you're up to it, Will?" Dupré had asked with a sly grin. "There's a lot of grunt work involved. It's not a glamorous job by any interpretation, but it's a great way to get your foot in the door . . . if you're interested." Of course Will had vehemently nodded his head and said yes. He had always wanted to get into politics and had always been fascinated by the goings-on up on Capitol Hill. Will started the job at Dupré's congressional office two weeks later and hadn't looked back since. He knew politics was his future, how he would spend the rest of his life.

Will climbed the last step and stood on the front porch, arriving early to their campaign powwow. Dupré had summoned his top managers to his vacation home to talk about their election strategy. He figured asking them to work during such a beautiful weekend would be less painful if boating and barbeque were involved.

Will got a halfhearted wave from George Kilburn, Dupré's campaign manager, who was furiously smoking a cigarette on Dupré's front porch. The front of George's Ken doll haircut was flapping in the breeze like a bird's broken wing as he slumped in one of the wicker chairs.

"Sara wouldn't let you smoke inside, huh?" Will asked with a cocked eyebrow, referring to Dupré's wife, Sara Dupré. The petite blonde spoke softly and moved gracefully, but she could be hard as nails when she wanted. Will suspected by the beleaguered look George gave him that Sara had shown her less than charming side the instant the chronic smoker dared to pull out a cigarette in her home.

"She said it would soak into the furniture," George mumbled with a roll of the eyes. "She doesn't care about my lungs, but I better not ruin her drapes."

At that, Will laughed.

"A smile . . . from *you*? I'm shocked," George said, taking one more drag before tossing his cigarette into the gravel several yards away. He raised one of his ankles to his knee and then slowly blew out a cloud of smoke.

Will narrowed his eyes. "What do you mean?"

George shrugged. "You've been a little surly lately. That's all. I was wondering if the pressure of the campaign was getting to you."

"Surly?" Will shook his head in confusion. "I haven't been surly. What are you talking about?"

"Well, you bit off that *Post* reporter's head last week during the phone interview."

Will scowled in annoyance as he crossed his arms over his chest. "Those questions that *reporter* . . . if you want to call him that . . . was asking were completely out of line."

George closed his eyes and sighed. "Fine then. What about Gretchen?"

"What about Gretchen?" Will exclaimed. He was on the defensive now and, quite frankly, pretty perturbed.

George sat forward, looking up at Will intently. "She said you've been snapping at her lately."

Will glowered again. Since the night that he had kicked Gretchen out of his house, she hadn't been the easiest to get along with. She could be nice one moment and spiteful and sarcastic the next, and, frankly, he couldn't take it anymore. Maybe he did snap at her but she had truly deserved it. Besides, why had she gone complaining to George about it? Why get him involved?

"If Gretchen has a problem with what I say, she should come to me, not go crying to you," Will argued, his eyebrows knitting together as he glared at George.

George rolled his eyes and sighed. "Will, it's not just Gretchen or that reporter. Even now you're raising your voice and—"

"I'm not raising my . . ." Will stopped as he heard his voice boom across the yard to the waterfront. He closed his eyes and took a deep breath.

George slowly nodded his head as he shrugged out of his windbreaker. "Look, Will, I've got to honest with you. I know in a campaign sometimes people get irritable. Sometimes tempers flare, but we all have to control those impulses if we want to continue to work as a team. Usually, you're pretty good at that. I count on you to be the level-headed one around here, but just . . . not lately. Something has changed and I've been trying to figure out what that is." George tilted his head. "Maybe you should take a day or two off to rejuvenate. Go on a day trip. Relax."

Will sighed as he leaned back against the porch railing. "I don't need a break, George. I'm fine. Really, I am. I'm just a little . . . frustrated and tired. But it'll pass," he said. He ran a hand over his face. "It'll pass."

Or at least he hoped it would. Will hadn't had a good night's sleep in more than a month. Every other day Will would wake up in the wee hours of the morning, his heart racing wildly, his muscles tense and his manhood hard. In his dreams, Will had explored just about every inch of Keisha's body and tried every position imaginable. He had tasted her, held her, and felt her tremble beneath him. But reality was a different story. It was exasperating to long for a woman in his dreams who totally ignored him when he was awake. He hadn't felt frustration like this since he was a teenaged boy.

It pissed him off. Why was he going through all this torture when he hadn't done anything wrong? He had planned to approach Keisha again and ask her out after the election, but now he doubted she would respond. Hell, in a perfect world, he could have had her already if it wasn't for Tanya. What stories about him had that little meddler exaggerated? What outright lies had she told? He was sure they had to be pretty bad to make Keisha give him the cold shoulder.

"Frustrated about what?" George asked with concern.

"The . . . the . . . Parker campaign staff," Will lied. "I've tried to set up a few meetings with them to talk about the debate in July. We still haven't agreed on the format."

George chuckled. "That's what's frustrating you? Oh, hell, I thought it was something serious, Will!" George leaned back in his chair and smiled. "They're amateurs. They require a lot more hand-holding than what we're used to, that's all. I can try making the calls myself if it's frustrating you that much. I can call Phil, the campaign manager, or Keisha Reynolds, his second in command." George smiled mischievously. "I wouldn't consider it too much of a chore to talk to her," he said with a wink, "but don't tell my wife that."

At the mention of Keisha's name, Will's eyes instantly narrowed. But he caught himself and forced a smile. "Your secret is safe with me," he assured George. He then cleared his throat. "So what's Keisha's story anyway?" he asked, trying his best to sound casual. "I heard she's new to all this."

George nodded. "*Very* new. In fact, I believe she was a high school teacher before she became Parker's deputy campaign manager."

Will frowned. *"A teacher?"*

"Yeah, I know. Which makes her highly qualified for the position, right?" George chuckled. "Parker's been telling everyone that he brought her on board because she worked for his mayoral campaign a few years ago when she was one of his students, but I've heard other theories for why she got the job this time around. I think I'm more inclined to believe them."

Will slowly pushed himself away from the front porch's railing. "Really? And what's that?"

George shrugged and smirked. "Well, she's a very attractive girl, Will, and I'm sure she's got lots of energy. Perhaps she was willing to do more than what the job description requires, if you know what I mean. Go above and beyond the call of duty to please her boss," he said with another wink.

"You . . . you think Keisha and Parker are having an affair?" Will asked, his voice ringing with disbelief. "Why?"

"Why *not?*" George exclaimed. "Wouldn't you? You have this sweet, young thing around you at all hours and you're telling me you wouldn't try to touch her? *Not once?*" He sighed. "I'm sure Parker is many things, Will. But a saint he is not," George said with a chuckle. "Look, she's completely inexperienced and has no business running his campaign. Why do *you* think she has the job?"

Will gritted his teeth. His nostrils flared. *George is talking out his ass,* one part of him shouted angrily. Will felt instantly as if he should punch George in the mouth for the things he was saying about Keisha. He had no right to talk about her like that, basically calling her an opportunistic whore, when he knew absolutely nothing about her.

But hold on there, another part of Will said—the logical voice that was so familiar to him. *You don't know for a fact that what George is saying isn't true.* Will's eyes lowered as he considered that possibility. Keisha's coldness toward Will . . . was it strictly based on what Tanya had told her about him or was it something more? Was this woman who frustrated him, who haunted his dreams, already spoken for by her married boss? The possibility appalled him.

"Will, I thought I heard your voice!" Dupré suddenly exclaimed as he threw open the front door. "How long have you been here?" His green eyes twinkled as he smiled broadly. The fifty-something gentleman, who was dressed in a white polo shirt and khaki pants, loudly clapped Will on his broad shoulder.

The years had been kind to Vincent Dupré. Though wrinkles and a lifetime spent in the sun did show his age, his physique was still trim and lean.

"I just got here a few minutes ago," Will muttered distractedly, now no closer to ridding himself of thoughts about Keisha than he was hours before.

"Well, why don't you come inside? I was just about to throw a few slabs of meat on the grill." Dupré leaned his head toward George and grinned. "Or you can stay out here and continue to watch George sunburn. It's up to you."

George cocked an eyebrow. "The last time I checked I'm not the only one on this porch in danger of turning into a lobster, Vincent," he said, alluding to Dupré's fair skin.

"Four words for you, George," Dupré joked as he held up four fingers. "S-P-F 30." He then turned to Will. "Come on, son. Help me start lunch before everyone else gets here. You comin', George?"

George dug into his jacket pocket to retrieve his pack of Marlboros. He then held one cigarette in the air. "I'll be in as soon as I finish this," he said, making Dupré roll his eyes and chuckle.

"Come on, Will," Dupré said, waving the younger, taller man through the front door into the lemon-scented, brightly lit foyer.

Will took a deep breath. He was no longer in the mood for their Saturday meeting. In fact, he was no longer in the mood to do anything that day besides go home and mull over what George had just told him.

But what good will that do me? he thought. He had wasted enough time thinking about Keisha Reynolds. He resolved, as he walked down the hallway in Dupré's home, that he would try his damndest not to waste any more time.

CHAPTER 8

."We need to take Northern Charles out of the locked column and shift it over," Will said. He reclined in his chair as he pointed at the projector screen.

"Why?" George asked, licking the last bit of pork rib juice from his fingertips.

Will slowly shook his head as he raised his beer bottle to his lips. "Because it's not locked, that's why."

"Will, we've carried Charles County for the past six elections!" George exclaimed. "Why isn't it locked?"

"Check the numbers, George. We've been winning by smaller and smaller margins each election year," Will insisted, leaning forward. "The demographics keep changing there and more and more diehard Democrats keep moving in. Put it in the soft column so we can allocate the right amount of volunteers to get out the vote and schedule more events so that Dupré's face is out there. I'm telling you, it's the right move."

Dupré chuckled as he gave Will's shoulder a fatherly pat. "Well, let's hope that the crappy housing market will work in our favor and the Democrats will stop moving in."

At that, the three men laughed and Will took another swig of beer.

It was after 11 o'clock. The rest of the campaign staff had left at least two hours earlier, but Will and George had lingered behind to go over more groundwork before they headed back home. Will could stay as long as he wanted . . . well, at least until Sara kicked him out. He had the keys to his parents' vacation home and luckily only had to drive a mile up the road to find a warm, soft bed for the night. He planned to head back to his place in Annapolis in the morning.

Meanwhile, George was getting cell phone calls from his wife every half an hour asking him where he was and when he was finally coming home. Will grimaced every time George rose from the table to have a hushed conversation with his wife in the corner of the room. *Any woman who calls that often must not trust you very much,* Will thought. He then wondered if George had ever given his wife any reason not to trust him.

Dupré sighed deeply as he considered the projector screen for several long seconds. He tilted his head. "All right. Move Charles out of the locked column," he muttered.

"What?" George exclaimed. "You can't be serious, Vincent!"

"No, George, Will's right," Dupré insisted, nodding his head. He tapped his cleft chin. "That area keeps changing and we shouldn't count on people voting the same way there as they have in the past. Maybe we should schedule a few more visits than usual down there. I'm sure the V.F.W. lodges are holding a few events. I can show up for the ribbon cutting ceremony for the business park they're opening around Waldorf."

"We're wasting resources, Vincent," George insisted. "I'm telling you. That money and time would be better spent somewhere else. Mark my words."

Dupré grinned. "And your words have been marked. End of discussion, George. Let's move on to the next topic," he said firmly as they heard a knock at the door.

"Come in," Dupré called out.

Sara poked her blonde head through the crack of the rec room door. She smiled. "Sorry to interrupt you guys but, George, your wife is on the line. She said she's been trying to reach you."

Will and Dupré exchanged glances. Both men smirked.

"Oh, yes, sorry about that," George mumbled. He quickly stood and took the cordless phone Sara held toward him. She exited the room. "I . . . I gave her your number just in case there was an emergency. I hope everything's all right." He loudly cleared his throat as he walked to the other side of the room. "Hello, dear," he said, less than cordially. "Yes, I turned off my phone . . . I turned it off because you kept calling me, Marjorie!" He quickly looked over his shoulder at Will and Dupré, then dropped his voice to a whisper. "I'm busy . . . Of course I'm working! What else do you think I'm doing? Marjorie . . . Marj, don't . . . don't act like this . . . Are you *trying* to ruin my career? Is that what you're trying to do?"

Dupré rose from the table. "Why don't we take a walk, Will? Give him some privacy."

Will quickly nodded and followed Dupré to the door. They shut it firmly behind them, leaving George to continue his argument with his wife.

Dupré smiled as they made their way up the staircase and into the living room. "I've got a little secret to show you, Will. Not even Sara knows about it," he whispered.

Will nodded and smiled. "And what would that be, sir?"

Dupré frowned as he walked over to dining room cabinet. "Oh, don't you start that 'sir' crap with me, Will!" he chided playfully as he opened one of the cabinet drawers. "It always makes me feel like a captain in the marines. You either call me Vincent, Uncle Vincent, or nothing at all."

Will chuckled as he crossed his arms over his chest. "Okay, Vincent, what do you have to show me?"

"These! I just got them in from Havana," Dupré said with a broad smile as he held up a wooden box. He peeked over his shoulder. "Sara isn't coming, is she?" he whispered. "Can you hear her?"

Will laughed. It was hard to believe that a man who ranked fourth in Congress was deathly afraid of his own wife. Will quickly shook his head. "She's not coming."

"Good," Dupré exclaimed as he opened the box's lid and beamed down at the stack of cigars. "I've been dying to try them but I haven't had the chance. Now I will. And you can have one, too."

Will shook his head. "I don't smoke, Vincent."

Dupré's face fell instantly. He frowned. "Oh, come on, Will. Don't break an old man's heart. You can fake smoking for one day, can't you? Come on, son!"

Will forced a smile. "Fine. Hand me one of those."

"Good job," Dupré said as he passed Will a cigar and got one of his own before returning the box to its proper hiding place in the dining room cabinet under a rarely used velvet tray of silverware. He grabbed a lighter from the dining room table and tilted his head toward the front door. "Let's smoke them outside."

The two men tipped-toed out of the dining room and into the foyer, careful not to disturb Sara, who was lounging on the family room couch, watching some murder mystery on their wall-mounted plasma screen TV. When Will and Dupré got outside and quietly closed the front door behind them, each man bit off the tip of the cigar, lit it up, and took a puff.

Will coughed a few times on his first and second try, but, by the third try, he got the hang of it. He slumped into one of the porch's wicker chairs, stretched his legs, and gazed at the waterfront as he took another puff from the Cuban cigar. He closed his eyes and savored the cigar. He exhaled deeply.

"Good, huh?" Dupré asked as he kicked off his deck shoes and fell into the chair beside him. He flexed his bare toes. "What'd I tell you?"

Will nodded in reply.

"I say it all the time. If there's one thing the Commies know how to do right, it's make a good cigar." Dupré sighed, then took his own puff and gazed at the full moon reflected in the murky black waters of the bay. "And there's nothing like a good cigar at the end of a long day." He then turned to Will, who could feel himself being lulled to sleep by the whir of the cicadas. "So tell me, Will. I haven't had a chance to catch up with you lately. How's your father doing?"

"You see Pop more than I do," Will murmured. "You tell me."

Dupré chuckled. "Well, he's irritated that he doesn't see more of you. But I told him I keep you busy."

Will took another puff from his cigar. "Yeah, I guess I should go over there and pay a visit. I've just haven't had the time."

"Oh, I remember how it is, son, the life of a single man," Dupré said with a wicked smile, bringing a twinkle to his green eyes. "It's still exciting, I hope."

Will slowly shook his head. "No, Vincent. Not too exciting lately."

"What? Not a different woman every night? I'm disappointed in you, Will," he chided playfully.

Will grinned. "I don't think I've *ever* had a different woman every night. They haven't invented a Viagra pill strong enough for that."

At that, Dupré roared with laughter, filling the night air with his deep baritone. He then nudged Will and slowly shook his head. "Well, I stand corrected, son," Dupré said. "I guess I've always taken you to be quite the ladies' man."

"Not during an election year, Vincent. No time."

"Well, enjoy it while you can, son," Dupré said. "Because once you get married and have kids, the party ends."

"Speaking of kids," Will said, frowning slightly, "where are Kendall and Paul anyway? I expected to run into them at least once today. Don't they usually come down with you guys to the Eastern Shore on weekends?"

Dupré shrugged. "Not lately. Kendall just started her junior year at Sidwell. She has a bushel of new friends and a new boyfriend. I think he's the son of some bigwig over at the British embassy." He shrugged again. "We don't see too much of her except when she wants to go shopping or needs cash. Just call me the Dupré Bank. I feel like a human ATM machine sometimes," he said ruefully.

Will didn't respond. Dupré believed in hard work, but it seemed that he hadn't instilled those same values in his daughter. Kendall, though a beautiful girl, had always come off to Will as amazingly self-involved and shallow even back when she was a five-year-old throwing a temper tantrum in her father's congressional office in the Rayburn building. She was like many of the princesses of Capitol Hill, all spoiled rotten by their parents, all behaving as if the lifestyle they had was owed to them. Will hoped if he ever had a daughter, she would never be like Kendall Dupré.

Will took another drag from his cigar and slumped back further in his chair. "So how's Paul then?"

"Oh, Paul's doing fine. He'll graduate from your alma mater, Georgetown, in May, you know."

"Really?" Will asked, raising his eyebrows in surprise. "Has it been that long? Does Paul know what he wants to do after school?"

"Not as far as I know," Dupré said, rolling his cigar between his thumb and index finger. "After four years you'd think he'd have more of a clue, but that doesn't seem to be the case. So far, all he knows is what he doesn't want to do. He doesn't want to go into politics and he doesn't want to go into law. Basically, he doesn't want to do anything where I could help get him a job." Dupré chuckled. "I think he's contemplating the Peace Corps, though."

"*The Peace Corps?*"

Dupré nodded and chuckled again. "I know. That was my reaction, too. But that's what he's considering. He wants to work with orphans somewhere in Africa or Guatemala, for all I know," Dupré said, shrugging. "I think he's just going through a rebellious phase. He wants to carve out an identity outside of his old man's image. I told him that I went through my own rebellious phase back in the '70s when I was as old as he is now. But I fell back in line soon enough. I guess he will, too. I'm still holding out hope that he'll be the second generation of Duprés on Capitol Hill, though right now he'd probably rather be dead than be a congressman."

"Wait. Back up." Will smirked. "*You* had a rebellious phase?"

"Don't look so smug, young man," Dupré chided playfully before vehemently nodding his head. "Yes, even *I*," he said as he pointed at his chest, "had a rebellious phase. I was just tired of everything. Tired of my classes. Tired of the law. I was burned out so I took off from law school back in '78 and worked at inner city community center in D.C. for a change of pace. I tutored kids and coached baseball." He chuckled. "There I was this skinny, rich white guy in one of the roughest neighborhood in D.C. My parents thought I had lost my mind! They were ready to ship me off to St. Elizabeth's psyche ward."

Will frowned. "I didn't know you worked in the inner city."

Out of the many stories Dupré had told him, this was the first time he had heard this one.

"Yeah, well," Dupré shrugged. "I didn't stay long. I did it for about a year and it was a whole 'nother world for me. While I was there I got an apartment in some rundown neighborhood in Southeast with one of the other instructors. She was eight, no, nine years younger than me. She was eighteen and absolutely gorgeous. She had ebony skin that was like running your fingers over silk and big brown eyes. She had this amazing, amazing body," he said wistfully before letting out a low whistle. "She grew up around there."

Will's frowned deepened. *Ebony skinned?* He hadn't thought that any woman that wasn't blonde and blue-eyed was Dupré's type. And rundown neighborhood? Will couldn't imagine Dupré ever living in a house that cost less than seven figures, let alone in an apartment building filled with poor people.

"We were so broke, Will," Dupré continued. "I think we ate beans and rice for dinner just about every night. We could barely afford rent. My parents completely cut me off when I moved in with her."

"I can imagine," Will muttered, quickly envisioning how Dupré's upstanding, rich Southern family reacted to the then-young man shacking up with a poor black girl.

" 'You're living in sin with this colored gutter tramp!' my mother said." He mimicked his mother's Southern drawl, grimacing as he recalled her words. " 'Colored gutter tramp.' That's what they called her. They told me that they'd help me if I got back to my senses but I didn't give a damn. I was poor for the first time in my life but, more importantly, I was happy and she . . ." He sighed. "Will, she made me feel like I could do anything. I was on top of the world when I was with her. We were so in love."

Will stared at Dupré, his cigar now forgotten. Who was this man? The one that was talking now seemed nothing like the Vincent Dupré he had known for the past two decades. "So . . . what . . . what happened?"

"She left me," Dupré said succinctly, taking another puff from his cigar.

Will quickly sat up in his chair. "She left you? Why?"

"It's way too complicated to explain now," Dupré said, waving his hands. "But she left. Just moved out one day and took all her fairy dust with her," he muttered sarcastically. "Two weeks later, I left the community center. It was just too much to stay there with all those reminders of her around me."

"What did you do?"

Dupré grumbled loudly. "What *could* I do? I went crawling back to my parents so I could pay tuition for law school and I went back to being a student," he said bitterly. "After I got back in school, I tried looking for her off and on for about two years, but no one knew where she was. It was like she had just . . . disappeared. Maybe she went to New York. She always wanted to dance on Broadway."

Will grimaced. "Damn, that's depressing, Vincent. That had to crush you."

Dupré smiled forlornly as he nodded his head. "Yes, it did . . . at the time."

"Did it make you bitter?" Will ventured.

Dupré sat silently for several seconds, contemplating the question. "It was a very . . . disillusioning experience," he finally said. "I'll put it that way. But eventually I moved on. I had to. In hindsight, I know now that it just wasn't meant to be. I loved her, but . . . we weren't meant for each other. That wasn't the life I was supposed to lead." He stared off into the distance at the dark waters of the bay, his cigar now forgotten. He fell into silence again. It was as if his mind was somewhere else, in the past, perhaps.

"You all right, Vincent?" Will asked, frowning with concern.

Dupré blinked and quickly shook his head. "I'm fine, son. I'm fine. It's just... it surprises me that after all these years it's still painful to talk about. I'm happily married to a beautiful woman. I have two wonderful children. But I still remember it like it was yesterday. So many memories . . . so many . . ." His voice drifted off. The two sat in silence for several minutes before Dupré abruptly broke his somber mood and forced a smile.

Will watched as Dupré began to wag his finger at him. "Let that be a lesson to you, Will. Don't fall for the wrong woman. Life has a way of knocking you on your ass and reminding you why it's such a bad idea."

Will gave a nervous chuckle. Suddenly, he thought of one wrong woman in particular. The image of Keisha quickly popped into Will's head and he was very, very grateful that Dupré couldn't read minds.

"Christ, it's getting cold out here," Dupré muttered as he doused his cigar, tossed it over the side of the porch and rubbed his shoulders. He shivered. "You think it's time to head inside, Will?"

"Probably," Will muttered.

"George should be done talking to his wife by now," the older man said as he rose from his chair. He stood and stretched. "Let's go find out if he's still married."

CHAPTER 9

"Tickets! Tickets! Buy your raffle tickets over here!" Keisha shouted, waving a blue ream of tickets in the air. "Tickets!"

"You're *way* too into this," Tanya muttered tersely. She leaned forward in her metal fold-up chair and smacked absently at a mosquito that was landing on her bare leg. "God, it's hot out here!" Tanya fanned herself with a flyer.

Keisha rolled her eyes behind her sunglasses and smiled. "It isn't that bad, Tanya."

"I guess you're right," Tanya muttered. "I've had root canals that were worse."

At that, Keisha couldn't help laughing.

Though Tanya was acting as if the day were her perfect imagining of hell on earth, Keisha couldn't help walking around with a slight hop in her step. She was actually enjoying herself.

Today was the opening day of St. Mary's County Fair and it seemed every Tom, Dick, Harry, and Betty Sue had shown up at the grand event. Keisha was happy with the turnout. She and Phil Levine, the campaign director, had long ago decided that Dr. Parker needed to get more face time in the more rural parts of the congressional district, and what better way to do that than to go to one of the county fairs and mingle with voters?

While Dr. Parker muddled his way through judging the baby calf 4-H contest, many of his staffers volunteered at a few fairground stands. Phil was sure it was a good way for them to better learn about the more rustic voters. But most of the staff, including Tanya, thought trying to appeal to the rural conservatives in the southern counties was a lost cause, and they weren't too happy about spending the day in "the sticks." Only Keisha had been excited at the idea. Having spent most of her life in the inner city, she had never seen a farm or been to a county fair. This was her first chance to do both.

"I'll take a ticket," a plump woman in a pink visor and fanny pack said as she waddled over to Keisha and Tanya's picnic table. Keisha leaned down to rip off a ticket, pushing her hair out of her face as she did so, and grinned.

"That'll be two dollars!" Keisha said.

She had foregone her emblematic chignon today, sparing herself the half an hour of toiling with the blow dryer to get her hair straight. Instead, Keisha had gone for a more casual look befitting a county fair. Her voluminous tresses were held back by a blue headband and casually fell over her shoulders and down her back. She had also traded in her normal clean-line suit for a crisp white button-down shirt, which was rolled up to her forearms and tied at the waist. Her denim shorts showed a lot more leg than she was used to, but it seemed suitable, considering the hot weather. Her casual look made her appear several years younger than her age. She seemed more likely to be a college volunteer or a staff intern than the deputy campaign manager.

"What do I win?" the portly woman asked.

"Well," Keisha explained as she pointed to a wicker basket on the table, "if we draw your number you could win this lovely gift basket and these spa coupons. It's a local business in Leonardtown and they'll do a facial and massage for two at half price."

The woman's blue eyes widened. "*Wooow*, that sounds nice! Doesn't it?"

"It does indeed," Tanya said drolly.

Keisha cut her eyes at Tanya before regaining her grin and returning her attention to the woman in front of her. "So come back at 2 o'clock for the drawing and see if you won."

"I sure will," the woman replied, nodding eagerly. She gave a quick wave. "You girls have a nice day!"

"You, too," Keisha and Tanya chimed.

Keisha glanced down at Tanya. "Could you *try* to look less bored?"

"Not without a lot of effort," Tanya muttered as she tugged at her tank top, glancing over her shoulder. She gave the first genuine smile she had given all day. "They're back!" she said as she nudged Keisha's leg. "So how were the calves?" she called out.

"Adorable!" Kelly, Dr. Parker's press secretary, answered as she walked over to the table. The petite blonde frowned. "Kind of makes me feel bad about the veal I ate last night."

Behind her trailed Dr. Parker and Phil Levine, their balding campaign manager, who was currently barking into his cell phone. At Dr. Parker's elbow was a photographer, who was furiously snapping pictures, and Javon Houston, a reporter from *The Baltimore Sun*. The newspaper was doing a profile on Parker and the reporter had been shadowing him for the past two days.

Keisha had been elated when she heard Kelly had talked to the *Sun* editors and set up the story. Once the profile was published and voters got to know Dr. Parker, Keisha was sure they would admire him just as much as she did.

"So how'd the contest go?" Tanya asked as she stood from the table.

Kelly shrugged. "Fine, I guess. This cute little brown calf won. They got a picture of Sydney feeding it with this big bottle," she said in a baby voice. "It was adorable!"

"It'll probably make a great shot above the fold," Houston said with a laugh as he politely broke away from Dr. Parker and stepped forward. He was tall and dark-skinned with a nice smile and dreads that hung in his eyes. He couldn't be more than twenty-five or twenty-six years old, judging from his baby face.

Keisha smiled up at him politely. "So how's the piece coming, Houston?"

He grinned. "Good, so far. I think I've got everything I need . . . with the exception of one or two things."

Keisha raised her eyebrows expectantly. "What one or two things?"

She watched as he glanced at Kelly. Kelly smiled tightly and anxiously cleared her throat.

"Actually," he began as he stared down at his feet and then met Keisha's eyes with a timid gaze, "I was wondering if *we* could talk."

"You need more background info about Dr. Parker, more anecdotes?" Keisha asked with a smile. She gestured to the picnic table. "Pull up a chair. I'll tell you whatever you need."

"Well," he said, licking his lips and giving a sly grin as he stepped closer to her, "I was hoping we could do it a little more . . . privately."

"Privately?" Keisha frowned in confusion. She stood silently for several seconds before laughing and slowly nodding her head with comprehension. "Oh! Oh, yeah. It is a little noisy out here, isn't it? Well, you can always call me at the office or—"

"Actually," he said, "I was hoping for something a little bit more private than that." He winked, making Keisha frown.

"Umm, Keisha," Kelly interrupted. "Could I talk to you for a sec?" She abruptly turned to Houston. "Could you excuse us?"

Keisha's frown deepened as Kelly cryptically leaned her head toward one of the stands several feet away before walking in that direction. She followed her while Tanya politely smiled at the reporter before turning and scurrying after them. By the time they all reached a popcorn stand, Tanya was almost hovering over Keisha's shoulder.

"What's wrong, Kelly?" Keisha asked quietly. She pushed her sunglasses to her crown. At this point she was more than just a little puzzled.

Kelly let out a puff of air that raised her bangs. She crossed her arms over her flat chest and frowned. "Look, just don't get angry at me when I tell you this. It isn't as bad as it sounds."

Keisha's eyes narrowed. "What isn't as bad as it sounds?"

"Just hear me out." Kelly held up her hands and sighed. "Look, I had a hard time pitching this story to the editors at the *Sun* and I knew we had a good relationship with Houston, so I asked if he could sell it to his editors for me." She sighed. "He agreed to do it under one or two . . . stipulations."

Tanya adjusted the straps of her tank top. "Oh, here it comes. There's always a catch." She frowned. "Let me guess. Everything's on the record? He's running it side-by-side with a profile about Dupré?"

"No, nothing like that. His requests have more to do with *who* he talks to than *how* it's done," Kelly insisted. "He wanted total access to Parker . . ."

Keisha nodded. "Well, that's understandable. You can't write a profile if you—"

". . . and to you, Keisha," Kelly said with a look of guilt in her eyes.

Keisha paused. She pointed at her chest. "To *me?*" she asked in bewilderment. "Why does he need total access to me? I'm not the one he's profiling." She glanced over at Houston, who was talking to Dr. Parker again. He turned to Keisha, Kelly, and Tanya, waved and smiled.

"I don't know," Kelly said with a helpless shrug. "I guess you made a good impression on him the last time you two talked. I told him tentatively yes, but I said I had to clear it with you first. But I forgot to ask you and I just really, *really* wanted him to do the profile, Keisha." She flapped her arms. "I was hoping he would forget the request once he started the interviews but it . . . seems like . . . he hasn't. I'm sorry."

Keisha stared at her, dumbfounded, and Tanya shrugged. "That's your big revelation?" She sucked her teeth and waved her hand dismissively. "Girl, I thought it was something that was serious."

Keisha's brows furrowed as she glowered at Tanya. "It *is* serious!" she shouted, finally regaining her words. She turned an angry gaze on Kelly. "So what's he expecting? What did he mean by 'total access'?"

"I have no idea! I was afraid to ask," Kelly mumbled, twisting her hands together. "Keisha, please, *please* just do this for me! Do it for Sydney!" she begged.

"Do what?" Keisha exclaimed.

Tanya shrugged. "Girl, it's not that big a deal. Hell, Keisha, maybe you'll even get a free dinner out of this," she said with a laugh. "Tell him you'll only agree to do the interview at an expensive restaurant on *his* tab. Make sure he has a good time, though, if you know what I mean." She winked. "We could use the good coverage."

Keisha gritted her teeth, ignoring Tanya's words. "Kelly, tell Houston that if he has any further questions *after* he talks to Phil, I'll be more than happy to answer them by phone or at my office," she said, taking on an officious tone. "But so far as 'total access' to me is concerned, he can forget it." She then turned on her heel.

"What?" Kelly yelled after her, her face red and crumpling with dismay. "But what if he won't finish the profile?"

"The story is about Dr. Parker, Kelly," Keisha said over her shoulder. "Not about me. And I don't appreciate anyone attaching conditions like that to his profile. If Houston wants another interview, he should talk to Dr. Parker and Phil. If he's just trolling for a date, I'm not interested."

"But, Keisha . . ." Kelly begged.

"Where are you going?" Tanya yelled after her.

"To the bathroom!" Keisha shouted back, but that was a lie. She was fuming and wanted to be left alone.

Houston caught her eye as she walked by him. He smiled. She frowned grimly in return.

Men, she thought angrily as she stomped her way through the crowd. This was why she had decided to keep them at arm's length during the campaign, and for most of her life for that matter. *Some of them can be so damn sneaky*, she thought with frustration. They were always trying to get something out of her. If it wasn't William Blake trying to get into her head, it was this guy Houston trying to get into her . . .

"Total access," she muttered as she pushed up her shirt sleeves against the heat. The day seemed to have gotten warmer.

And Keisha could only imagine what "total access" meant. No man had gotten "total access" to her since she was a naïve seventeen-year-old college freshman who had slept with the school basketball team's point guard. She lost her virginity because he had played her emotions off those of another girl and made it seem like the only way Keisha could have him was if she had slept with him. But a week later, he still left her. The experience had been both physically and emotional painful and humiliating, but, more importantly, eye-opening for Keisha. That night when she limped home alone from his dorm room, she had promised she would never allow herself to be manipulated by any man again, and so far she had stayed true to her promise.

Keisha's mother thought she was "inexperienced", but, quite frankly, Keisha had chosen not to be very experienced. Of course, she dated men. She'd even kiss them. But that was where the intimacy always ended. She had never found one with whom she was willing to go past that point, willing to trust and let in again.

CHAPTER 10

Minutes later Keisha rounded another corner and began a new row of stalls. She was still fuming and needed time to cool down a little. Squinting against the bright morning light, she lowered her shades over her eyes. She walked through the fair and passed a stand filled with basket weavers. Another was filled with home-made quilts. She made a mental note to stop there on the way back. Her mother loved folk art and crafts. Maybe Keisha could find something for her there. Her heart rate slowed and her temper abated as she inhaled the scent of crab stew, corn on the cob, and fresh baked bread. She smiled as her stomach grumbled loudly. She'd probably have to stop at one of those stands on the way back, too.

Keisha rounded another corner and began a new row of stalls but abruptly stopped in her tracks when she saw an all-too-familiar face hovering behind a podium. She sighed and her shoulders slumped. It seemed that Dr. Parker wasn't the only one who was using today as a way to rub elbows with potential voters.

Vincent Dupré was decked out in starched jeans and a polo shirt and waved to the boisterous crowd gathered around the small wooden stage. Beside him stood a petite blonde woman in a matching polo shirt and a khaki skirt. Keisha recognized her from photos as his wife, Sara.

Behind them stood a gangly dirty blonde in tight white shorts and powder blue tank top who gazed at the crowd with the look of sheer teenaged boredom. Beside her stood a young man who could only be described as a younger version of Dupré. Keisha guessed that the girl and the young man were Dupré's son and daughter, Paul and Kendall.

"The perfect cookie-cutter family," Keisha muttered dryly. However, a deep part of her envied them. Life had been easy for Vincent Dupré, and she imagined fortune and power would come just as easily for his blessed offspring.

She watched as Dupré motioned for the crowd to silence its loud applause. Then he thumped the shoulder and shook the hand of the man who stood on the other side of him. "I want to thank County Commissioner Willard for that wonderful introduction," Dupré said, following his words with his usual broad smile. "I greatly appreciate the invitation for my family and me to come here today and meet the wonderful people of St. Mary's County," he said, drawing more applause. Dupré took a deep breath as County Commissioner Willard and Sara Dupré stepped aside, giving the congressman ample room at the podium. "For nearly eighteen years, I have represented the great people of St. Mary's in Congress. I have represented your values, your American pride," he said, making Keisha roll her eyes heavenward again in exasperation. "I have fought to clean the Patuxent River. I fought to build new bridges and new roadways," he said, pointing into the distance. "And let me tell you, ladies and gentlemen, in these hard economic times it hasn't been easy."

Keisha crossed her arms over her chest and frowned. The organizers of the fair had specifically told her team that all candidates should refrain from making campaign speeches during the event, and here was Dupré using an open mic to make a stump speech. Keisha guessed the same rules didn't apply to the great Vincent Dupré.

"Why am I not surprised?" she murmured.

"Not surprised by what?" a baritone voice suddenly asked.

Keisha blinked, stunned speechless.

Will Blake gave her a wry smile. Like her, he had foregone his usual business attire today. He had traded it in for a gray T-shirt and blue jeans that showed off his lean, muscular frame. Paired with his work boots, Will looked almost rugged. All he needed now was a Stetson and he'd look like a black cowboy who had taken a break from toting bales of hay and herding cattle.

Keisha's eyes widened as her heart skipped a beat. *In a park filled with hundreds of people, why did I have to run into him today,* she silently lamented. She then took a deep breath and cleared her throat.

"I'm not surprised your candidate is flagrantly ignoring the rules that were given to us by the fair organizers," Keisha said with false calm. She crossed her arms over her chest, hoping to give no hint to the nervousness that lurked inside. "We were told there would be no political speeches."

Will's smile quickly disappeared. "Well, this isn't a political speech. Congressman Dupré is merely sharing his *eighteen*-year record with the audience." He shrugged. "When you've achieved so much, it's hard to be humble."

"I bet," Keisha muttered before turning on her heel.

"What? Not going to listen to the whole thing?" Will asked as he trailed behind her.

"No," she answered, picking up the pace. For some reason he was following her.

"You might want to," he said with a grin as he fell into step with her. "In fact you should send your speech-writer over. They might learn a thing or two."

Keisha glared at him.

"You know, you're a fast walker," he remarked as they strode past a cotton candy stand.

Keisha continued to walk swiftly, though keeping up her heart-racing pace was making her winded. "I don't know about . . . you, Will. But I have lots . . . to do today," she said between huffs of breath. "I didn't think strolling was appropriate."

Will stopped walking. "Are you sure you aren't just trying to avoid walking with me?" he called after her, stopping her in her tracks. "Maybe if you walk fast enough you could lose me?"

Keisha turned, tilted her head and smiled. "Will, why would I ever want to lose you?" she asked sarcastically.

He crossed his arms over his chest and took a deep breath. "I don't know, Keisha. You tell me. Or is that type of honesty beyond you *already*," he challenged. "You better watch out. There are lots of bad habits you can pick up in politics. Habitual lying is one of them."

"Don't talk to me about 'bad habits!' " she spat. "You've got no right to talk, especially when you've written the book on how to deceive and manipulate!"

"Well, it's about time!" he exclaimed with a smile. "Now we're having it out. Finally!" He then took several steps toward her, looming over her. Keisha glared up at him. "I was wondering why you've been acting like you have a stick up your . . ."

She silently dared him to finish the sentence, but he grinned instead.

"So tell me, Miss Reynolds, how did I 'deceive and manipulate' you?" he asked.

She gritted her teeth and pointed her finger up at him. "When we met, you didn't tell me you worked for Dupré!"

"So? You didn't tell me you worked for Parker," he said, shrugging.

"But you knew who I was! You were just trying to fool me and it backfired when Tanya showed up."

"Prove it," he dared. "Prove that I knew who you were."

Keisha opened her mouth then abruptly shut it. She balled her fists in frustration.

"You can't, can you?"

"I don't have to prove anything to you!" she yelled, drawing a few stares. "I know what I know!"

He chuckled. "You know what you know? That's your argument?" He shrugged again. "I'm sorry, Keisha, but if this is the best you can come up with, you're not going to last in politics very long. By that reasoning I could argue that you knew who I was and tried to deceive me. I've got absolutely no evidence to support that, but 'I know what I know.' Who could argue with logic like that?" he asked mockingly.

Her nostrils flared. Oh, she wanted to punch him! She wanted to punch him so bad! He was talking to her as if she were an idiot and, worse, she couldn't think of a way to come back at him.

"Now come on, Keisha. We both know why you're *really* angry," he said. His voice and face softened as he took another step closer to her. "And it has nothing to do with me deceiving you. You're frustrated . . . just like I am." He raised his hand to her face and lightly trailed his fingers along her cheek, sending tingles up her spine. "You feel the tension, too, don't you?" His eyelids and voice lowered. "You want me . . . and I want you."

Keisha's eyes widened. A rush of blood began to sing in her ears. The world around her seemed to disappear and all she could hear were the words Will was whispering to her.

"You don't have to be afraid. I won't bite. I swear," he said with a wicked smile as he cupped her face and began to lower his mouth to hers. "Unless . . . you want me to."

Will's lips brushed her own just as Keisha jerked back. Her eyes glinted with outrage. She wasn't sure what she found more offensive; how he seemed so assured that she was attracted to him, or the fact that he was so close to the truth. The pesky tingle that had started at her cheeks now radiated across her body.

"I bet it's hard to imagine that a woman wouldn't want you, isn't it?" Keisha spat before gathering the willpower to shove his hands away. "You know, it's good we're outside, Will. I doubt all your ego could fit into one room!"

He cocked an eyebrow. "I may have a big ego, but that doesn't mean I'm not right about this."

"You're delusional!"

It's just another one of his tricks, Keisha thought angrily. He wasn't really attracted to her. He didn't feel any "tension." He was just manipulating her, using her emotions to his advantage.

"No, I'm being honest with you, Keisha!" Will shouted back, drawing even *more* stares. "So be honest with me!"

"You know, Will, you were right before," she said as she nodded and gave an evil smile. "I don't want you to walk with me. I don't even want you to *talk* to me!" she spat. "In fact, I bet we'd be better off pretending we never met. Just forget my name, okay? Because I'd rather not be associated with a man like you."

"A man like me?" he asked in disbelief, pointing at his chest.

"Damn right, a man like you," she said, curling her lips. "I don't like what you stand for! You work for bigots and hypocrites and, quite frankly, I don't see how you can look at yourself in the mirror every morning."

"So that *is* the reason why you're fighting this?" he asked. "I thought you were smarter than that, Keisha."

She gritted her teeth. "I am smart! And I'm not 'fighting' anything," she lied.

"Once again, all of this is based on what you heard about me. It's all speculation, right?"

She pursed her lips. "You can call it speculation if you want, but I trust my sources."

"So by that token I should trust what my sources say about *you*?" he asked quietly, tilting his head.

Keisha paused. Her face fell. "What?"

He gave a sly smile. "Well, if what they say about *you* is true, quite frankly, I don't see how you can look at yourself in the mirror in the morning . . . ," he paused, ". . . knowing that you're having an affair with a married man."

Keisha blinked furiously. Her mouth fell open in shock. "An affair with a married man?" she exclaimed. "What *married man*? What are you talking about?"

His smile widened. "Oh, don't play innocent, Keisha. That cat's been out of the bag for a while now. Everyone knows about you and Parker," Will said casually as he shoved his hands into his pockets and slowly walked away.

"Me and . . . and . . . ," she sputtered. "Are you *serious*?" she shouted after him with disbelief.

"As serious as a heart attack," Will said with a cold laugh. "Did you think something like that would stay a secret forever?" he asked casually as he walked off, leaving her both angry and befuddled.

Keisha cringed. *Me and . . . Dr. Parker?*

CHAPTER 11

Will was nearing the end of his cardio workout. As he jogged to the crest of the hill, sweat ran down his brow and back. The thudding beat of the music from his mp3 player filled his ears, matching the sound of his heart. It was an exhausting routine, and he wanted to pump his fists in the air in triumph, like Rocky did when he reached the top of the Museum of Art's stone steps.

Not only had he finished four laps around his neighborhood in record time, but he had also had several good nights of sleep for the first time in months.

If he had known he would feel this good after putting Keisha Reynolds in her place, he would have done it sooner.

"Oh, yeah!" he shouted, throwing punches into the air. One of his elderly neighbors stared in bewilderment as she pruned a rose bush on her front lawn.

Will had needed to redeem himself that day at the St. Mary's County fair. He'd had to regain his pride somehow. Lusting after Keisha had been bad enough, but, once again, he had not walked away from her when he knew he should have. Instead he had followed her around like an annoying little brother and prodded at her just to get *some* reaction out of her.

When she lost her temper with him, he definitely should have taken the hint, but he still couldn't help himself. When he was around her, there was some inexplicable magnetic force that drew him to her. And he'd finally given in to that pull, that impulse to touch her. Hell, he had been a millimeter away from *kissing* her!

Will had been relieved to realize the attraction he felt between them the day they met hadn't disappeared. In fact, it was downright palpable. But Keisha had stubbornly denied that she felt anything for him in return. Worse, she had insulted both him and Dupré. What else could he have done but insult her back? Yes, he admitted, it had been a low blow to tell Keisha the rumor about her and Parker having an affair, especially when he knew for sure based on her reaction that it wasn't true. But she had pissed him off. Keisha had turned out to be a self-righteous, naïve, hot-tempered little . . .

"Bitch," Will said as he ran another block.

And she'd needed to be knocked down a peg or two . . . maybe even three. She was nothing like the alluring, demure creature he had met at the hotel in Greenbelt all those months ago. That woman had obviously been an illusion. Now that he knew the truth about Keisha, he no longer felt that she had a hold over him. He could finally move on and, with any luck, he would never have to speak to her again. The idea couldn't have made him happier.

As he neared his block, Will peeled off his T-shirt, which was soaked in sweat thanks to the blistering heat. He slowed down his pace and tugged off his earphones, placing his index and middle fingers to his throat, checking his pulse.

He slowly climbed his front steps. As he neared his front door, he heard his phone ringing. Will frowned and glanced down at his watch. It was only 6:15. Who was calling him this early in the morning?

"Will?" George said when he answered. "Sorry about calling you at the crack of dawn, but I wanted to know if you could get in a little bit early today. Tried catching you on your cell phone but you didn't answer."

Will leaned against his kitchen counter and frowned. "I was jogging and didn't have my phone with me. Why? What's up?"

George sighed. "The damn Parker campaign. We've had about five million conference calls about this debate and we still can't agree on just the basic terms. It took some wrangling, but Phil and I agreed that a face-to-face meeting is the only way we can resolve it at this point."

Will sighed. "A face-to-face?"

"Yeah, you and me, Phil and Keisha Reynolds, maybe a few more staffers. We thought we should all meet tonight to discuss this. We're supposed to work out the place today. Does that sound good to you? I want to go over a few things with you and Dupré first before we head over there, though."

Will clinched his teeth and closed his eyes. *Great*, he thought. Now he would have to see *and* talk to Keisha again, and a lot sooner than he had intended. "Can't wait," he muttered morosely.

CHAPTER 12

Keisha walked down the darkened corridor of the campaign headquarters, every now and then peering into doorways in search of Phil. She glanced at her watch and slowly shook her head. The meeting with the Dupré campaign was supposed to start in less than an hour. They would have to leave soon if they wanted to get there on time. She continued down the hallway, sighing when she saw that Phil's office was empty and both the lights and his computer were turned off. She loudly sucked her teeth.

"Where the hell is he?" she muttered. She perked up when she heard Phil's voice coming from the end of the corridor, from Dr. Parker's office.

"Phil?" Keisha called out. She quickly walked toward the shaft of light spilling from the doorway. The click of her heels was the loudest sound around her. "Are you ready to leave? We should get going if we're gonna—" and stopped in surprise.

"Oh." She stepped into the room and saw Phil standing on one side of a grand oak desk and Dr. Parker on the other.

Dr. Parker looked more than mildly irritated. Keisha frowned as she glanced at both men.

"I'm sorry for interrupting, guys," she said hesitantly. "Dr. Parker, I didn't know you were still here."

Dr. Parker glanced at her from behind his horn-rimmed glasses. "I'm not. I was driving home and realized I'd left a few things in my office." He held up a thick hardback book and a notepad. "I just popped back in to get them but got trapped into a one-hour conversation," he murmured sarcastically, nodding to Phil.

"A candidate's work is never done . . . at least not until Election Day," Phil muttered.

"No, my friend," Dr. Parker said as he began to walk around his desk, "that's when the real work begins."

"Sydney, I wouldn't talk about this now if it wasn't serious. Look, if we could just talk about this juvenile crime issue one more time," Phil pleaded as he followed Dr. Parker towards the door. "I'll let you go. I swear. I know the Dupré campaign will want to highlight it during the debate to prove that Dupré's harder on crime than we are, and I just think it's foolhardy for you to take the stance you're taking. It's not going to play well with the Southern Maryland crowd. Either I tell them tonight that we're avoiding the topic entirely during the debate or—"

"I change my opinion?" Parker said, exchanging a look with Keisha.

Phil sighed tiredly. "I prefer to call it 'reworking your stance.' "

You mean flip-flopping, Keisha thought. She gave Dr. Parker a knowing smile.

Phil could be relentless when he wanted to make a point. But he faced a noble adversary in Dr. Parker. Her professor couldn't be bullied into changing his opinion, particularly if someone told him it was an unpopular one.

"I don't care what you do, Phil," Dr. Parker said firmly. "But I'm not 'reworking my stance' on this."

Phil's face reddened. He pursed his lips. "I think that's a big mistake, Sydney. I really do."

"I appreciate that, but I'm not changing my position," Dr. Parker murmured as Keisha stepped aside to let him pass. She gave him a reassuring pat on the shoulder that made him smile.

"Now if you'll excuse me, you two," he continued. "I told my wife I'd be home for dinner on time tonight. She's making my favorite meal."

"Chicken and waffle special?" Keisha asked with a grin.

Dr. Parker smiled. "Of course. I'm a sucker for the old Southern favorites." He turned to Phil. "Good luck with the meeting tonight. I'm sure—"

"You can't budge on this one thing, Sydney? This *one* thing?" Phil suddenly burst out, widening his eyes as Parker paused. Keisha anxiously glanced at her watch.

"Despite the advice I've given you?" Phil continued. "You know, you hired me for a reason. I thought that was to help you get elected! We need a leg up in Southern Maryland, and so far they're painting you as a liberal who's loose on crime and big on taxes. And everything you're saying supports that!" Phil closed his eyes and pressed his fingers to his temples, as if overcome by a seismic headache. He took a deep breath. "Look," he began softly, "if you admit that the justice system in

Maryland should be a little, just a *little,* harder on juveniles that commit serious crimes, the voters will—"

"No, Phil."

"But we can—"

"I said no, Phil!" Dr. Parker boomed, making both
Phil and Keisha flinch. "The system shouldn't be harder
on juveniles because those kids deserve a second chance.
I would be a hypocrite if I said anything different. I got
my second chance and look where I am today! Why
shouldn't they?"

Keisha frowned and Phil stared at Dr. Parker in confusion. The room fell silent.

She had tried to keep quiet during their conversation.
She agreed with Dr. Parker, of course, but she was always
leery of choosing sides and taking any position against
Phil. The campaign manager had already made jealous
mutterings about how Dr. Parker and his prized, former
pupil were always in lockstep together. She didn't want to
make him feel any further like an outsider.

But Keisha couldn't keep silent this time. What Dr.
Parker had just said definitely required an explanation.

"What do you mean? What second chance?" she
asked.

The older man sighed gravely as he shoved his books
into the crook of his arm. His gaze fell to the office floor
before returning to Keisha, who stared at him worriedly.
"It happened a long, long time ago, Keisha," Dr. Parker
said tiredly.

Phil narrowed his eyes. "What happened a long time
ago?"

Dr. Parker took a deep breath and closed his eyes. When he opened them again, he looked as if he were debating the words he was about to say. "I was a very different person then, a very angry, *confused* young man," he began. "I was poor and needed money and unfortunately . . . I took the shortest, easiest route to get it." He cleared his throat. "That route . . . also happened to be illegal."

"Illegal?" Phil suddenly squeaked. "What do you mean *illegal?* What the hell did you do, Sydney?"

Keisha turned to Phil with exasperation, silently pleading with him to shut up so Dr. Parker could finish his story. But Phil wasn't looking at her. His eyes were bulging and he seemed on the verge of passing out or throwing up. She wasn't sure which. His skin had turned from an angry shade of red to a sickly shade of white. He visibly gulped for air as he clutched the back of a chair.

"When I was fifteen, I . . . ," Dr. Parker paused, ". . . I stole a few cars. Broke into a few houses and stole things. I did it for stupid reasons, for the thrill and because a bunch of thugs in my neighborhood gave me cash if I brought that junk to them. I got pretty good at it, but one night I got cocky and . . ." He closed his eyes. ". . . And the police caught me. It landed me two years in juvenile hall." He slowly shook his head. "That was by far the worst moment in my life, but it scared me straight. I had a lot of time for self-reflection and I came out of there a man, not a dumb kid anymore." He sighed. "I know if I could change, anyone can change. They just need a *chance*. That's why I can't say that the justice system should be harder on juveniles. I couldn't say that and not feel like the biggest hypocrite that ever walked the earth. "

Keisha's eyes widened at his confession while Phil began to mutter, "Oh, Christ! *Jesus Christ!*" as he fell into one of the chairs opposite Dr. Parker's desk.

She couldn't believe it. *Dr. Parker had served time in jail,* she thought with amazement. Looking at the reserved, almost saintly man before her, such an idea seemed ludicrous.

"Believe me, I'm not proud of what I did," Dr. Parker murmured. "Not even my wife knows about this."

"Who cares if your wife knows about it?" Phil exclaimed. "*I* should have known about it!" He jumped from his chair and pointed at his chest. "Why am I just now hearing about this?"

Dr. Parker opened his mouth but then abruptly closed it. His nostrils flared as he looked at the floor with embarrassment.

"Do you honestly expect to win an election with a criminal record, Sydney?" Phil asked. "The press will rip you apart if they find out! They'll chew you up and spit you out!"

Keisha frowned and stood between the two men. "Wait a minute, Phil," she said, holding up her hands as she came to Dr. Parker's defense. "All this happened when he was *fifteen years old!* He was a juvenile! Practically still a baby, in my book. And when you're that young those records are sealed by the courts, aren't they?" she said.

"Besides, it happened almost forty years ago! No one can hold him to something he did when he was a kid! He said he was sorry and that he regrets it. What more can people ask of him?"

"He said he was sorry!" Phil yelled with disbelief. He glared heavenward. "*Are you kidding me?* You both are so naïve! This isn't some mayoral election in a small college town like it was last time. You're running for Congress, dammit! And the closer we get to the election and the closer we get in the polls to Dupré, the dirtier this race is gonna get. And, with this little bombshell, you've just made their job a lot easier! This is a game changer!" he shouted before pushing his way past Dr. Parker and Keisha and storming out of the office.

"Phil. Phil!" Keisha shouted after him.

He shook his head as he stomped down the darkened corridor. "The campaign's over! We lost! We're done!" he yelled over his shoulder. Seconds later, the front door to the headquarters slammed behind him.

Keisha turned to Dr. Parker. Her shoulders slumped.

The older man looked completely stricken. He was almost shaking. For the first time in the years that she'd known him, Dr. Parker looked scared. Keisha instantly reached out to touch his shoulder and reassure him.

"Don't worry, Dr. Parker. Phil's just . . . just . . . ," she halted, ". . . upset because he was caught off guard. It's really not that big of a deal." She forced a smile. "Really, sir."

"Isn't it?" Dr. Parker asked softly, his gaze wavering. "Phil doesn't seem to agree. He said I've lost this for us."

"No, you haven't!" Keisha said angrily. She closed her eyes and took a deep breath. She opened her eyes again and said more calmly, "Phil is just worried. It's his job to be cautious, sir."

Actually, she had been pretty appalled by Phil's reaction. It was his job to encourage Dr. Parker, not to have a temper tantrum and act like the campaign had entered the apocalypse.

"Phil just tries to consider the worst-case scenario in every situation." She paused. "That's what you hired him for, right?"

When he didn't respond, Keisha looked him firmly in the eyes. "I can assure you, Dr. Parker," she said, mustering as much authority in her voice as she could, "that this is not a problem. Phil and I will take care of it. Right now, we're the only three people who know about this, right?"

Dr. Parker slowly nodded his head. "Right," he said quietly.

"So there's nothing to worry about," she declared. "And if by some crazy, far-out chance someone does find out . . . we'll handle it, okay? We'll make up a contingency plan for this. Trust me, we've got it covered, sir. We've come too far to give up now."

It felt like an eternity before Dr. Parker finally gave a half-hearted smile and nodded his graying head. "Okay, I'll let you handle it."

"Good." Keisha grinned. Then she glanced at her watch. "Wow, we're running behind. Look, I've got to go, but I want you to head home, not worry at all about this, and enjoy your chicken and waffles, all right?"

Dr. Parker nodded. "Will do."

"Bye," Keisha said as she scuttled toward the door, hoping that Phil hadn't driven off in a huff and left her behind.

CHAPTER 13

So much for me worrying about being late, Keisha thought. She stood near the catering table with Jason, Phil's assistant, at her side. They had rushed to get to the meeting at the community center, but, judging from how empty the room looked, it seemed that most of the Dupré campaign wasn't there yet. Eight or so of Parker's staffers were milling about, though, glancing at their watches or helplessly shrugging their shoulders.

"So is this thing still on or what?" Jason asked impatiently, adjusting his tie.

"I guess it's still on," Keisha muttered. "No one's told me any differently."

Keisha slowly glanced around the room. Her eyes settled on Phil, who was busily scanning his BlackBerry. At least he had calmed down a little.

Keisha had found him in the headquarters parking lot twenty minutes earlier with his head resting on the steering wheel. It had taken a few minutes to "talk him off of the ledge." He'd said the campaign was doomed, that Parker never trusted him. He had threatened to quit. It had taken some pleading and arguing, but Keisha had finally convinced him that the campaign was not doomed and that they could not win without his help.

Her words had appeased him enough to get him to agree to come to the meeting. Hopefully, now that he had calmed down, he would no longer consider leaving the campaign. If he did that at this late date, it would make Dr. Parker look bad and the D.C. rumor mill would start whispering about the possible reasons why Phil left. The campaign didn't need that drama.

"You want one?"

Keisha blinked as she was suddenly pulled from her thoughts. She glanced down at the bottle of water Jason was offering to her and she thanked him. Taking a sip, she glanced around the room again, hoping that the meeting would start soon. Maybe she could still catch one of the late night shows on television if they got out by 10 o'clock.

"Reggie showed up at my place yesterday," Jason suddenly blurted out before popping a cube of Swiss cheese into his mouth.

Keisha braced herself. It looked like she was going to hear the latest installment of *The Gay and the Restless,* the "on again, off again" relationship of Jason and his boyfriend, Reggie, an ad executive who was still firmly in the closet. Keisha and Jason had been talking about it for months. She figured Jason thought it was cheaper to talk to her than a therapist.

She sighed. "You didn't let him spend the night, did you, Jay?"

Jason's pale face reddened as he gave a bashful nod.

"Jason," she whispered, "I thought you said you wouldn't have anything to do with him anymore. Remember how he hurt you the last time."

"I know. I know," he muttered. "But I was in a dry spell. It's been two months since the last time he came over and I've been so busy that I haven't met any other guys and well . . ." He shrugged again. "Look, I'm not proud of it. You . . . you just don't understand!"

"Trust me. I understand," Keisha said glumly. She reached for another hors d'oeuvre. *If you think two months is a long dry spell, imagine twelve years,* she thought.

Her eyes suddenly darted to the conference room doorway as Dupré and his campaign manager, George, walked in. They were conversing quietly. Seconds later, Will entered. The instant Keisha saw him, her heart skipped a beat. She almost forgot the pigs in a blanket hors d'oeuvre that hovered near her mouth.

The man who had haunted her dreams for months had materialized. Though she kept trying to deny it, she knew she still felt an instinctive attraction to the handsome politico. Tonight he practically oozed smoothness and self-confidence in his crisp black suit and red tie while everyone else stood about tiredly in business clothes wrinkled from the workday. She watched as he did an almost jaguar-like pace around the room, pausing only to talk to one or two of Dupré's other staffers. Finally, his gaze settled on her. To her frustration, her legs went wobbly and her heart raced. Keisha bit her lower lip as he strode toward her. After the county fair, she had resolved to never speak to him again. He had tried to seduce her and then had the gall to accuse her of sleeping with Dr. Parker.

You hate him, she told herself as he drew closer. *Remember? You hate him. You hate him. You* hate *him!*

"Hey," he said with an irresistible, dimpled smile.

She gave a hesitant grin and, despite her earlier declarations of hatred, started to return his greeting.

"Hey, did you just get in?" a female voice asked over her shoulder.

Keisha frowned and turned to find Gretchen, Dupré's press secretary, loudly sucking barbeque sauce from her fingertips before taking another nibble from a chicken wing.

"Yeah. Traffic was pretty bad on the way up," he muttered as he walked around Keisha, bumping her shoulder as he did so. He seemed to look right through her as he reached for a nearby cocktail napkin.

Can I get an 'excuse me'? Keisha thought with exasperation.

"And this place is in the middle of nowhere," Will continued. "I had a hard time finding it even with my dashboard navigation system."

"I know what you mean," the redhead said with a nod. "I got lost *twice.*"

"So what kind of spread do we have here?" Will frowned at a tray of Swedish meatballs.

"*We* didn't pick the caterer," Gretchen said derisively.

What were you expecting? Wolfgang Puck? Keisha thought sarcastically.

"I guess it'll do for tonight," Gretchen continued. "I hope they give out complimentary antacids with food like this, though."

Keisha blinked as she watched the two continue their conversation. Had she become invisible in the past five minutes? Will was completely ignoring her, and, despite her desire not to care, it bothered her that he was acting as if she wasn't even there.

And who does this chick think she is? Keisha frowned, suddenly hit by a pang of jealousy. Will and Gretchen were acting rather chummy, chuckling and whispering to one another. Keisha watched as Gretchen tossed her red locks over her shoulder and grinned adoringly up at Will. He smiled in return. Keisha rolled her eyes when the redhead giggled.

"I think I'm going to puke," Keisha muttered under her breath. She guessed Tanya was right after all. Will did have a particular taste in women: all cream, no coffee.

"Are you all right?" Jason asked with a concerned frown.

Keisha turned to him and forced a smile. "I'm fine." She popped her hors d' oeuvre into her mouth and wiped the grease from her hands with a cocktail napkin. "It's just getting a little crowded in here."

Jason nodded his blond head. "Yeah, we probably could have used a bigger room, but I think Phil thought a space like this would lend itself to a sense of intimacy. You know, to make the negotiations easier."

"Negotiations," Keisha murmured with a sigh. "It sucks that we even have to use that word. Why do we have to do this at all? All this stuff should have been worked out two months ago."

Jason leaned toward her. "It could turn out to be a tight race," he whispered. "Dupré knows that. I'm sure his people," Jason said, glancing toward Will and Gretchen at the other end of the food table, "know that, too. They want to make sure this debate works in their favor. That's why they're against the town hall format. It's not to Dupré's advantage to have random questions from the audience."

Keisha slowly nodded. She guessed she shouldn't be surprised. The longer the campaign progressed, the more she learned about political maneuvering: how one side always tried to outdo the other in gaining some strategically advantageous position. It could get downright ridiculous sometimes. Who got the better venue? Who got more speech time? Who was seated with the right people at a banquet? It could all be so tiresome.

"Will. Gretchen," Dupré said with a smile, suddenly snapping Keisha out of her daze. He motioned for the two of them to come toward him.

Keisha felt herself being nudged aside again and it took all her willpower not to turn and snap at Will and tell him to learn some damn manners. She watched as he and Gretchen walked around her toward Dupré and George. Phil even made his way over to the group and shook each of their hands.

"Oh, God, it looks like they're starting introductions," Jason said before he took his last gulp from his water bottle. "Do I have anything in my teeth?" he asked, turning to her with bared teeth.

Keisha laughed with bemusement. "Your teeth are fine, Jay."

"Okay, good." He shrugged. "Well, I guess we should head over there now."

"Fine, if we have to," she replied. She tossed her paper napkin into a nearby trashcan and took a deep breath, hoping to calm her nerves as they slowly crossed the room.

"Oh, I don't plan to stay!" Dupré loudly proclaimed. "I just wanted to come in and introduce myself to everyone and thank you for doing this. I'm sure both sides will be able to reach an agreement. I have faith in all of you," he said, giving his usual amiable grin. He suddenly turned to Keisha and Jason. "And more staffers! Dr. Parker seems to have an ever-expanding payroll. His fundraising must be better than I thought."

Keisha pursed her lips, ignoring the obvious sideswipe at Dr. Parker.

"Dupré, let me introduce you to Phil Levin's executive assistant, Jason Wheeler," Will said. "He and I met a few months ago."

Jason smiled in surprise and shook Dupré's hand. "We did, but only briefly in a room of nearly a hundred people." Jason chuckled, blushing slightly. "I'm surprised you remember my name!"

Was he actually giggling? *Oh, good God*, she thought. It seemed that no one was immune to Will's charms.

"And this is . . . is . . . ." Will turned to Keisha and paused. "I'm so sorry but . . . your name escapes me," he said, tilting his head and giving her a seemingly innocent smile.

Keisha's own smile tightened. He knew damn well what her name was. She supposed this was his payback for when she had told him at the county fair to forget who she was. He obviously was finding it very amusing to take her words literally.

Keisha took a deep breath, ignored him, and focused all her attention on Congressman Dupré. "Keisha Reynolds, sir," she said as she extended her hand. "I'm Parker's deputy campaign manager. We've spoken a few times by conference call. It's pleasure to meet you."

"Ah, Keisha, good to finally meet you in person," Dupré said as he shook her hand and smiled politely. She had expected him to move on to the next person waiting to be introduced, but Dupré's grip on her hand suddenly tightened, making Keisha wince in pain.

Confused by the unexpected change, she followed the path of his gaze, which currently led to her breasts. Keisha fought the urge to curl her lips in disgust and to roll her eyes. *So much for him being a family man,* she thought sarcastically. *What a pervert!*

"Keisha . . . Reynolds," he repeated, his eyebrows furrowing.

Keisha slowly nodded her head, wondering when he was going to finally let go of her hand. "Yes, that's right. Keisha Reynolds."

"That locket, Keisha," he said slowly. "It's a very unique antique." His eyes suddenly flashed to her face. "Where did you happen to get it?"

She frowned. Could she have her hand back? "My mother gave to it to me. It's an old birthday gift."

"Your *mother*?" He paused for a long time, then took a deep breath and licked his lips again. "And who . . . who gave it to her?"

Keisha shrugged. "I don't know. I guess she bought it somewhere, maybe a yard sale. I've never asked."

"Is there . . . is there a...anything inside of it?"

He finally let go of her hand then. Keisha flexed her now-sore fingers and pursed her lips, wondering why Dupré was acting so strangely. Even Will frowned slightly, as if he were wondering where this conversation was leading. Keisha reached down and opened the locket's clasp. "Nope," she said as she held it up to Dupré. "It's totally empty."

Like a thunderstorm departing, Dupré's intense expression finally softened. He nodded his head. "Th-thank you for showing it to me," he said quietly. "It's . . . very lovely."

"Thank you for saying so," she muttered.

"It was . . . nice meeting you, Keisha."

She nodded politely, still feeling ill at ease as he gazed at her for several seconds longer, studying her features before finally turning away to face the next person waiting to shake his hand. Keisha sighed, slowly shook her head, and looked up at Will. She guessed she wasn't invisible after all. He was staring at her openly now and causing the same pesky reaction she always felt whenever he fixed those dark eyes on her. Her pulse instantly quickened and she could feel the hairs on the back of her neck standing on end. Annoyed, Keisha didn't fight the urge to roll her eyes this time. Then she abruptly turned and switched to the table in the center of the room.

"All right, everyone grab a chair. Grab a chair," Phil said. "If you haven't introduced yourselves already to the person sitting next you, now would probably be a good time to do it before we start."

Keisha slowly dragged one of the aluminum fold-up chairs from beneath the plywood table. She frowned. It was a long table, but there still wasn't enough space for Dupré's campaign to sit on one side and Parker's campaign to sit on the other. *Someone's going to have to get really cozy with the enemy,* she thought with a smirk as she sat down. Keisha pulled out a legal pad and pen and watched as a few other people did the same. She began to scan a few emails on her BlackBerry but looked up when she heard the loud squeak of metal scraping over linoleum tile. She glared at Will as he removed his suit jacket and plopped down beside her.

He cracked open a canned soda and made himself comfortable, stretching his legs and placing his laptop on the table, nudging her pad aside as he did so. "Pardon me," he muttered. After several seconds he turned to her, meeting her glare with his own.

"Yes?" he challenged.

"Why aren't you . . ." . . . *sitting with Gretchen,* she wanted to ask. But she stopped herself. Keisha gritted her teeth, deciding to ignore him. She had no desire to repeat their confrontation at the county fair here, in front of all of these people. Even if he decided to act juvenile, she wasn't going to be baited. He was just trying to get into her head and mess with her mind. She knew his game plan.

Keisha loudly cleared her throat and crossed her legs, then returned her attention to her notes. The more she knew about Will Blake, the more she felt justified in her behavior toward him.

"Should we begin?" Phil asked. He glanced around the table as the loud talking died down to a soft murmur. "Okay, first, I think we should discuss the format of this debate since that seems to be the biggest issue of contention."

"I wouldn't say it was a matter of contention, Phil," George insisted, leaning back in his chair. "I think we can have a disagreement without it being described as 'contentious.' "

Phil's face reddened noticeably. "Fine," he said tightly. "Then let's address our biggest *non*-contentious disagreement. Our campaign was under the impression that this was going to be an open town hall format with questions submitted from the audience, but . . ."

Keisha instantly lost her concentration as she felt the heavy weight of Will's leg fall against her left thigh. She looked over at him only to find that he was sitting casually with his legs akimbo as he seemed to focus all his attention on his laptop screen. Will was taking up an enormous amount of space beneath the table and seemed completely oblivious to that fact.

"Do you mind?" she whispered.

Will cocked an eyebrow and looked up at her. "Do I mind what?" he whispered in return.

"Your leg," she said as she pointed down at his knee. "Do you mind moving it over?"

She watched as he shifted his leg away from her by a few centimeters. Keisha sighed and slowly shook her head. She shifted slightly to her right to increase the distance between them and returned to her notes, trying to focus again on what Phil and George were saying. Five minutes later, she could feel Will's leg again. Keisha grumbled and shifted even more, turning slightly sideways in her chair. It was an uncomfortable angle, but she didn't want Will touching her. Jason gave her a worried glance. He was sitting to her right and she was nearly in his lap.

I'm not going to let Will piss me off, she thought. *I'm a grown woman who knows how to ignore this childish—*

When Keisha felt Will's leg the third time, she almost lost it.

"Will!" Keisha whispered shrilly.

He glanced at her. "What?"

"Stop, please," she mouthed, making him frown.

"Huh?"

"Please stop," she mouthed again.

"What? I can't hear you."

"I said, 'Stop!' " she shouted.

"Yes, Keisha?" Phil asked, frowning slightly. Everyone at the table turned to look at her. "Did you want to say something?"

Keisha's eyes widened and her mouth fell open as Will quietly snickered beside her. "Uh . . . ummm....I . . . uh," she uttered, feeling her face redden as she tried desperately to think of something to say. She had been so preoccupied with Will that she had no idea what they had been talking about. "I . . . uh . . . just wanted you to stop . . . a-a-and repeat what you said," she muttered before turning to Will, who was presently grinning from ear to ear. "I was a little distracted and didn't catch what you guys were saying. Sorry."

"I guess when you said holler if you don't understand something, some of us took it more literally than others, huh, Phil?" George said with a chuckle. A few people at the table joined him and started laughing.

Keisha slumped down in her chair, now thoroughly embarrassed. She kept her eyes focused on her notepad from that point on, refusing to look up.

CHAPTER 14

"I guess we've made a little progress," Phil mumbled two hours into the meeting. "If everyone wants to stretch their legs, now would be the time to do it. Smokers, you can go take your puffs."

A few of the campaign staffers sighed in relief, immediately leaping up from the table to run to the restrooms down the hall or to head outside to smoke. Keisha was the only one left in the room by the time she decided to wander into the hallway.

Keisha slowly walked down the corridor of the almost deserted community center, feeling downtrodden. *Why do you let that man get to you? He knows how to press your buttons and you fall for it every time,* she thought as she glanced through the windows of vacant rooms.

Keisha pushed on one of the double doors at the end of the hallway and cautiously peered inside. Thankfully, the gymnasium was dark and empty. She yawned loudly and headed to one of the bleacher stands. Most were pushed against the wall but a few near the basketball hoops were not. She climbed a few orange steps and plopped down. Keisha kicked off her heels and flexed her toes. She yawned again.

Maybe that's why he gets to me, she thought as she shrugged out of her suit jacket. She then stretched, lay on her back, rested her head on her balled-up jacket, and gazed up at the gymnasium ceiling. Keisha wrapped her hand around her locket, closed her eyes, and sighed. *I'm always exhausted. I'm always irritable. That's what happens when you get only four hours of sleep a night.*

And what little sleep Keisha did get was filled with tormenting dreams. If her dreams weren't about the election, then they were about Will. "Damn him," she muttered. She just needed some peace from her thoughts of him. *Why can't I get him out of my mind?*

"No, that won't work for end of this week, Rob," she heard Will's voice boom. The gym door loudly slammed behind him. "You said you'd have it done by tomorrow. Tomorrow is what I'm expecting from you."

Keisha's eyes instantly popped open. She cursed under her breath as Will drew nearer.

"I understand things happen, but things happen on my end, too. That doesn't change our obligations," Will said as Keisha scrambled to rise from the bench. "So you'll get it done then?" He paused as Keisha's shadowy figure came into view. "That's good to hear. Look, Rob, let me call you back . . . All right . . . Yeah . . . Okay . . . Bye."

He slowly smiled as he returned his BlackBerry to his jacket pocket. "Did I disturb your nap, Sleeping Beauty?" he called into the darkened gymnasium.

She could hear that annoying laughter in his voice again. Keisha shoved her arms back into her jacket sleeves, refusing to answer him. She reached down to retrieve her shoes.

"Hey, don't let me stop you," he said as he slowly walked over to her. "It's going to be a long night. You might want to catch a few minutes of shut-eye before you head back."

"I wasn't sleeping," Keisha muttered as she finally found her right shoe, stepped into it, and rose to her feet. "I was just leaving. You can have the gym all to yourself."

She quickly walked down the bleachers and around him, adjusting her collar as she did so. She refused to meet his gaze even though he was staring at her again.

"Why leave? It's a big space," Will exclaimed, spreading out his arms. "I'm sure I won't *offend* you by accidentally bumping into you in here."

That stopped her in her tracks. Keisha turned to face him. "*Accidentally* bumping me? You know damn well what you did in there wasn't accidental."

"No, it was," he argued, raising his eyebrows. "It was an accident and you're being petty, as usual," he said, provoking her even more, "overreacted. Though I wonder if you would have reacted the same way to your friend Jason?"

Keisha frowned. "What? What does Jason have to do with this?"

He tilted his head and shrugged. "You two seem rather . . . friendly. That's all. I wasn't sure if I was interrupting anything by sitting near you two."

Friendly? She and Jason? Will was talking about the same Jason that she had counseled an hour ago about the tumultuous relationship with his ex-boyfriend? He was talking about *that* Jason, right?

Keisha chuckled. "Well," she said, deciding to play along, "you know me. I like to multi-task. While I'm having an affair with my fifty-two-year-old boss I thought keeping a younger man on the side would be a good idea, too. You know, to spice things up a bit," she said, giving an exaggerated wink. "Jason seemed like a good choice, considering that we're on the same campaign and all. We meet up in the copy room twice a week. Catch a few quick minutes on the copier. The whole arrangement works well. I'm on my feet twelve hours a day and on my back eight hours," she said with a cold smile. "I barely have time to sleep."

"I admire your energy level," Will muttered derisively.

Keisha crossed her arms over her chest. "You know, I'm surprised you noticed Jason and me together, Will, considering how chummy you were with Gretchen. Have you two shared a few hours in the copy room yourselves?"

At that, Will gave a barely discernable flinch. His nostrils flared. She could see the look of guilt all over his face.

God, I was right, Keisha thought with disgust. *He is sleeping with her! Typical! Just typical!* She angrily turned on her heel and strode to the door.

"Gretchen and I aren't together, Keisha," he called after her.

"That's not what your eyes said," she barked over her shoulder.

"We are not together. Not anymore. And even if we were, what do you care? You said before you're not attracted to me. Besides, you and Jason—"

"Jason and I have nothing, Will!" Keisha shouted, turning to face him. "Jason and I have nothing, like Parker and I have nothing!" She took a deep breath, well aware if she continued to yell at him, someone in the hallway was bound to hear. Keisha clenched her fists and quickly walked over to Will. She pointed up at him indignantly.

"One week you accuse me of having an affair with Parker and the next week you say that I'm 'friendly' with Jason. For some reason it's impossible for you believe I can have platonic, professional relationships with men around me, though I'm not sure why. Dr. Parker is a happily married man and Jason is gay!"

"*Gay?* Jason's gay?" Will frowned. "I didn't know that."

She sucked her teeth. "He doesn't wear a damn sign! And I don't carry a 'Not the Campaign Ho' sign, either, but maybe I should!"

She watched as he took a deep breath. "I'm sorry. I didn't mean to insult you. I just—"

"How could I not be insulted?" she almost shouted in disbelief.

"Look, I was only trying to bring you down a few notches. That's all. It's obvious that we both keep misunderstanding each other, Keisha. I wasn't trying to—"

"*Excuse me?* 'Bring me down a few notches'?" she squeaked. "Why, Will? You get a kick out of embarrassing me? Screwing with my head?" She put her hands on her hips. "Look, there are plenty of other staffers in there for you to target your bionic mind-meld on. So why do you keep picking on me, huh? You see me as an easy target? Is that it?"

He slowly shook his head. "No, Keisha, I—"

"I'm young and inexperienced. Why not, right?" she barked, cutting him off. "I obviously must be stupid! It's impossible for me to know what the hell I'm doing! Is that what you think?"

He sighed. "I never said—"

"Well, let me tell you something, Will Blake," she said, pointing a finger into his chest. "I'm not dumb! Nor am I as much of a pushover as you think I am, okay? If you shove me into a corner, I'll fight my way out of it!" she yelled. "So don't think that—"

Her words were abruptly cut off as he lowered his mouth to hers.

Keisha was suddenly taken aback, not only by the feel of Will's warm mouth against her own, but the intensity of the kiss. *What the hell,* her panicked mind suddenly exclaimed as he wrapped his arms around her, locking her against his chest. This time she couldn't shove him away. Keisha fought to regain her bearings but the world around her seemed to swirl and dip as his lips parted and something inside her urged her to do the same.

She obeyed that urge and opened her mouth, suddenly feeling his warm tongue inside it. Keisha welcomed the sensation and met his tongue with her own. As he loosened his hold, she wrapped both arms around his neck. Her heart pounded wildly and they both tilted their heads at a better angle to deepen their hungry kiss. Keisha could feel her feet leaving the ground. *Am I floating?* No, Will had hoisted her higher, pressing her harder against him so she couldn't let go even if she tried.

Suddenly, Keisha wished that they were no longer in a gym. Suddenly, she wished that they were no longer wearing clothes. It wasn't enough to feel his warm fingers kneading against the back of her shirt or cupping her behind. She wanted them on her skin, on her breasts, and running along the inside of her thighs. *Oh, God,* this *is what I've been dreaming about for months,* she thought as their tongues danced. Tasting him. Inhaling his scent. She was being overwhelmed with so many sensations that she almost felt high.

And just as unexpectedly as the spell began, it ended. Will abruptly pulled his mouth away from her, almost making her whimper. He lowered her to the floor, stepped back, and took a long, steadying breath. She stared up at him drunkenly, pushing hair out of her face. She watched as he cleared his throat and adjusted his tie.

"We should get back," he said flatly. He walked around her and headed toward the gym door.

Keisha blinked in shock. *Get back? What the hell just happened?*

If it wasn't for the fact that her lips were now swollen and felt almost scorched, she would have sworn that the kiss was all in her imagination.

"Are you coming?" he asked as he held the door open for her.

Keisha frowned. *Am I coming or going?* She walked over to him and the gymnasium door. *I don't know.*

She angrily stalked out of the gym and into the corridor, refusing to meet his gaze, feeling duped again.

After all these years, you'd think I would have learned, she thought.

CHAPTER 15

The auditorium in Towson University crackled with an unshakeable sense of electricity as the two men stepped up to their respective podiums. The chatter of the audience quickly died down to a whisper as the crowd waited in anticipation. The auditorium lights dimmed and the stage lights came up, revealing a blue back screen and a series of American flags.

The mood two floors above in a classroom that had been converted into a makeshift greenroom was just as tense as the seconds to air were counted off. Will took a deep breath, leaned forward in his padded chair, and adjusted his tie and then his collar. He checked his watch, checked his BlackBerry, and, finally, to stop fidgeting, he clasped his hands in front of him. He watched as the moderator began the introductions for that evening's debate.

After agreeing on the format of the debate, the campaign staff had been prepping Congressman Dupré for the past two and half weeks. They had tried to throw him every curve ball imaginable, coming up with any possible question that could come from the audience. But Dupré had not minded the constant practice and endless drilling. He had given it his all. He knew what was at stake.

Will clinched his fists as Parker was called on first to answer the moderator's question. He watched as Parker adjusted his glasses and cleared his throat.

"First, I would like to say thank you," Parker began, "to Congressman Dupré for agreeing to tonight's debate. It is an honor to spar with you, and I hope that tonight will prove to be a meaningful exchange. Secondly, I would like to thank Towson University for sponsoring this event . . ."

Will wondered how many people Parker planned to thank before actually answering the question.

"Just get to the question already!" someone shouted in the greenroom.

Will couldn't agree more.

Everyone knew that Dupré had to do well tonight. For the first time in a long time, he was losing ground in the polls to an opponent. Somehow, Parker had pulled ahead. The voters were responding to Parker, and, subsequently, tonight's debate had given a sense of urgency to Dupré. He knew that he had to use this platform to sell himself to his constituents, remind them of all he had done as their congressman, and why he should be reelected. He'd also have to point out Parker's faults.

Will now thought back to a conversation he had with Dupré an hour earlier.

"I've had enough of this crap," Dupré muttered as he and Will rode alone in the back seat of a Lincoln Town Car on the way to the auditorium. Dupré had just finished reading the latest glowing editorial about Parker in one of the local papers and tossed the broadsheet aside in disgust. "I've got to take him down, Will. No more playing around."

Will slowly nodded his head in agreement.

"When I leave Congress, I want to leave on my terms," Dupré said angrily, pointing at his chest. His green eyes seemed almost glacial. "I want to leave when *I* say I've had enough. Not because I've been kicked out by the Nutty Professor!"

Will didn't say anything in response. He didn't have the heart to tell Dupré that a decision like that wasn't always left up to the candidate. Sometimes in life people get kicked out of the party before they realize the party is over.

Dupré groaned as he ran his hands over his face. "Things don't look too good, Will," Dupré admitted, his voice faltering as he slouched back against the seat. "I know they don't. But I can pull it together. I know I can. I've gone through worse challenges in my life and I have always, *always* pulled it out in the end. It just means buckling down, working harder. This election just . . ." He sighed. "It just isn't going to be a coast to victory." He turned to look at Will, fixing him with a penetrating gaze. "Can I count on you, son? If the terrain gets rougher, you'll stick around, won't you?"

Will frowned. He sat in disbelief for several seconds. "Of course I will, Vincent," he answered adamantly. "Why would you ask me a question like that?"

Dupré sighed again. "Politics can be a tricky game, Will," he said softly, returning his gaze to the window. "You think you know who your friends are. You think you know loyalty, but every now and then . . . every now and then people surprise you." He quickly shook his head. "I wasn't trying to insult you, son. I just wanted to make sure . . . that . . . that I can count on you."

Will nodded his head. "I can promise you that there won't be any surprises from me, Vincent. I swear."

∽◌∾

Will now watched Dupré on the television screen. The older man looked confident and calm, not giving any hint of the desperation that lurked inside him. Dupré cleared his throat and began to speak. Will couldn't help critiquing his boss.

He should have paused there, Will thought as Dupré gave his rapid-fire answer. *He looks angry now, not authoritative.*

Will frowned. *Take a deep breath, Vincent. Take a deep breath and slow down.*

Suddenly, Will found himself needing to take a deep breath.

"Anyone want any water? I'm getting some water," he said, suddenly leaping out of his chair and heading toward the green room door. He drew only a few curious gazes from the rest of the staff before they returned their attention to the television screen.

Will sighed as he walked down the corridor toward one of the floor's convenience machines. He reached into his pocket and managed to find a few quarters and dimes. He shook the coins listlessly, wondering if Dupré would indeed make a comeback tonight.

There's no reason for him not to, Will thought. *There's no reason why he can't.*

But as Will told himself this, he felt more and more as if he were trying to ward off doubt. He had always imagined Dupré would end up like the age-old Senator Robert Byrd, only leaving office when he was carried out. But something had gone wrong this year for Dupré. Something was different, and success did not seem as certain as it had been five election cycles ago. It did not seem certain at all.

Will rounded the corner and abruptly stopped in his tracks. His stomach clinched.

Keisha loudly banged her open palm against the glass face of the snack machine. He watched as she pressed several plastic buttons before throwing back her head, sending a lock of hair flying from her carefully constructed chignon.

Will knew the Parker campaign had one of the other classrooms on this floor and should have expected to run into her at some point. Just looking at her still tied him in knots.

Dupré wasn't the only one who had been knocked off his game this election season. Something had changed this year for Will, too, and that something was named Keisha Reynolds.

"Come on," she exclaimed. She took off her snug suit jacket and tossed it over the top of the vending machine, then knelt on the floor and shoved her hand through the flip door. He watched as she closed her eyes and bit on her lower lip in concentration, as she felt her way inside.

Kissing her had been one of the biggest mistakes Will had ever made and he had wanted to kick himself the minute after he had done it. The kiss had been impulsive, an itch he had yearned to scratch for *so* long. But kissing her had only made things worse for him. Now the yearning for her was stronger than before, almost unbearable.

He wasn't in love with Keisha. He couldn't be. He barely *knew* her, and yet something about her still tugged at him. *Lust*, he thought cynically. *Old-fashioned lust, and you can't give in to it.*

"Need some change?" he blurted ineptly.

Her eyes opened and narrowed when her gaze settled on him. She quickly pulled her arm from the flip door and slowly rose to her feet. She didn't look embarrassed that he had caught her trying to pilfer from the vending machine. Instead, she gave him a look that could have frozen boiling water.

"No thanks," she said icily, wiping the dust off the front of her skirt and then retrieving her jacket. "It's a candy bar I didn't need anyway." She tossed her suit jacket over her arm and began to walk toward him.

His gaze was instinctively drawn to her full mouth.

God help me, he thought as she came near. He wanted to kiss her again.

"Keisha," he said softly before reaching out to touch her. His fingers tingled in anticipation.

He watched with dismay as she stepped out of his reach and continued her long strides down the corridor.

"Keisha," he called after her again, but she ignored him.

CHAPTER 16

"Great job, Sydney!" Phil exclaimed as he gave Dr. Parker a loud slap on the back.

Dr. Parker wrapped his arm around his wife, Suzanne, gave her an affectionate squeeze, and kissed the plump woman on the cheek.

"Did I do well, honey?" he asked her.

Suzanne pursed her red lips, looked up at him, and gave him a wink. "I think you did okay."

"Okay?" Phil nearly shouted. "He did wonderful! He kicked Vincent Dupré's butt!"

This led to a burst of laughter from the other staffers. Some in the green room then chimed in with their congratulations, but Keisha remained conspicuously silent. She masked her emotions with a tight smile, not giving any hint to what she was really feeling.

"I say we have a toast! There's no champagne, so everyone hold up your soda cans and water bottles," Phil ordered with a chuckle. "Hold them up! Hold them up!"

Keisha held her half empty Coke can in the air, though her heart wasn't in it. She was in a dark mood, and so far the only one she had revealed it to was Will.

Will, she thought angrily. His handsome, deceitful face suddenly came to mind. *Don't get me started on that one,* she thought.

"To Sydney, for taking us a hundred steps closer to victory," he said with a grin. "Cheers!"

"Cheers!" Everyone shouted in unison before clinking cans and filling the room with chatter.

It was nearly midnight, but the staffers were still pumped up. Keisha, on the other hand, was exhausted and ready to head back to her hotel. She gazed at Dr. Parker, a man whom she idolized, and wondered what he was thinking right now. He seemed so happy and unmistakably proud. Did he have any idea how much he had disappointed her?

Dr. Parker had done well tonight—in a conventional sense. In her opinion, he had dominated the debate and come off as both articulate and knowledgeable. But there was something about his answers that had left Keisha unnerved. In fact, one answer in particular had rendered her speechless.

Ten minutes into the debate, the moderator had asked the dreaded question about mandating higher sentences for juveniles. When he did, Keisha watched as Phil closed his eyes, bracing himself for the worst. Both of them knew what Dr. Parker's answer would be. She remembered the heated argument between the professor and Phil weeks earlier. Dr. Parker wasn't going to back down, but she wondered how diplomatically he would pose his answer now that he was being put on the spot. Thousands of potential voters were watching, after all. How would he convey the complexity of his position on the issue without discussing his checkered past?

Keisha had waited eagerly for his answer. Her heart went out to him. This wasn't an easy spot to be put into.

"I am . . . I am *completely* for giving our wayward juveniles a second chance," he began slowly, "but . . . but there must be . . . ," he paused, ". . . there must be no misunderstanding of how our laws operate. As the saying goes, 'If you do the crime, you must do the time.' " He frowned uncomfortably after he said that, as if the words had been forced out of his mouth. He then glanced down at the podium. "Juveniles should be held accountable for their actions. Our citizens should not be held hostage by the tyranny of crime, whether that crime is committed by someone fifty-six years old or sixteen," he said, pounding the podium, his voice gaining more vigor. "We have to shore up our education system to keep our youth off the street so they won't be drawn to crime, but juveniles also have to understand the law. If we go too light on them, they'll never learn to respect the law. That is why . . . ," he paused and cleared his throat, ". . . that is why I-I support higher . . . mandatory sentences . . . for juvenile offenders."

At those words, the greenroom had fallen silent. Dupré had gaped openly on camera while Keisha's face had crumpled in dismay. She had looked over at Phil, only to find him grinning like a hyena and giving the thumbs-up sign to the television screen.

What the hell just happened? Keisha had thought. Had Phil engaged in some arm-twisting behind the scenes that she wasn't aware of? Why had Dr. Parker suddenly changed his stance? But as the debate progressed, she noticed several changes to Dr. Parker's answers. Positions that he had held for years now were more tempered. They were more moderate than the liberal views she thought he had. Question after question, Keisha was left to do nothing but helplessly shake her head. What in the world had happened to him?

Keisha now stood silent in the greenroom as staffers buzzed around her. She was filled with a sense of unease and desperately needed answers from her mentor.

Keisha gritted her teeth and wrung her hands nervously. She really wanted nothing more than to go to back to her hotel room and sleep, but she knew she wouldn't get a minute of rest until she talked to Dr. Parker. She had to resolve this. She had to find out what had happened between the last time they had spoken and the debate. Keisha took a deep breath before walking across the room and tapping Dr. Parker on the shoulder.

"Dr. Parker," she said quietly. "Dr. Parker, sir," she said again.

He finally turned to her and smiled. "Keisha, are you still here? I thought you'd be heading off with the rest of them to get drunk and be merry," he said with a chuckle.

She gave a pained smile. "That's not really my style, sir." She cleared her throat. "Actually," she began quietly, "I was wondering if I could talk to you for a few minutes . . . privately. I wanted to talk about tonight's debate and—"

Dr. Parker let out an exasperated sigh. "Keisha, is that why you haven't gone?" His smile widened into a grin as he waved his hand dismissively. "Believe me, we can save the recap for tomorrow. Go ahead and enjoy yourself."

Keisha opened her mouth to argue, but he quickly shook his head and placed his hand on her shoulder. He gave it a fatherly squeeze.

"Keisha, tonight is a night when we can enjoy ourselves. You all have worked very hard; no one harder than you, it seems," he said with a chuckle.

"Mandatory sentences," she blurted out, now meeting his eyes. "Mandatory sentences for juveniles. You said you supported it but . . . but you told me . . . you told *us* that you didn't." His smile faded. "And the other things you said tonight, Dr. Parker, I just . . . I just don't understand why you said them."

"Keisha," he said with a loud sigh, "tonight was a televised debate. That's all. It was just a bunch of sound bites and talking points. If the constituents really want to know my position on the issues, they can go to my web site. They can come to *me!* But I can't be expected to fully articulate my opinion in two minutes. I realize that in that type of venue, I'm allowed some wiggle room. I'm allowed to—"

"Rework your stance," she said bitterly, recalling the words that Phil had used, that she *thought* she and Dr. Parker had both staunchly opposed.

"Keisha," he began quietly. "We're winning now, and that was something I had not anticipated. When the Dems asked me to run, I had no idea that I'd actually have a chance of beating the great Vincent Dupré, and now I do. You don't just give up a lead like that."

"But what about *principles*, Dr. Parker? Sure, it's one issue here, one issue there. But what about . . ."

She stopped when she felt Dr. Parker's grip on her shoulders tighten. He released his hold and dropped his hands to his sides.

"Keisha, it's been a *long* day." He tilted his head. "Please go out. Have fun. Any discussion like this can be, *should* be, saved for tomorrow, okay?"

When she didn't nod her head, but instead opened her mouth again, he held up his hand.

"O-*kay*?" he repeated slowly.

Dr. Parker was smiling but the smile did not reach his eyes. It was futile to protest. She knew that now. Maybe she should just save her questions for tomorrow. Maybe she *was* being too hard on him. They should be celebrating their victory, not arguing about principles and meaning.

"Yes, sir," she said finally, forcing a half-hearted smile. He nodded then turned to his wife and several people who stood around them.

Keisha stared at Dr. Parker's back and sighed deeply.

Let it go, Keisha, she silently told herself. *Just let it go. He said you'll talk about it tomorrow.*

So why did some nagging part of her suspect that despite Dr. Parker's promise, the conversation would never happen?

❧

Keisha obeyed Dr. Parker's request and walked downstairs with the other staffers to head to one of the local bars to celebrate. It wasn't until she hopped into her Ford Focus that she realized she had left her binder upstairs. She called Jason on her cell phone and told him that she would probably be late to the bar. Lucky for her, the security guards had not locked all the doors to the building. One of the side entrances was still open, allowing her to get upstairs.

Keisha walked back alone to the greenroom, hoping that her leather binder was still where she had left it, perched on one of the coffee tables. She was frustrated with herself for leaving something so important behind.

Thankfully, it was right where she left it. She tucked it into the crook of her arm and glanced at her watch. If she hurried she could still make it to the bar only fifteen or twenty minutes after the other staffers. She turned and headed towards the door. When she saw a dark figure looming in the doorway, she yelped in surprise. Her binder fell to the floor.

"Sorry," Will said as he quickly pushed away from the doorframe and walked toward her. "I didn't mean to scare you."

"Dammit, Will!" Keisha shouted. She raised her hand to her chest, feeling her heart thud against her ribs. She cursed under her breath. "Do not sneak up on me like that!" she said as she bent down and retrieved her binder.

He licked his lips. "I wasn't trying to sneak up on you, Keisha. I just happened to walk by and I saw you were in here. So I thought—"

"—that it would be a good idea to scare me *half to death*?" she exclaimed, shooting back to her feet.

"No," he said. "I thought . . . I just thought that we should . . . talk."

Keisha pursed her lips and slowly shook her head. "We have nothing to say to one another, Will."

"Oh, we don't?" he asked incredulously as she attempted to walk around him.

Keisha sighed. "Besides 'good night'?" she asked, pushing a loose tendril of hair behind her ear. "No. Not really."

"Good night?" He raised his eyebrows in disbelief. "That's all you have to say to me?" He grabbed her arm, stopped her, and turned her around to face him.

She pulled out of his grasp with irritation. "What am I supposed to say, Will?"

"Something, *anything*," he spat. "Just don't ignore me. Don't act like what happened a few weeks ago didn't happen."

"Are you kidding me?" She glared up at him with outrage. "What do mean, don't act like it didn't happen? What about *you*? *You* didn't say a damn thing after we kissed! You just walked away like we had just shaken hands."

He sighed and shrugged. "I was . . . confused."

"You were confused?"

He gritted his teeth and threw up his hands. "I'm sorry. I hadn't expected it to play out that way. I had planned to ignore you the whole night. I had planned not to talk to you, but then I saw you standing alone in the gym and then . . . and then . . ." His voice trailed off.

"Will," she began as she stared up with bemusement, "*you* kissed *me*. You initiated it. How could you not . . ."

Enough, she thought while shaking her head. *You should know better by now, Keisha. You're not going to win with him. He's too smart and too good at playing these games. It's not worth it.*

She closed her eyes and rubbed her temples, feeling a headache coming on. She barely knew him, yet he seemed to know her so well. He knew which buttons to press, what levers to pull. Will was like sandpaper, shredding away at her outer layers, leaving her bare and worn down. She had to get away from him.

"I've got to go," she said quietly, feeling the urge to run from the room.

"Tell me what I've done," he said as she began to walk to the door again. "What have I done to you that would make us go on like this, Keisha?"

She could hear the desperation in his voice. *It's a trick*, she suddenly thought. *It's all a trick.*

"Don't shut me out because of what other people told you about me!" he argued.

Keisha stopped, leaned against the door jam and sighed. When she finally turned to face him, she couldn't deny it. He looked desperate. He was gazing at her earnestly, holding out his hands like a hopeless beggar.

"How can I not shut you out, Will, when I don't know the truth? I don't know who you really are. You say one thing and . . . they say another."

"So why don't you just *ask* me?" Will asked impatiently, making his voice boom in the darkened room. "Why don't you just *ask* me for the truth?"

Keisha tilted her head and gazed up at Will. "If I ask," she began quietly, "will you really tell me?"

Will firmly nodded his head. "Anything you want to know."

She pursed her lips and stood silently in front of him for several seconds. "The people you used to work for said that premarital sex causes cancer," she finally ventured. "Do you really believe that?"

"*That's* your first question?"

She pursed her lips indignantly. "Yes."

"No, I don't believe it causes cancer. Of course I don't. And there are about 30 percent of things at America's Bright Future I don't believe or agree with. But I don't think it's necessary to agree totally with someone to work for them. I liked and respected their overall objective, which is to hold parents and schools accountable for children's education." He shrugged. "So occasionally they put out a press release about some stupid medical study. There are worse things."

The answer was well articulated, but, from him, Keisha had expected as much. She narrowed her eyes again. "Like outing someone to win an election?" she asked, making Will frown. "Is that a worse thing?"

"What?"

"I'm talking about the 2002 election, Will," she said in annoyance as she brought her hands to her hips. "How could you possibly forget? You worked for Congressman Taylor the year that he was running against Mitch Waldren in Wisconsin. Mitch was ahead in the polls and, somehow, three weeks before the election, the press found out that Mitch was gay. Not only did he lose the election but he almost lost his foster kids, too!" Keisha said angrily as she pointed up at him. "There've been rumors for years that *you're* the one who did it, Will. You called the reporter and you leaked that information!"

Will stared down at the accusatory finger she jabbed up at him. "Are you telling me I did it or asking me if I did it?" he asked, pushing her finger aside.

Keisha recoiled from his touch, not wanting the distraction. She adjusted her suit jacket and shrugged her shoulders. "Asking, I guess."

"Okay then," he muttered. "Well, first of all, whoever told you that rumor—and I suspect I know who did— needs to get her facts straight," he said curtly. "I didn't work for Taylor's campaign that year. He hired me as a legislative aid for his office on the Hill, so legally I couldn't be on his campaign staff." Will sighed. "But I'll admit that I didn't like all the guys who were running things over there. The campaign got pretty ugly toward the end. I saw the articles and the TV coverage. Taylor was losing and I could tell they were getting desperate."

"Desperate enough to trash Waldren?" she asked.

"Probably," he admitted. "Look, Keisha, I wanted just as much as everyone else in our office for Taylor to get re-elected. I wanted to keep my job. But I realize some things shouldn't be compromised. I didn't like how Taylor handled the election. I didn't like what it turned into. I didn't think Mitch deserved what happened to him. It was hard to watch." Will slumped back against the edge of a nearby desk and closed his eyes.

"Hard to watch but you kept watching, right?" Keisha asked reproachfully, making his eyes flash open. "You didn't do anything to stop it, did you? Did you talk to Taylor? Did you tell him how you felt?"

Will glared at her for several seconds, not saying a word. Finally, he slowly smiled, catching her off guard. "You've got a lot to learn, Miss Reynolds."

"Excuse me?"

"You've got a lot to learn," he repeated slowly. "Look, I *did* tell Taylor how I felt and almost lost my job because of it. I discovered it's really hard to fight the tide of fifty other people who are telling your boss one thing when you're saying another. You'll figure that out, too, one day when you're on the wrong side of a debate."

Keisha crossed her arms over her chest. She would never tell Will but she suspected that, for the first time, she was *already* on the wrong side of the debate. Dr. Parker was a winner now and that had changed him. Her advice no longer reigned supreme with him, either. She was already starting to feel shut out.

"You know . . . it hurts when people disappoint you like that," Will murmured slowly. He was saying the words aloud that she had been thinking all evening. "You think you know a person. You respect them and then suddenly they just . . . change." He sighed. "Like I said before, I don't think it's necessary to agree totally with someone to work for them, but Taylor pushed me past my limit. I can only look the other way but so many times. So after the election was over, I tendered my resignation. He didn't have to fire me because I didn't want to work for him anymore."

Keisha stared at Will, dumbfounded. *He had quit over what happened during the election?* Tanya hadn't told her that part of the story. Keisha could feel the walls she had erected between her and Will quickly tumbling down with each thing he told her. It was easy to hate him when she believed him to be a monster, but it was much harder now that he was proving otherwise.

"So does that answer all your questions?"

Keisha dropped her defensive stance and shrugged. "I guess so."

At those words, Will took several steps towards her. Keisha took a few hesitant steps back toward the door, ready to bolt at a second's notice. His eyes were growing intense again, making her pulse quicken. He was staring at her mouth and he looked as if he wanted to kiss her.

Wait a minute! Wait a minute, a voice yelled in her head as her stomach began to tie itself into knots. Her eyes widened as he took her right hand and then her left within his own. Tanya had warned Keisha to be on her guard with Will, that things weren't always what they seemed with him. Will was a great tactician. He knew how to play people. "He'll say and do just about anything to win, girl," Tanya swore.

Keisha blinked rapidly as he abruptly tugged her towards him and wrapped an arm around her waist. *He's winning! He's winning,* she thought with panic, feeling herself falling underneath his spell, unable to pull away from him. Her breathing quickened as he lowered his mouth to hers.

"You don't like coffee, only cream!" she blurted out against his lips.

Will leaned back, squinted down at her and frowned. "What?"

Keisha swallowed loudly. *Okay, that didn't come out right*, she thought.

"I mean," she cleared her throat. "I-I-I mean I-I heard that when it . . . comes to women, you don't take your coffee black, if you . . . know what I mean. You just . . . prefer . . . cream." She winced at Tanya's phrasing.

His grip around her waist loosened. "I see."

"Th-th-that's . . . that's what I heard anyway," she stuttered. She attempted to step out of his grasp but Keisha suddenly felt his hold tighten around her waist again. He pulled her back toward him, tilted his head, and smiled.

"Not so fast," he said, running his thumb along her bottom lip. "Don't you want to hear the truth about that, too?"

She blinked and slowly nodded.

"Well, let me correct you by saying I do 'take my coffee black' . . . more than you think," Will said as he toyed with her chin. "Black coffee, cream, coffee with cream—it makes no difference to me. I have and will always be an equal opportunity coffee drinker," he muttered with a smirk.

Despite herself, Keisha laughed, and Will joined her. It was a good and hearty chuckle that made all the tension between them disappear. She opened her mouth to give some quip in return but the words never made it past her lips. Will leaned down and kissed her with enough force that it almost knocked the air out of her.

The kiss was ravenous and deep and sent enough chills throughout her body that it left her weak-kneed and almost in a daze. Their heads twisted for better access. Their tongues danced. Keisha's nipples swelled with arousal against the silk of her shirt and she felt the overwhelming urge again to disrobe and have him touch and kiss the skin beneath her clothes. Just as she moaned, her stomach grumbled loudly, filling the quiet space with noise. Will pulled back his head and smiled.

"Are you hungry?" he asked.

"Yes," she whispered languidly against his lips. She tried to bring her mouth back to his.

He grinned. "I meant for *food.*"

"Oh," she exclaimed. Her eyes widened as she loudly cleared her throat. "Umm, yeah. I mean . . . yes, I'm . . . I should eat." She gazed down at her feet with embarrassment. "Sorry about the stomach noise. I skipped dinner."

Will released his hold around her and nodded. "Don't apologize," he said reassuringly. "If you're hungry, you're hungry. I know a nice Italian place that is twenty minutes from here, if you'd like to go. They stay open pretty late."

Keisha looked up at Will. She slowly smiled. "Are you . . . are you asking me out on a date?"

He shrugged. "Shouldn't I? You need to eat, and, besides, don't you think we should rack up one date before we end up in bed together?" he asked casually as he took her hand and led her toward the door.

Keisha blinked in astonishment. *Excuse me?* Now she remembered why she found him so egotistical in the beginning.

"Wait a minute. Wait a minute," she insisted. "What makes you think we're going to end up in bed together?"

Will smiled confidently as he gazed back at her and chuckled. He tugged her toward the open door and into the hallway. "Trust me. We will," he said.

Her eyes widened as she gulped nervously.

CHAPTER 17

They dropped off her car at her hotel before heading to dinner together. Will was eager for some alone time with Keisha. He wanted to get to know more about her, but, to his dismay, the ride in his silver Audi Roadster to the restaurant was carried out in silence. Will kept glancing over at Keisha, who for some reason sat motionless in the passenger seat beside him with her hands in her lap. He wanted to say something to her but didn't. He wanted to touch her again but felt he could not. He had sensed this tension between them before, but tonight it felt as if it had been turned up several notches. This was no longer a mix of flirtation and frustration that left their stomachs in knots. Tonight something was going to happen, one way or the other.

When they arrived at Lugiano Ristorante, Will held the door open for Keisha and motioned for her to step inside first. As she passed him, he tried to lock eyes with her but she avoided his gaze and smiled nervously. That worried him.

Keisha had asked Will to be honest with her, but maybe he had been a little *too* honest. He knew his confidence often came off as cockiness, but there was no way he could deny the attraction he felt between them; tonight they had the choice of either walking away or finally acting on those emotions. He could feel it. She had to feel it, too. Was acknowledging that being cocky?

He let his gaze trail over Keisha's back as the maître d' guided them through the maze of candlelit tables in the bustling restaurant. Will's eyes lingered on every curve of her body, from the slope between her neck and her shoulder to her plump backside. He watched as she lowered herself into the chair the maître d' held out for her, crossing her legs and carefully adjusting her skirt as she did so. She fidgeted, adjusting the water glass and cutlery, as Will sat down in the chair across from her. She turned and smiled as a waiter handed them both brown leather-bound menus. "Thank you," she murmured.

"And what can I get you to drink," the wiry waiter asked, leaning forward slightly as he clasp his hands behind his back. "May I suggest our sauvignon blanc? It goes well with many of our staple dishes. Or perhaps the pinot grigio? That's a popular choice."

"I'll take the blanc," Will answered quickly, keeping his eyes firmly fixed on Keisha.

She tucked her hair behind her ear, a nervous tick, he assumed. Keisha smiled. "Then I guess I'll try your pinot grigio."

The waiter nodded. "Good choices. And would you like to order your meal now or will need a few more minutes to review the selections?"

"I don't know about you, Will, but I think I'll need a few minutes to look over everything," Keisha said demurely. She gave a helpless shrug.

"That's perfectly fine. Take your time," the waiter insisted. "I'll be back with your drinks." He quickly departed the table.

Keisha examined the menu, slowly flipping each page. "I'm glad you chose this place. I've wanted pasta for a few days now," she murmured, gnawing on her lower lip, a lip that begged to be kissed again, in Will's opinion. "I can tell I'm going to have a hard time choosing which dish to order, though."

He watched as she picked up the locket around her neck. Keisha then began to toy with the long silver chain, unwittingly drawing Will's attention to the shadow between her cleavage and then the swell of each breast, both of which were currently showing over the low-slung baby blue silk top she was wearing.

"Everything looks so good," she murmured.

I couldn't agree more, he thought. This dinner is going to be torture of the worst kind. He hoped Keisha would show some mercy and skip the appetizers and dessert.

She must have instinctively felt Will's heated gaze upon her for she hesitantly looked up from the menu and gave a shy, crooked grin. "What? What are you staring at?" she asked.

Uh-oh. Busted, Will thought. He had been caught ogling again. He had to come up with a good excuse for this one. Will cleared his throat and smiled. "Your locket," he lied as he pointed at the silver jewelry piece around her neck. "I notice that you wear it all the time."

Keisha nodded as she looked down at the silver dollar-sized locket and took it in the palm of her hand.

"Yeah, it's pretty old. I should probably send it to a professional to get it cleaned, but I feel so weird not wearing it. I've had it for so long that I'm . . . I'm kinda attached to it."

"You said that your parents gave it to you, right?"

"My mom gave it to me," she clarified before tucking her hair behind her ear again. "I never met my father. He died before I was born."

Will flinched. "Oh," he murmured. "I'm sorry. I . . . I didn't know."

Keisha shook her head and smiled. "It's okay. How could you have known if I didn't tell you?" She shrugged. "It's not that touchy of a subject. I never knew him, and it's hard to grieve over someone you didn't know. But I'll always wonder what he was like, what he could have been like as a father." She fell into silence as she smiled at the locket, fingering its clasp. "You know, when I was little, I used to pretend that my father *did* give me the locket. People used to ask me all the time if he left me anything when he died, but, of course, he didn't. He was twenty-eight. Someone that young wouldn't make up a will. But everyone kept asking, so I had to come up with something. I lied and said it was the locket."

"Well, it's very pretty," Will said. "Even Dupré noticed it."

Keisha's smile abruptly disappeared. She dropped the locket back to her chest and returned her attention to her menu. "I don't think *that's* what got Dupré's attention," she muttered.

Will frowned. "What do you mean?"

"Your wine, sir," their waiter said, seeming to materialize out of nowhere. He placed a glass of white wine in front of Will. "Your wine, ma'am," he said as he turned to Keisha. Will slowly drank from his glass. When he lowered it back to the table cloth, he found Keisha glaring down at her menu.

"Are you ready to order now?" the waiter asked.

Keisha didn't respond.

"We're going to need a few more minutes, I think," Will muttered.

The waiter tightly smiled and nodded before disappearing again.

Will sighed. Something he had said had pissed her off, though he could not fathom what it was. They sat in silence for several seconds. "What's wrong, Keisha?" he finally asked.

He watched as she clapped shut her menu and leaned across the table toward him. "Will, you're a decent guy," she began. "I had my doubts before but . . . I can see it now. I just don't understand how . . . *how* you can work for a man like Vincent Dupré."

Will rolled his eyes. *More questions?* He thought he had addressed everything back at Towson. His frown intensified. "What do you mean, 'a man like Vincent Dupré'? There's nothing wrong with Vincent."

"There's nothing right with him, either!"

Will closed his eyes. He should have anticipated this. Their old debate was once again rearing its ugly head.

"Vincent is a politician, Keisha, just like any other," he said calmly, though he could see her opening her mouth to argue again. He held up his hands to stop her. "Yes, you may disagree with him on some issues, but Vincent hasn't done anything to you personally. He's a pretty good guy. He's a great father, a loyal husband to Sara, and a good friend. He and Pops were in the same law firm. I've known him for years. Hell, Vincent was the one who helped me get into politics! He's been honest and honorable as long as I've known him," Will insisted, making Keisha snort and roll her eyes. "I don't understand what you find so repugnant about him."

"Would you like the full list, or should I summarize?" she spat. "I mean, honestly, Will. How can you be so naïve?"

How could I *be naïve?* Will's nostrils flared as he fought back his burgeoning anger. This . . . *this* was the part about Keisha that irritated the hell out of him! Her foolish self-righteousness was one of her worst traits.

"Look, it's not like Parker walks around with a halo over his head, either," he argued. "I disagree with Vincent on some things. I know he isn't perfect and I'm willing to accept that. Unlike you! You may worship at the altar of Saint Parker, but I'll tell you something, he's *not* perfect."

Keisha quickly shook her head. "I never said he was perfect, Will. In fact, his imperfections are . . . ," she paused, ". . . they are . . . what make him a . . . a complex human being. They're what make him a man I . . . ," she paused again, ". . . deeply respect and look up to."

Will cocked an eyebrow. *Looking for a daddy figure, are we?* Keisha was the classic case. She hadn't grown up with her father and it was starting to sound like Parker had filled that role for her in her mind.

"Great," Will muttered sarcastically. "Parker's imperfections make him a 'complex human being' and Dupré's imperfections make him Satan incarnate. You have heard of the phrase 'double standard,' right?"

"Parker," she growled, "has had a much harder life than that rich, self-entitled hypocrite that you call a boss and Parker has still made something of himself!"

Will leaned back in his chair and glared at Keisha. He slowly counted to ten. "Let's drop this," he finally said as he unfurled his dinner napkin and laid it across his lap.

"No, Will."

"Keisha, drop it," he said through clinched teeth.

"No!" she exclaimed indignantly, drawing the attention of a couple at a nearby table. "Why should I? Because you don't want to hear the truth?"

"No, because I'm sick of arguing with you," he blurted out as he slammed his napkin back to the table. Will closed his eyes and sighed. "You don't care about the truth, Keisha. You care about being *right*, which is why you won't stop arguing with me. It's like you're addicted to it! You don't know a damn thing about Dupré besides what you've read and what you've heard through the liberal rumor mill. How the hell do you know if Dupré is self-entitled? Have you ever had a conversation with him? Have you ever exchanged more than four sentences with him? How the hell do you know if Parker's had a harder life?"

"Because I know Dupré didn't live on food stamps when he was a child like Parker did!" she barked as she pointed at her chest. "I know that Dupré didn't have to wash dishes to pay his way through college! And I know Dupré didn't get dumped in a jail as a fifteen-year-old boy who was only trying to survive and make some money! Tell me what the Great Almighty Vincent Dupré went through that was worse than that!"

Will frowned. There was a long pause as he stared at her in amazement. Had he heard her correctly? *"Jail?"* he repeated vaguely. "When did Parker go to jail?"

Keisha gaped. Her face reddened as her eyes widened with alarm. Her gaze fell to her lap as she nervously adjusted her skirt.

"Have we made a decision?" the waiter asked loudly as he reappeared. "Are we ready?" He looked eagerly from Will to Keisha and back again.

Will stared at Keisha. She looked as if she wanted to throw up.

"Five more minutes," he muttered, making the waiter grit his teeth in frustration and walk away from the table again.

Will reached across the table top and placed his hand over hers. She was trembling.

"This is why," she murmured. "This is why I shouldn't have come."

Will frowned.

"I knew . . . I *knew* I would end up blurting out something. Please tell me this isn't going to come back to haunt me, Will," she pleaded softly, now on the verge of tears. "I'm not going to hear on the news tomorrow night the story about Dr. Sydney Parker serving jail time when he was a teenager, am I?" She leaned forward. "He really is a good man! He regrets what happened when he was younger. It was a mistake. He knows that. Please, don't tell anyone. Don't let it be held against him. Please, Will. I—"

"Keisha," he whispered, squeezing her hand reassuringly, "you can trust me. Whatever is said between us, stays between us."

She sniffed, took a deep breath and slowly shook her head. "I'm damned if I do and I'm damned if I don't. One minute it seems like if I put as much distance between us as possible, if I walk away, the safer it is for both of us. We wouldn't have to worry about anyone finding out. I wouldn't have to worry about saying anything stupid." She shrugged. "Well, anything *else* stupid. I wouldn't have to worry about disappointing Parker or worse, getting fired. But the next minute, it all changes. I can't stop . . ." She sighed and finally locked her eyes with his. "I can't stop thinking about you, Will. I've tried to but I can't. I can't walk away." She dropped her head into her free hand. "I'm so confused. I'm almost thirty and it's like high school all over again."

Will slowly smiled. He tugged her hand away from her face so that he was holding both of her slender, soft hands in his own. He rubbed his thumbs over her knuckles and gazed at her, trying to lock with her doe-like eyes which were still downcast. He was touched by her confession.

"Keisha, look at me. Look at me, please."

She finally did, begrudgingly. He could see the vulnerability in those dark eyes. He leaned across the table to kiss her but stopped midway, making her frown. He cocked an eyebrow and gave her a lopsided grin. "The only way this is going to work is if you meet me halfway," he whispered.

Keisha slowly smiled. She caught his double meaning, and it was true. Nothing between them could happen if she and he weren't both willing to take a chance. If she really wanted to do this, she did have to meet him halfway. Keisha slowly leaned across the small bistro table and they joined in a kiss, feeling the warmth from the candle flames on their faces. Like before, the kiss started off sweet and tender but Will quickly lost all sense of where he was, allowing the kiss to become more earnest and passionate, despite the fact that he and Keisha were in the middle of a crowded restaurant. She held his face in her hands and tilted back her head, opening her mouth to him, making his heart thud in his chest. If it wasn't for that damn table between them, he could get at her even better. By the time the waiter loudly cleared his throat and they both reluctantly pulled away, Will was fully aroused.

"Excuse me but . . . have you decided?" the waiter asked, his voice now filled with irritation.

"Can we just get the check?" Keisha murmured seductively before licking her swollen lips.

Will nodded, quickly dug into his pocket, pulled out his wallet and removed a $20 bill. "That's for the wine," he muttered to the waiter as he grabbed Keisha's hand. "Keep the change."

She giggled as Will tugged her to her feet. They both left the table and the bewildered waiter standing there as they swiftly walked to the restaurant's front door, eager to get back to the hotel.

CHAPTER 18

The fact that they made it upstairs to Keisha's floor at all was a miracle in itself. In the car, in the lobby, in front of the hotel elevators, and in the elevators, every touch turned into a kiss and every kiss turned into a caress. Keisha had never in her life been so overwhelmed by heady lust. It was almost like being drunk. She felt disoriented and completely dazed. It was *wonderful!*

They stumbled out of the elevator with lips still locked. Keisha smiled as she tugged her mouth away and pointed down the hallway. "I'm over here," she said, quickly digging into her purse in search of her room's key card.

Will grinned and ran his hands over her hips. "Lead the way."

It's really happening, Keisha thought with excitement as she walked down the hotel room corridor with Will trailing at her heels.

It sure is. And you have absolutely no idea what you're doing, a warning voice in her head said in return.

Keisha paused. The voice was right. This would be the first time she had slept with a man since college. What if she seemed awkward? What if she couldn't do it? Her hands began to shake as she inserted the plastic key card into her hotel room door. She repeated the step over and over again, too nervous to notice that the green light had flashed.

"I think you can open it now," Will whispered against her ear. Exasperated, she quickly nodded before tugging the brass handle down and pushing the door open.

Great, I can't even open a door by myself, she thought glumly. *Get it together, Keisha!*

The room was dark save for a desk lamp in the corner that she had left on before heading to the debate. Keisha turned on the overhead light, swallowed loudly and walked to the other side of the room, leaving a now confused Will to awkwardly stand in the center of the brown paisley carpet. He frowned.

"Are you okay?"

"Oh, I'm fine. Just fine. M-m-make your . . . make yourself at home," she said with false cheeriness. She tugged off her suit jacket and placed it on the back of the desk chair, then tossed the hotel room key on the table. Keisha couldn't meet his eyes though she could feel his gaze on her as she clumsily circled the room, trying to think of something to say, something that would calm her nerves. Or better yet, she hoped for some way to dissipate the cloud of heat that seemed to be enveloping her.

What am I doing? What the hell am I doing?

"I'm sorry about the room being so hot," she blurted out as she flapped her hands in front of her chest. "I've called maintenance but I still can't figure out how to lower the thermostat."

He shrugged. "I feel fine."

"Well, good for you. But I'm burnin' up!" She then laughed and snorted.

Oh, God, I'm snorting, she thought. *Stop snorting, Keisha! Stop snorting!*

"W-w-would you like a drink?" she asked. She turned her back to him and rushed over to the leather-bound hotel menu that sat near the big-screen television. "It's a three-star hotel, so no bar in the room, unfortunately. But," she said as she ran her fingers over the wine list, "I think they have a decent wine selection downstairs that room service could—"

Keisha finally stopped talking when she felt herself being whipped around. Will lowered his searing mouth to hers, parting her lips and kissing her as hungrily as he had in the elevator. She sighed, all nervousness evaporating as she wrapped her hands around his neck. She stood on the tips of her toes, leaning into him, firmly kissing him back. He tilted back her head and their kiss deepened. After several seconds she could no longer determine where her mouth and tongue ended and his began. Keisha was sinking into him, into lust again, and she made no attempt to pull herself back to the surface.

She almost whimpered when Will abruptly pulled his mouth away. She stared up at him, completely dazed.

"Your phone's ringing," Will said.

"Huh?" she murmured dreamily, her hands still wrapped around his neck.

"Your phone is ringing," he repeated slowly as he tapped the BlackBerry on her hip.

The spell now broken, Keisha reached down to remove the device from its holster and looked at its glass screen. "Oh, hell," she muttered as she scanned the number.

Will quickly shook his head. "Don't answer it."

"Will, it's Phillip," she said as the BlackBerry continued to buzz. "I have to answer it."

"No, you don't," he replied, He snatched the BlackBerry out of her hand and tossed it across the room, making her mouth drop open in shock.

"Hey!" she exclaimed. "That phone cost me almost $200!"

Will pulled out his BlackBerry from his suit jacket. "And this cost me $300," he said. He hurled it across the room in the same direction as her phone, making her laugh in amazement. "No phones tonight," he pronounced, fixing her with a steady gaze. "No campaign managers. No elections. None of that crap! Tonight it's just about us." He pointed his finger at his chest and then hers. "You and me. That's the only way this is going to work. Agreed?"

She slowly smiled and took a deep breath. "Agreed."

"Good," he said.

Keisha yelped in surprise as Will wrapped one hand around her waist and, with the other, gripped her bottom as he hoisted her onto the cherry wood desk behind them. The table groaned slightly under her weight. He kissed her again, towering over her, gripping the back of her neck with one hand while the other snaked its way to the small of her back, pressing her against him. She could barely breathe as their tongues danced. It sounded as though a freight train was going past the hotel window but it was really her heart thudding wildly, making the blood pound in her ears. Keisha's eyelashes lowered just as Will's hands moved nimbly to her thighs. In a matter of seconds he hoisted her skirt to her waist, parted her legs, and forced himself between them in one fluid move. He then pushed her thighs further apart, dragging her knees to his waist. Keisha's eyes flashed open again. Alarm bells went off in her head the second she felt the crotch of her white silk panties being roughly pushed aside. She then watched in horror as Will began to tug at his pants zipper. Suddenly, decade-old reruns of the college point guard and his dorm room started to play. *Not like this*, Keisha thought. *Not like this!* Frightened that this would turn out the same way, Keisha attempted to grab Will's hands.

"Stop," she said against his mouth. "Please, *stop!*" she pleaded, pushing against his chest.

They lurched to a halt again. Will pulled away, gazing down at her angrily. "What?"

"I need you to . . . to stop, Will," she said slowly. "Please."

"But why the hell should I . . . We've come this far and now you just want to . . . This is . . . This is just bull . . . ," he sputtered, before turning away from her to regain his calm. She watched as Will took a deep breath. "I'm sorry. I'm sorry. I didn't mean to yell at you. It's just . . . I thought . . . I thought you wanted this, too," he said quietly.

"I did . . . I mean I do . . . I just . . ." She sighed as she pushed back down her skirt and slid off the desk. "I just need for this to move a little . . . slower."

He gazed at her with disbelief. "*Slower?*" he asked, as if the idea was preposterous, as if he had already been pushed to the brink too many times.

"Just be patient with me. Okay?" she pled softly. "It's not you. It's just that I'm . . . I'm out of practice . . . with all of this. It's been a while."

He stepped aside and let her walk over to the hotel bed. Keisha sat on the tan comforter, keeping her eyes firmly fixed on the carpeted floor as she held her head in her hands.

"How long is 'a while'?" he asked, adjusting his pants so that his protruding manhood wasn't quite so uncomfortable.

She closed her eyes and sighed, now thoroughly humiliated. "Twelve years," she said in a barely audible voice.

"*Twelve years?*" His eyes widened. "You haven't had sex since you were . . . what?" He narrowed his eyes as he counted in his head. "*Seventeen years old?*" She could hear the disbelief.

"I've been really busy, I guess," Keisha joked with a wry smile, though her heart wasn't in it. She slowly shook her head. *Good job, Keisha,* she thought. He wasn't going to have the thrill of having sex with a virgin, and she doubted that a guy like him would be willing to slog his way through a refresher tutorial with someone whose entire sex life to date had lasted for ten painful minutes.

163

"I'm sorry," she mumbled as she pushed dark tresses out of her face. "I know I should have told you earlier but . . . I didn't know how to . . . approach something like this." She hesitated. "Look, I understand if you want to leave."

"Why would I want leave?" he asked as he shrugged out of his suit jacket and loosened his necktie.

She shrugged. "It's obvious you expected things to go a lot faster. Now you have me turning on the red light. It has to be frustrating for you."

She watched as Will dropped to his knees and knelt in front of her. He placed his index finger under her chin and raised it, so that he could look her in the eyes. "I'd say that it's more of a yellow light than a red light," he joked. He then gently rubbed her legs and smiled, teasing her as he let his long fingers trail up her calves and then along the outside of her thighs, making her tingle. "Look, Keisha, we'll take this as slow or as fast as you want to go. All right?" He then lightly kissed her lips, gliding over them softly. "We've got all night and I'm not going anywhere. I promise."

She lowered her lashes and leaned her forehead against his own, so grateful that he understood. He was willing to be gentle with her, to go slower—if that was what she needed. It wouldn't have to be a hurried consummation on a hotel desk.

Keisha sighed. She could feel herself opening up to Will Blake, and not just sexually. She closed her eyes as she hesitantly brought her mouth back to his, cupping his face in her hands as she did so. Within seconds, she resolved herself to an undeniable fact. She was losing her heart to Will. There was no point in fighting it anymore.

They slowly fell back against the mattress and instead of Will kissing her hungrily as he had before, he toyed with her mouth for several minutes, slowly licking the inside of it, lightly tugging on her bottom lip with his teeth. Keisha could feel her breath leaving her as she closed her eyes. Her heart pounded wildly and a warm wetness pooled between her thighs as he showered her with languorous kisses and caresses and raked his fingers over her body. She was so lost in the sea of sensation that she barely noticed when he pulled her shirt out of her skirt. "Raise your arms," he whispered against her ear. She did as he ordered and watched as her shirt was tugged over her head and tossed to the hotel floor, revealing the white lace bra underneath. Will paused. His eyes darkened. Keisha suddenly realized that he was the first man in a decade to see her in her underwear.

He didn't unhook the back clasp of her bra—at least not initially. Will simply tugged the bra up, pushed it higher so that her breasts were exposed. He then lowered his mouth to one dark, taut nipple, causing Keisha to breathe in sharply. She wrapped her hands around the back of his head, running her nails through his hair as she arched her back to meet his mouth. He toyed with each breast, flicking his tongue over each nipple, suckling them gently and then at times tugging them with his teeth. Just when she felt she couldn't take any more, Keisha felt her skirt being hoisted up again. Her legs tightened instinctively as his large hand reached between her thighs. "It's okay," he whispered. "I won't hurt you." She took a deep breath and relaxed slightly, allowing his hand to search there. Within seconds he was past the silk of her panties, touching the slick, quivering flesh underneath. She moaned as she felt his fingers gently kneading the warm spot, coaxing it open to him, while his mouth continued to play at her breast. *Oh, God, this is torture*, Keisha thought, gazing up drunkenly at the hotel's popcorn ceiling. But whoever thought torture could feel this good?

Minutes later, he pulled his mouth away from her and she gazed up at him, completely dazed. Keisha blinked. She was halfway naked while Will, with the exception of his discarded necktie and open shirt, was completely clothed. "Raise your hips," he ordered gruffly. Keisha complied, knowing that at this point if he told her to jump on one foot and bark like a dog, she probably would. He unzipped her skirt and tugged it off, along with her panties, pulling them both over her hips and then tossing them over his shoulder. They landed on the same heap as her discarded shirt. She wondered as he loomed over her what he planned to do to her next. She got her answer when he lowered his mouth to her stomach, leaving a languid, wet trail down the center. She allowed herself to enjoy the sensation but immediately cried out in surprise when his head dipped lower and his mouth nestled between her thighs.

Keisha's heavy moans grew louder as his mouth and tongue caused the throbbing at her center to radiate upward, downward, all over her body. Her legs and hips tensed, trembled and bucked helplessly as if she were in pain, though this was the sweetest pain she had ever felt. Keisha bit down hard on her lower lip to try to stifle the moans but she couldn't, feeling her chest rapidly rise and fall each time Will flicked his tongue or moved his mouth. Is *this* what she had been missing for the past eleven years? *Good God*, she thought. *Don't stop, Will. Don't stop.* She had a lot of years of lost pleasure to make up for.

But he did stop, leaving her with an ache that made her let out a soft whimper. Keisha rose from the bed, no longer afraid. Like a wild woman, she clawed at him, ripping at the buttons of his shirt and reaching for his belt buckle as she kissed him eagerly. She was too blinded by hunger to notice that Will had only paused to reach into his pocket to retrieve a condom. He was just as eager to remove his clothes as she was and did so within seconds. Keisha finally felt Will's warm body against hers, the taut muscle and skin now slick with sweat. She raised her leg and felt his manhood jerk against it. This time she didn't tense up when he slid her thighs apart and nestled his body between them. She arched her hips in anticipation.

But the sharp pain that followed as he entered her was unexpected. Keisha cried out against his lips and dug her nails into his back. She breathed in and out sharply, feeling betrayed by the sudden change in sensation. *This wasn't her first time!* Why was her body betraying her this way?

"You have to spread wider, wider," he murmured breathlessly, looking down at her. "That's the only way I'll get in."

Despite the pain, she nodded and spread her thighs as far as they would go. Will then cupped his hands under her bare bottom, raised her hips, and tried again.

This time, she moaned. He was right. The feeling was much smoother. With his lips and his body on top of hers, Keisha felt that she was gliding, floating even. Her cries and moans of delight were answered with his grunts and then cries of his own. The couple joined in a primal dance, their hips moving rhythmically as they met one another with each thrust. Keisha's heart thudded like a bass drum. Her spine arched. Her eyes rolled back and she shouted when she came. She went limp as Will's entire body jerked. He then did the same before collapsing on top of her.

The two lay in silence for several minutes. Keisha tentatively kissed Will's shoulder and gently rubbed her head. He sighed as he flopped onto his back.

"Twelve years, huh?" he murmured.

She smiled and nodded. "I know. What a way to make up for lost time."

At that, he chuckled.

Keisha then turned onto her side. She let an elbow rest on Will's chest, trailing her fingers along the light, curly hairs that lurked on his chiseled stomach. "Sorry you had to do all the work."

He vigorously shook his head, chuckling again. "Don't apologize. You did absolutely fine. Great, in fact. I was just happy to be there."

She tilted her head. *"Really?"*

"Really. Trust me."

Keisha smiled mischievously. She tossed her hair over her shoulder and slowly climbed on top of Will, straddling his waist.

"Imagine how good I could be if I actually tried," she said seductively as she lowered her mouth to his. "Care to see?"

CHAPTER 19

Will woke up the next morning slightly sore but satiated. Last night, in a matter of hours, he had fulfilled just about every fantasy with Keisha that had kept him awake at night for the past several months. Of course, it had taken some tutoring on his part. Her inexperience had caught him off guard, but she had been a willing student. Keisha had needed only little whispers of guidance and encouragement before she became confident enough to take the reins herself. And when she did, that night became everything he had hoped for and more.

So you finally got what you wanted, he thought, remembering the way her body had trembled under his. *Now what?*

That was the million-dollar question.

He had known going into this that a relationship with Keisha had no long-term potential during the election while he worked for Dupré and she worked for Parker. Trying to develop this into something more now would just be too complicated, and, quite frankly, the risks were too high. Last night had no permanent implications. It was just supposed to satisfy a need that had been plaguing the both of them for quite some time. It was just about sex . . . *right?*

He gazed at Keisha, who was still lost in a blissful sleep.

"Yeah, sure it was," a voice inside his head mocked. If he remembered correctly, he had told her at least twice last night in the throes of passion that he loved her. *So much for it being just about sex.*

Will gritted his teeth and pulled back the covers, deciding that this battle between emotion and logic would have to be left for another day. He had too much to do today, even if it was a Saturday. One meeting was scheduled for this morning, two for this afternoon, and he probably had about fifty voicemails and a hundred emails waiting for him that had to be answered on his discarded BlackBerry.

Will slid off the bed, hoping that he didn't wake Keisha as he did so. He walked in the dark—tired and naked—to the bathroom. He turned on the vanity's fluorescent lights and squinted against the brightness. Pulling back the shower curtains, he stepped inside the stall and turned the stainless steel knob, feeling a hot blast of water. He washed with the hotel's complimentary bar of soap, figuring that by the time he finished his shower, he would have his head on straight again. He then would get dressed, give her a kiss on the cheek, and leave. There was no need for discussion or a melodramatic goodbye. Keisha understood the circumstances. Hopefully, she would respect the way he handled their situation.

Will emerged from the bathroom almost fifteen minutes later with a bath towel wrapped around his waist.

The hotel room was no longer completely dark. The sun had begun to rise and shafts of light were starting to peep between the curtains and dance on Keisha's exposed shoulders. Despite all the noise Will had made, she still slept soundly, her chest rising and falling with each breath she took. This would be the perfect opportunity to make an exit. It could be another hour before she woke up and realized that he was gone.

Will reached down to remove his shirt from the hotel floor but paused when he saw her stir and let out a soft moan. She turned onto her stomach and kicked aside the white, cotton bed sheet, exposing a honey-brown calf and thigh in the process. Will gazed at her hungrily.

Put on your clothes, Will, he thought. But he couldn't help himself. He inched toward the bed as she let out another soft moan. He wondered what she was dreaming about, but as he lowered himself to the bed and saw her pelvis shift and her thighs tense up, he had an idea. Will smiled impishly.

He pushed aside her hair and lowered his mouth to the back of her neck. He pulled the bed sheet downward, leaving light kisses along her shoulder blades and the small of her back. Keisha stirred, wiggling and whimpering each time that he kissed her, though she never fully roused. *She certainly is a heavy sleeper,* Will thought with amusement. When he dragged down the bed sheet further, revealing the tantalizing curve of her bare bottom, he lowered his head and nipped one cheek playfully.

"Oww," she murmured. Keisha stretched, opened her eyes, and slowly raised herself to gaze bleary-eyed over her shoulder at Will, who was reaching for one of the few remaining condoms on the hotel night table. "What are you doing?" she asked before yawning loudly.

"Waking you up," he muttered with a naughty grin. He removed the towel from around his waist.

"Huh?" she murmured sleepily. He nuzzled the back of her neck again and then raised her hips and crouched behind her. Will guided her hands to the headboard so that she could brace herself.

"Will, what are you doing?" she repeated, frowning with unease. He didn't respond and just continued to nuzzle her neck.

Keisha let out a cry of surprise as he entered her. The knuckles of her hands whitened as she tightly gripped the wooden headboard while his hands cupped her breasts. She turned her head slightly and he met her mouth. They kissed eagerly. After hours of lovemaking, their bodies knew one another. In a matter of seconds they quickly fell into the same familiar rhythm, bucking rapidly until a time bomb exploded inside of them. Both Will and Keisha fell back to the mattress, completely spent.

After regaining her breath, Keisha rolled onto her back and slowly smiled. "Well," she said as she stretched, now fully awake. "A good morning to you, too."

"I'm sorry." He chuckled. "I didn't say good morning, did I?"

She slowly shook her head. "No, you didn't. But you could make up for it by buying me breakfast."

Will's smile tightened. *Breakfast? So much for a quick exit,* he thought.

As if reading his mind, Keisha raised herself to her elbows. She looked at him and shrugged. "Or you can just have your way with me and leave me here," she said. "It's up to you."

Her voice was shaking, but she smiled as if trying to sound lighter and saucier than she felt. He could tell he had hurt her feelings. *Christ, the least you could do is buy her breakfast, Will,* he thought.

"What would you like to eat, Keisha?" he asked quietly.

She gave a tentative though genuine smile. "Waffles with blueberries and a side of bacon would be fine. Maybe some orange juice."

He nodded his head. She rose from the bed, attempting to take the sheets with her as she made her way across the room, but he tugged at them firmly, stopping her in her tracks.

"Excuse me!" she exclaimed with a laugh. "You mind letting go?"

He cocked an eyebrow. "Why? You don't need a sheet to take a shower."

"No, but I'd prefer not to walk around the hotel room buck naked!"

"But why not?" he challenged. "I've seen you already. I know what you've got."

Keisha contemplated his words for several seconds. "Fine," she murmured and shrugged. She then dropped the sheets to her ankles. Will breathed deeply as he watched her cross the room, her hips swaying, her pert bottom shimmying with each step.

"The menu's beside the television," she said casually. She turned slightly, revealing one of the full breasts he had held earlier. She swept up her long hair from her neck and shoulders, raised her arms and began to twist the unruly tendrils into a bun atop her head. "You should look through it, too."

Will sighed as she shut the bathroom door behind her. In another life, Keisha could have made lots of money off a body like that. If he didn't watch himself, he could develop a real addiction to this woman.

Get a hold of yourself, Will, he suddenly thought. *Order her breakfast and end it at that. You have a lot to do today, and screwing around in bed with Keisha ain't one of them.*

By the time she emerged from the bathroom, smiling ear to ear, Will was already dressed. He shrugged into his suit jacket as her gaze drifted to the breakfast tray perched on the edge of the bed. One lone plate and glass sat on it. Keisha's smile instantly faded.

"You're not going to eat anything?" she asked, frowning deeply, looking crestfallen.

Will adjusted his tie and cleared his throat. "Uh, no," he said, forcing a smile. "I don't usually eat breakfast anyway. I had some of your O.J., though. I hope . . . you . . . don't mind."

He watched as Keisha's expression suddenly changed. She steeled her back and gave him a glacial stare as she slowly strolled over to the bed. She tightened her towel around her then sat with one leg dangling over the edge and the other tucked beneath her. "Considering what we've already shared, I don't think drinking my orange juice is that big of a deal, Will," she said before slicing into one of her Belgian waffles.

Will grimaced. "Sorry I have to rush off," he mumbled, refusing to meet her gaze. "I just have a lot of . . . things on my plate today and—"

"Sure, I understand," Keisha said quickly, shrugging her shoulders as she bit into a slice of bacon, "it's election season. You don't have to explain." She reached over to grab the television remote and turned on the TV, filling the bedroom with the morning banter of the *Today* show.

"Maybe I'll . . . give you a . . . call later," he muttered.

"Yeah, okay," she said with another shrug, keeping her eyes focused on the television.

Will gritted his teeth. It shouldn't be this hard to walk away. Keisha looked dejected, but at least she was willing to give him an out. It was an election and he *did* have lots of work to do. She probably did, too. But the truth was Will didn't give a damn about the work. He didn't care about the messages that were in his email box or on his voicemail. He didn't care about the meeting that would start in forty-five minutes that he was supposed to attend. He didn't want to leave her—not yet.

"Can I have a slice of that bacon?" he asked, surprising himself.

Keisha lowered her fork and blinked in shock. "*Bacon?* I thought you didn't—"

She stopped as he took a slice from her plate before ripping it in half and popping some of it into his mouth.

"Not bad," Will murmured. "How are the waffles?" he asked, before sitting on the mattress beside her.

"Good . . . I guess," Keisha said slowly. She gazed at him with open suspicion.

"Can I have some?" he asked, glancing at the fork that hovered near her mouth.

Keisha frowned. "I thought you didn't have time for breakfast, Will."

"I don't," he answered succinctly before taking the fork out of her hand and having a bite of her waffle.

"And I thought you said you had a 'full plate' this morning," she interjected. "You know, 'lots of stuff to do.' "

Will wiped at the dollop of syrup near the edge of her mouth and smiled. "I do."

"Will, please," she said sternly. She pushed his hand away and glared at him. "You said you had to go. Either you do or you don't." She paused. "Or were you just saying that because you want to get out of here?"

He frowned, now genuinely offended. "What do you mean? You think I'm lying?"

Her gaze faltered as she sighed. She didn't answer his question. Instead she stared down at her lap. "Look, I'm a big girl, okay? This . . . this isn't the first time this has happened. I can . . . handle it. If you have to go, then go. We both had a good time. It was nice while it la— "

Keisha stopped when he lowered his mouth to hers, tasting the sweet syrup on her full lips as he did. He gave her a long, sweltering kiss that made her yelp in surprise and then moan in delight as she pressed against him and wrapped her arms around his neck. He had wanted to silence her, to take her breath away. But he hadn't meant the kiss to steal his breath, too. When she finally broke their kiss minutes later, they were both panting heavily.

"Oh, man, that was good," Keisha murmured as she loosened her arms from around his neck and raised her hand to her brow. She slowly shook her head, trying to pull herself out of her lust-induced haze. "Wait . . . W-what was I saying?"

"If you can't remember it must not be important," he muttered as he pulled her toward him, preparing to lower his mouth to hers again.

She frowned. "No, I was saying . . . something . . . important, very important." She twisted her head away from him before he could kiss her again, making him sigh impatiently. "I was trying to make a point."

"There's a festival in Baltimore today," he blurted out, hoping to distract her again.

Keisha blinked, now thoroughly confused. "What?"

"Do you like crabs as much as you like blueberry waffles?" he asked with a sly grin.

Her frown intensified. "Yeah, I guess I do, but—"

He cocked an eyebrow. "You guess you do? Either you're a Maryland crab cake fan or you aren't, Keisha," he chided playfully. "There's no guessing involved."

Despite herself, she smiled. "Yes, I like crab cakes. I *love* crab cakes, but—"

"So why don't we go to Baltimore today? I'll head home, change out of this suit and tie, and come back to pick you up," he said. "I promise you all the crab cakes you can eat and corn on the cob and coleslaw."

Are you on drugs? What the hell are you doing, Will, a panicked voice said inside his head. *Staying to eat breakfast with her was one thing but you're taking her to Baltimore? Have you forgotten everything you have to do today?*

But Will ignored that voice. Instead he gazed eagerly at Keisha, silently willing her to say yes. She was now giving him a bemused look. She shook her head.

"Will, you don't have to ask me to go to Baltimore with you," she said quietly.

"I know I don't have to, but I *want* to. Will you go with me today?"

She rubbed her temples. "Will . . ."

"Will you go with me today?" he repeated.

She chuckled softly. "You're not going to give up on this, are you?"

"Will you go with me today?" he asked insistently.

He held his breath until her cautious smile broke into a full grin.

"Okay. Okay, yes," Keisha said. "Yes, I'll go to Baltimore with you. Now go home and change."

They both rose from the bed and he held her hand as she walked him across the room to her hotel door.

"I'll be back in an hour in something a lot more casual, probably a T-shirt and shorts," he said as he stepped into the hallway. The drone of the cleaning woman's vacuum filled the corridor.

Keisha nodded. "Well, by then I should be wearing something a lot *less* casual." She glanced down at herself, tilted her head, and gave a bashful smile. "More than a white bath towel, I hope."

"Frankly, I'd prefer you in a lot less," he said with a mischievous grin. Wrapping his arms around her waist, he lowered his mouth to hers to give her a memorable goodbye. She stood on the tips of her toes and tilted back her head as they teased one another's lips and then let their kiss deepen. Will could feel the hunger building up inside him again. He wanted nothing more than to rip that towel off Keisha, dig his fingers into her hair and drag her back into the room to the hotel bed. But thankfully, Keisha ended their kiss before he was pushed any further.

"Go home, Will," she whispered as she pulled away, licking her now-swollen lips. She placed her hands against his chest and gave him a light shove. "I'll be ready to leave by the time you get back. I'll meet you downstairs, by the concierge desk."

He swallowed loudly and quickly nodded. "Concierge desk. I'll be there. See you in an hour."

Will watched as Keisha let out a low whistle and fanned herself before shutting the door. He smiled as he walked toward the elevators. He could totally sympathize with her. He was feeling rather overheated himself.

A door slammed, making Will turn his head. He looked down the corridor but saw no one there. "Humph," he murmured, shrugging his shoulders and continuing toward the elevators.

So how are you going to explain this one, the pesky voice inside his head asked as he pressed the down button. *You're going to pull a no show for a whole day's worth of appointments? You aren't planning to call anyone back? What's going to be the big excuse?*

"I was sick, *really* sick," Will said aloud and let out a hearty cough for good measure.

During election campaigns you travel a lot, eat at lots of places that don't have the cleanest kitchens, and you shake lots of hands, he reasoned. There was no telling what virus he could have contracted, what contaminated food he could have consumed. He'd just tell George that he fell ill and couldn't do anything about it. He was allowed one sick day, wasn't he? He was only human, not a machine.

I was just sick, Will thought as the elevator doors opened and he stepped inside. With that decision now made he could now focus totally on spending another romantic day with Keisha, and he was eagerly looking forward to it.

Have you fallen for this girl, Will? the pesky voice asked.

He didn't answer.

CHAPTER 20

"That bastard," Gretchen muttered between gritted teeth. "That *bastard!*" she shrieked, hurling the ice bucket across the hotel room at a desk chair. The bucket ricocheted off the chair and hit a nearby wall.

George emerged from the bathroom barefoot with a towel wrapped around his hairy potbelly and a toothbrush dangling out the side of his mouth. "What's the matter, sweetheart?" he gurgled through frothy lips.

She whipped her head around, sending her red locks flying as she faced him with her fists balled at her sides. She was almost snarling. Gretchen opened her mouth to tell George exactly what she had seen when she tried to leave his hotel room a minute ago to get more ice, but she stopped herself. The wheels in her brain began to spin slowly, then rapidly. Information like this was important. Maybe she could use it for ammunition later. Blurting it out now to George would be a waste.

Gretchen closed her eyes, took a calming breath and then opened them again.

"Nothing," she said quickly. "It was nothing."

He frowned as he watched Gretchen stomp across the room to the bed that was still disheveled from their lovemaking the night before. She began rummaging through her purse.

"It didn't sound like nothing," he murmured, wiping the toothpaste from his mouth with the back of his hand. "You sounded pretty upset."

"Dammit, I know it's here somewhere," she muttered, ignoring him as she dumped the contents of her purse on the bed. "Where the hell is it?"

"What on earth are you looking for, Gretchen?" he asked, his frown deepening.

"George, dammit! Stop distracting me!" she shouted. She then rifled through the pile of lipstick, hair brushes, and business cards that were now spread on the wrinkled sheets. "Just . . . go do . . . something!" she spat, shoeing him away with her hand. "Shouldn't you be calling your wife by now? I thought you had to check in every thirty minutes."

"Is that what this is all about, honey?" He sighed and slowly walked over to her. He rubbed her shoulders. "Look, I told you that this is only temporary," he whispered against her hair, raising one of his hands to her breasts. "At least until the election is over. I'll leave Marjorie when—"

"This is not about your wife!" she shouted, shoving him away. "Your phone is ringing," she said, tilting her head toward his cell phone, which perched on the night table. "Go answer it!" She then quickly began to check business card after business card.

He pursed his lips and blushed, looking at her with the sad eyes of a kicked puppy as he answered his cell phone.

George sighed. "Hi, Marj," he said quietly. "No, honey, I was just about to call you. How are the kids?"

Usually Gretchen would apologize and placate him. She'd make George feel that she wanted him for the sexy, virile man that she assured him he was. But Gretchen wasn't in the mood to placate him today, and was only five seconds away from blurting out what she had been holding in for months: that she didn't find George sexy or virile, that it was to her advantage to sleep with her boss. In fact, she could think about a hundred other men she would rather have in her bed. And one of those men had just left the hotel room of Keisha Reynolds . . . of all people!

How Will could choose that girl over me is mystifying, she thought.

While in the hotel lobby last night, waiting to get the okay from George to come upstairs to his room, she had thought she saw Will in the distance, kissing some woman in front of the elevators. But the kiss had been so torrid she knew it could not be Will. Cool and reserved, *tight-assed* William Blake was not into PDAs, especially one that passionate. She was sure of it. But a few minutes ago, she opened George's hotel door to find Will down the hall kissing Keisha Reynolds, Parker's deputy campaign manager. The kiss was just as passionate as it had been in the lobby, maybe more so. Gretchen had been outraged as she glared at them through the crack of the door. *He never kissed me like that!*

And it was obvious that Will and Reynolds had exchanged a lot more than a kiss, judging by the wrinkled suit he wore that looked like the same suit he had had on night before. It took all Gretchen's willpower not to hurl her ice bucket at the back of his head. In a fury, she had slammed the hotel door shut instead.

I can't believe he would do this to me, she thought angrily. She had practically thrown herself at that man and he had turned her away because he claimed to be in a "serious relationship." *So I guess Reynolds was the "serious relationship" he was referring to*, she thought. Not only had he chosen that girl over her, but he had chosen the opposition over his *own campaign*.

Who the hell does he think he is?

Oh, she would make him pay. That was for sure! But she'd take care of his little tart first.

"Yes! I've got it!" Gretchen exclaimed as she grabbed one of the business cards.

George watched her with bewilderment as she grabbed her cell phone and rushed across the room to the sliding glass doors that led to the balcony.

"What are you doing?" he mouthed as his wife droned in his ear.

Gretchen ignored him as she slipped onto the concrete balcony and shut the sliding glass doors behind her. She smiled from ear to ear as she leaned against the steel railing and quickly punched in the number on the business card. She was practically humming when someone picked up on the other end.

"Hello?" Phil answered.

"Hi, Phil, it's Gretchen Chase at the Dupré campaign. How are you doing today?"

The phone line went silent and Gretchen had to keep herself from laughing. She could tell that she was probably the last person in the world Phil expected to be on the other end of the phone line. She could imagine him frowning intensely, trying to regain his bearings. "Uh, yes." He loudly cleared his throat. "Well, hello, Gretchen, how . . . how can I help you?"

"Well, Phil, I just wanted to find out from you how long you think your meeting is going to run over today?" she asked as she twisted a lock of hair around her finger. "We understand that you guys are tied up . . . but we have our own meeting scheduled and I'm just trying to figure out how far back to push it since we need Will Blake there. I wanted to know how long he's going to be with you guys."

"Pardon me, but . . . ," he paused, ". . . I think you're mistaken, Gretchen. I don't have a meeting today with Will," Phil said. "In fact I've never had *any* meetings scheduled with Will, at least none that I'm aware of."

"Oh, really," Gretchen said, putting on her best imitation of surprise. "Well, I was under the impression that you all had a meeting this morning, at least that's what they told me."

"They?" Phil said, sounding even more confused.

"Will and Keisha Reynolds, your deputy campaign manager," Gretchen exclaimed. "I ran into them here at the Biltmore Hotel as they were just about to board an elevator heading upstairs. I felt bad interrupting them since they seemed like they were in a deep conversation. But I wasn't sure if it was related to the campaign. When I asked them what they were up to, they said they were having another meeting and you would join them later."

"*Another* meeting?"

"Yes, I think this is the third one they've had." She shrugged. "Well, anyway, the last time I saw them was about an hour and a half ago. I've been calling and calling but haven't been able to get Will on the phone, so I thought I'd try to reach you."

I should get an Oscar for this, Gretchen thought mischievously. Who else could ad-lib so well without any professional training?

Phil cleared his throat again. "Let me get this straight. You saw Keisha and Will at a hotel together?"

"Yes, I did but . . . but," Gretchen gave a dramatic pause, "I thought you guys had a meeting today. Are you saying you don't?" Gretchen's eyes widened as she forced a deep sigh. "But I'm pretty sure that's what they told me. Why else would they be at the hotel together?" She sighed again, letting Phil come to his own conclusions. "Well, I am just totally confused now."

"So am I," Phil said quietly.

"This just doesn't make any sense. I don't think Will or Keisha would lie," she said with a forced giggle. "I guess I just misunderstood. Well, sorry, Phil! I'll let you get back to work. I'll just clear this up later with Will. You have a good day."

"Uh," he murmured, sounding a little shell-shocked. "You, too."

She quickly disconnected and clapped her hands gleefully.

That couldn't have gone more perfectly, Gretchen thought to herself. Her little story about finding Will and

Keisha Reynolds at the hotel was bound to make Phil suspicious. Keisha's loyalty to her campaign would be drawn into question. Gretchen wished she could see the look on Keisha's face when Phil confronted her. Maybe he would even tell Parker what Gretchen had just told him. At the thought, Gretchen almost died from laughter. She'd love to see Keisha try to talk her way out of this one. Now Gretchen's next step was to figure out the best way to get back at Will.

"What's so funny?" George asked with a frown as he slid the glass door open.

Gretchen turned and smiled. "Everything," she sang giddily before skipping across the balcony and leaping into his arms. She then kissed him with a loud smack on the lips before wrapping her arms around his neck.

"You're acting very strange today, Gretchen." His frown intensified. "What are you up to?"

Gretchen gave a wicked smile as she tugged his bath towel open. *"Everything."*

CHAPTER 21

Keisha stood against the back wall of the meeting room at the senior citizens center in a crisp brown suit with her arms crossed over her chest. She shifted constantly from one three-inch heel to the other so that her feet would hurt less. For at least a half an hour, she, Tanya, and Phil had been standing near the continental breakfast table, observing the throng of retirees who sat in fold-up metal chairs. She sipped lukewarm coffee from a Styrofoam cup while Dr. Parker gave his campaign stump speech. Keisha gazed at the riveted crowd and then at the stage where Dr. Parker stood.

"We can take back this country!" he shouted. "And if you choose me as your representative I can assure you that I will listen to you and you *only*, ladies and gentlemen," Parker said as he pointed to faces in the crowd. "Not some lobbyist that wants to rob you of your health care or of your social security. Their voices have been listened to way too long!"

Keisha gazed up at him. Dr. Parker had the same commanding presence that he had had as a full-time college professor, but on the campaign trail he had certainly become a lot more polished, almost debonair. She observed him in his charcoal Ralph Lauren suit and his fresh $100 haircut. It was definitely an improvement over his past look. She could tell from the enthralled expressions on the older women's faces in the audience that they not only liked what they heard, but now liked what they saw. But part of Keisha missed her scruffy old professor.

Tanya smirked as she leaned toward Keisha. "Girl, they are eating out of his hands. He has got this," she whispered into Keisha's ear as the room filled with applause during a break in his speech.

"It definitely looks like he does," Keisha murmured and then glanced down at her hip as her BlackBerry gave a loud buzz. She frowned, wondering who would be trying to reach her this early in the day. She lowered her coffee cup to the breakfast table, unhooked her BlackBerry and glanced down at the text message on the screen.

"When can I see U?" the message read.

She could tell from the phone number that it was Will. It took all her strength not to break into a grin.

"I'll be right back," Keisha whispered. Tanya quickly nodded while Phil narrowed his eyes at Keisha.

"Is something wrong?" he asked.

"No, nothing's wrong," she said quietly, pointing toward the meeting room's double doors. "I'm just going to take this outside. I'll be back in a few minutes."

He gazed at her without saying a word for what felt like eternity before slowly nodding his head. "Okay," he whispered.

Keisha quickly began to walk toward the doors but glanced over her shoulder only to find Phil still staring at her suspiciously.

He's not suspicious, Keisha. You're just being paranoid, she thought as she walked into the corridor. *Why would he suspect anything? Only you know its Will's number.*

With thumbs flying, she quickly typed a reply text message, smiling as she did so. "Not 2day. I've got plans. Sorry ☹"

Within seconds she got a phone call from Will. Keisha chuckled as she answered.

"Yes?" she said with a laugh.

"What do you mean, you have plans?" he asked indignantly over the phone line in his deep baritone. A chill went up her spine at the sound of his voice. Keisha clinched her legs together to steady herself and to halt the throbbing that radiated from between them. She cleared her throat, trying her best to hide all signs of the spell he cast over her.

"I'm sorry, Will, but I already have something scheduled for tonight," she said as she strolled toward a floor-to-ceiling window facing the parking lot.

Today was her birthday. Keisha initially had planned to treat it like any other day but because she was turning thirty, her mother had insisted they make a big deal out of it. Lena had reserved a table at one of their favorite restaurants in downtown D.C. to celebrate.

"So cancel it," Will ordered playfully, making her laugh again. "Seriously, though, I want to see you. I *need* to see you. It's been too long."

"*Too long?* You just saw me three nights ago!" she exclaimed.

And the night before that and the night before that, Keisha thought. Since that night at the hotel almost four weeks ago Keisha had been a permanent fixture at Will's house. She had decided to give him a break for the past two days by not driving to his home in Annapolis, figuring that he'd quickly get bored with her if she spent the night too often. Her lack of romantic experience made her rely on conventional wisdom, and conventional wisdom said that distance made the heart grow fonder, right? But judging from the way Will was behaving, distance only seemed to irritate him.

"*So what?* I don't care if it's been three days. It feels longer," he said impatiently. "Well, when does your workday end today?"

Keisha shrugged. "I don't know. Five, I think."

"And when do your plans for this evening start?"

She gave a wry smile as she slumped against a window frame. She knew where this was going. "They start at eight, Will."

"*Eight?* That's three whole hours when you aren't doing anything."

She sighed. "I wouldn't say that I'm not doing anything. I'm driving from—"

"Three hours," he repeated. "And you're telling me you can't pencil me in anywhere?"

Keisha slowly shook her head and laughed. "Will, it'll take me thirty minutes to get to your place. That leaves us two hours together, maybe only an hour and half, tops. That's not enough—"

"Don't worry," he insisted, cutting her off again. "That's plenty of time for the surprise I have for you."

Keisha cocked an eyebrow and frowned. "Surprise? What surprise?"

"Well, I guess you'll just have to come and find out, now won't you?"

"Let me guess." She tilted her head. "Does it involve a French maid costume and a feather duster?"

Will chuckled. "I'm not revealing any of my secrets until you get there."

"Will," Keisha said, laughing again, "I told you that I can't make it. It's not enough time! I have *plans*!"

"Come over between five o'clock and eight, all right?"

Her eyes widened. "Will, did you hear what I said?"

"Look, I've got to go. I'll see you tonight."

"Will," Keisha whispered shrilly. "Will!"

The phone went dead, making Keisha slowly shake her head.

"I can't believe him! He will *not* give up," she thought with bemusement. But in all honesty, the idea that Will wanted to see her that badly made her downright giddy. Keisha had been longing desperately to be with him, too. She refused to entertain the thought that he was falling in love with her as she had fallen for him, especially this soon. But butterflies fluttered in her stomach at the idea that he could possibly, maybe, feel the same way about her that she did about him.

"What are you grinnin' about?"

Keisha jumped at the sound of Tanya's voice. She turned to find the older woman gazing at her with a cocked eyebrow and a smile. Keisha blinked. "Huh?"

"*Huh?*" Tanya mimicked in a high voice. She put her hands on her hips and walked toward Keisha. "I said, 'What are you grinnin' about?' That must have been a good phone call, judging from the smile on your face."

"Umm, my mom called. She . . . she . . . just wanted to finalize plans for t-tonight," Keisha stuttered while tucking her BlackBerry back on her hip. "She's taking me out to dinner."

Keisha's smile tightened as she tried her best to control the muscles in her face. Despite her efforts, Tanya narrowed her eyes. Keisha felt almost as if she were at a police station being questioned by a detective about some capital crime.

It's not like I murdered anybody, Keisha thought anxiously as her palms began to sweat under Tanya's penetrating gaze.

"You are such a horrible liar," Tanya said with a slow shake of the head.

Keisha blinked. "What?"

"Please, girl, from all that whispering and the gigglin', that did not sound like you were talking to your mother," Tanya insisted. "No, that sounded like you were talking to a man. Your new man, I suppose." Tanya suddenly grabbed Keisha's hand and smiled eagerly. "So what's his name? I want all the details: when you met, how you met, what he does for a living, and, more importantly, how fine he is! Tell me everything!" she ordered, bouncing enthusiastically on the balls of her feet.

Keisha's eyes widened. She loudly cleared her throat as she tugged her hand away from Tanya. She nervously began to fidget with one of her jacket buttons. "I-I don't know what you're talking about Tanya. I'm not dating anyone."

Tanya's smile abruptly disappeared. "What do you mean, you aren't dating anyone?"

"I'm just . . . not . . . dating anyone," she said, forcing a tight smile and adjusting her suit. "I wish I were, but I told you before that I really don't have time for dating right now. Gotta stay focused." She turned toward the doors where several of the senior citizens had started to file out one by one. "Is Parker's speech over already?" she asked as she began to walk toward the meeting room. "I guess we should probably get back in there and—"

She stopped when Tanya tugged her arm.

"Don't try to change the subject." Tanya crossed her arms over her petite chest. "Are you really telling me that you aren't seeing anyone? That all the laughing and smiling you've been doing lately is just my imagination?"

Keisha took a deep breath and shrugged. "I guess so. Sorry to disappoint you," she said with a forced smile. She turned again and quickly walked back to the room before Tanya could ask her any more questions. "I swear to you, Tanya," she called over her shoulder, "the instant I meet the right guy, you'll be the first to know."

Keisha continued her swift strides away from her friend. She sighed with relief. *That was close.*

∽◦∾

Keisha quickly pulled bobby pins from her hair, trying to undo her chignon as she raced up the driveway to the front door of Will's house. She knew Will preferred her hair down. He liked to play with her locks when they lounged on the couch and to run his fingers through it when they made love.

She tried to look at herself in the stained glass panel window beside his front door. It was hard to see her reflection in the dying light of early evening but Keisha did her best. She reached into her purse to quickly apply lipstick. She pinched her cheeks for color and sighed. *You look tired*, she thought, running her fingers over the bags under her eyes. But Keisha guessed there was no helping that. The election was picking up and she was getting even less sleep. Plus, it had been a long day and the truth showed on her tired face.

"Just make sure you don't stay long," Keisha told herself. She would have to tell Will this again as soon as she saw him. She had dinner tonight with her mother and it had taken her longer to get to his place than she had expected. Keisha could only stay thirty minutes, an hour at the most. He would just have to accept that.

Keisha rang the doorbell and waited to hear Will's heavy footsteps coming toward the front door. After a long interval, she heard nothing. She rang the doorbell for a second time and waited but once again, there was no response. Keisha glanced over her shoulder to look at Will's driveway and frowned. His silver Audi Roadster was parked there. He should be home. Maybe the bell was broken.

Keisha loudly knocked on the door once and then twice with more gusto. It slowly creaked open. She hesitantly peeped inside. All the lights in Will's foyer were off, though an orange glow came from the kitchen. "Will? Will?" she shouted before pushing the door open further and stepping inside. "You left the front door unlocked. You . . . oh!"

Her eyes drifted to his hardwood floors and what she found beneath her feet dumbfounded her. A lush trail of red and pink rose petals—hundreds of them—led from the foyer through the living room and into the kitchen. At the sight of them, Keisha covered her mouth and grinned so hard that her cheeks hurt.

"Follow the trail," Will finally said to her through the darkness.

"Is this my surprise?" Keisha asked as she set down her purse, removed her shoes, and shut the front door. She goose stepped through the rose petals, feeling their lush softness beneath her stocking feet.

"Part of it," he teased in return as she drew closer to the kitchen.

From the doorway, Keisha could see the tea light candles and the three vases filled with roses, calla lilies, and orchids, but she didn't spot the chocolate cake with the single birthday candle in the center until Will turned around and stepped from in front of it. Keisha raised her hand to her mouth again, nearly blinking back tears as she gazed at him. She could never have imagined that he'd orchestrate something so sweet for her.

"So you managed to pencil me in then, birthday girl?" he asked with a lopsided grin. He looked rakishly handsome with his loosened tie and unbuttoned collar. He had even rolled up the sleeves of his dress shirt. "I told you three hours was plenty of time," he said as he strolled forward, uncorking a bottle of Moet & Chandon. "You know, I almost forgot what today was but I remembered you mentioning it when—"

Keisha couldn't help herself. She quickly ran over to Will, hitting him with such force as she leapt into his arms that she knocked the air out of him and made him almost tumble backward against the kitchen sink and drop the champagne bottle. Keisha then planted on Will the hottest kiss she could muster, despite the tears trickling down her cheeks.

"I take it that you like your surprise then," he said with a chuckle when their kiss ended. Will then gazed down at her, frowned, and placed the bottle on the kitchen counter. "Keisha, what's wrong?" he asked, wiping the tears away with his thumbs. He pulled her closer to him.

Keisha quickly shook her head, too overwhelmed to say anything. She couldn't explain why she was crying. She guessed she was just that happy.

"I just . . . I just," she said finally, sniffing loudly. She gazed up at him with tearful eyes. "No one's ever done something like this . . . for me . . . before. It's all so beautiful. I never . . . I never would have guessed you'd do this, Will."

He gave a nervous smile. "Well," he cleared his throat, "that was the point."

"No, you don't understand! Seeing all this makes my . . . my heart feel like it's gonna burst out of my chest!" she exclaimed, starting to weep again. "Because it's so wonderful. You're so wonderful, Will." She raised her hand to cup his face. "Will, I . . . I just love you so—"

Keisha watched as Will's eyes widened. His Adam's apple bobbed as he swallowed loudly.

Oh, God, what am I doing? They had only been dating for a few weeks and Keisha had already blurted out the l-word. She was gushing and blubbering uncontrollably, like some love-struck school girl. Will didn't seem to be taking her behavior well either. In fact, he looked absolutely terrified.

Keisha slowly pushed away from him and reached for a paper towel to wipe away her remaining tears. She had to clear this up somehow and get that look of fright off his face. She loudly cleared her throat and forced a smile as she balled the paper towel in the palm of her hand.

"I just love your surprise so much, Will. I love so much that you . . . you did this f-for me, I mean," she lied as she sniffed again. "You were right. I never would have guessed it. Good job!" Keisha's eyes darted to the kitchen table as she tried desperately to change the subject. "Chocolate! My favorite! Did you bake it yourself?"

He stared at her warily, not saying a word. After several uncomfortable seconds, Will gave a wry grin and finally spoke.

"I can't bake a cupcake," he said as he filled two glasses with champagne and handed one flute to her. "There's no way I could have baked this."

Keisha giggled as she tipped the champagne glass to her lips, happy that they had changed the subject to lighter things. The champagne bubbles tickled her nose, making her sneeze. She watched as Will gulped the rest of his champagne and grinned.

"All right, time for you to blow out your candle," he said as he reached into his pocket and pulled out a silver lighter. Then he leaned over and lit the candle in the center of the chocolate cake.

She frowned. "Only one?"

"I thought if I put all thirty on there I might set off the kitchen smoke alarm," he chided her playfully with a chuckle. "*Owww!*" He yelped in surprise as she smacked him on the arm. "I was just kidding!"

"Very funny," she said.

He gave her a wink. "Go ahead. Make a wish, birthday girl."

Keisha smiled and gazed down at her cake and then up at Will. She didn't have to think about the wish she wanted to make. She knew it instantly. She had fallen for Will Blake, heart and soul. She hoped that in the near future, he would fall for her, too. She looked forward to the day when she could tell him she loved him and see that same love in return in his eyes, not fear.

Here's hoping, Keisha thought as she held back her hair, leaned down and closed her eyes. She took a deep breath before making her silent wish and blowing out the flickering flame on the candle.

"What did you wish for?" Will asked casually as he poured himself another glass of champagne. "Fame? Fortune?"

Keisha quickly shook her head and smiled mischievously before bringing her mouth back to his.

CHAPTER 22

Keisha yawned loudly as she closed her eyes, feeling herself falling asleep against Will's chest. "Wake me up in a half an hour . . . no, twenty minutes, please," she murmured as he gently trailed his fingers along her back. "I want to take a quick nap."

The second bottle of champagne, the fresh strawberries, and chocolate cake sat mostly untouched on the first floor. Keisha and Will had not been back to the kitchen since he carried her upstairs a half an hour ago. Part of her wanted to sample the rest of her birthday treat before she left for her dinner date with her mother, but she was too tired. After all that lovemaking, right now Keisha wanted nothing more than to sleep.

"Why do you want me to wake you up?" he asked, running his fingers through her hair. "Why don't you just stay tonight?" He smiled. "I'll make you breakfast in the morning. I've got fresh blueberries, and we both know how much you like waffles and blueberries."

"It's tempting, but I can't," she muttered tiredly with a smile, snuggling against him to get more comfortable. "I told you that I have to be somewhere later."

He frowned. "But you're already late. I thought you had to be there at eight."

"I do have to be there at eight." Keisha's eyes instantly shot open. "Wait . . . what time is it?"

Will reached over and raised the digital clock on the night table beside him. "It's 8:15."

Keisha sucked her teeth as she pushed herself off his chest. "Oh, hell! I didn't know it was that late! I thought it was 6:30!" she exclaimed as she quickly pulled back the sheets and climbed out of bed. "Why didn't you tell me?"

She had arrived at his house at a little after 5:30. How could they have possibly been in his bedroom for more than two and a half hours? *Time certainly flies when you're having fun, I guess*, Keisha thought.

Will raised himself to a sitting position and propped a pillow behind his back. He shrugged his shoulders. "I lost track of time just like you did. Just call them and tell them you're running late, or, better yet," he said, lowering his voice as he reached for her, "tell them that you can't make it."

Keisha didn't answer him. Instead she stared over his shoulder at the alarm clock, cursing under her breath. It was indeed 8:15 p.m. She should have been at the restaurant meeting her mother. She could envision the older woman anxiously checking her watch as she waited for her daughter.

Keisha stepped out of Will's reach as she scrambled to grab her underwear and blouse. It would be an hour's drive from Annapolis back to D.C.

"Why don't you just *call* them?" Will asked again, frowning as she hurriedly climbed into her underwear. "Does it have something do with the campaign?"

"No," Keisha said as she fastened her bra clasp.

"Well, then what is it?" He cocked an eyebrow. "What? A date?" he asked sarcastically with a smirk.

She quickly shoved her arms into her shirt sleeves. "As a matter of fact, it is . . . kinda," Keisha said as she buttoned her blouse. "It's for my birthday. I was supposed to meet someone for dinner."

"*That's* what you had to do this evening?" Will gazed at her, dumbfounded. "Are you kidding me?"

"Does it look like I'm kidding?" Keisha asked, frowning at his tone. She turned and saw that his face had morphed from an expression of surprise to one of anger. The muscles along his chests and arms were tense.

"Why the hell didn't you tell me that when you got here, or when I talked to you *twelve* damn hours ago, Keisha?" he asked with hot indignation.

Her eyes widened.

"Who is he? Were you planning to tell me about him or were you just—"

"It's a date with my *mother*, Will," Keisha quickly clarified. "She's taking me out to dinner for my birthday. So calm down, all right?"

"Oh," he said. She watched the muscles in his arms and chest relax as he sighed. "Why . . . why didn't you say that in the beginning?"

Keisha rolled her eyes and walked around the bed to grab her skirt. "Goodbye, Will," she said, leaning down and kissing him on the cheek. "I'll call you this weekend," she yelled over her shoulder as she hopped into her skirt. She then sprinted down the hall and the staircase.

Seconds later, Keisha climbed inside her car. She reached into her purse and turned on her BlackBerry. There were several voice messages waiting for her, two of which were from her mother. Keisha quickly dialed Lena's number.

"Keisha Reynolds, where are you?" her mother's perturbed voice answered. "You didn't tell me you were going to be late. Are you parking now?"

Keisha frowned sheepishly. "I'm sorry, Ma. A meeting with Phil ran over," she lied as she put the car into reverse and backed out of Will's driveway. "I couldn't . . . I couldn't get out of it to call you, but I'm on my way now."

Her mother sighed. "Well, maybe they can hold the reservation a little longer. How far away are you?"

Keisha drove down the tree-lined street, making a left turn at a stop sign. "I'm about an hour away, Ma. I'm in Annapolis."

There was a noticeable pause. "*Annapolis?* Why are you in Annapolis?"

"It's for work," Keisha blurted out impatiently. "It's hard to explain. Look, Ma, I'm on the road so I should get off the phone."

"Keisha," her mother said before letting out another heavy sigh, "I made these reservations two months ago. You knew what time—"

"Ma, I couldn't get out! What do you want me to do?"

"Fine. Fine," she said quietly. "Just meet me at the house. I don't think the hostess can hold our reservation much longer. I guess I'll just heat up something quick at home. It's not the same as a four-star meal, but it'll have to do. Drive carefully, honey."

"Sorry, Ma. Bye," Keisha said, ending the connection. She tossed her BlackBerry onto the car seat beside her, tightened her grip on the steering wheel, and pressed down the accelerator.

She sounded so disappointed, Keisha thought guiltily.

Keisha hated lying, particularly to her mother, but she seemed to be doing it all the time now. How many fibs had she told in the past week to cover up some afternoon rendezvous with Will? At least a dozen, she surmised. She wondered if Will had told just as many lies so no one would find out about her.

We should stop this, she thought. *I know we should.* But it was so hard to do it. For the first time in her life Keisha could say she was helplessly in love, in every sense of the word. Physically and mentally, Will had a magnetic hold on her and she suspected she had a hold on him, too. How was it their fault that by sheer coincidence they worked for the opposing candidates? Why should she go without being happy just because of some dumb election?

Some dumb election, a voice inside her head mocked. *That election was once really important to you. You have a lot invested in that election, Keisha!*

Keisha quickly reached over and turned up the music on her car radio to drown out that voice. "I'm happy, damn it," she mumbled aloud to herself. "Why can't I be happy for once?"

Why couldn't she enjoy the moment?

∽◦∾

Thanks to a beltway accident, it actually took more than an hour to make it to her mother's house. When she arrived, it was a little after 9:30. Keisha ran up the front steps and quickly opened the front door.

"Sorry I'm late, Ma!" she shouted as she nearly sprinted down the hall and into the kitchen. "Sorry about dinner! Like I said, the meeting ran longer than I expected. I hope you started eating. Please tell me you didn't wait for me again."

She had to pause to catch her breath from running so fast.

Lena slowly looked up from her dinner plate. She scanned Keisha for several seconds, not saying a word. She then pointed across the kitchen table to a plate sitting on the bamboo place mat across from her. "It's okay, Keisha," she finally muttered, taking a bite from her fork. "That's yours. I left a chilled glass for you in the freezer."

"Thanks, Ma," Keisha said with a quick nod. She walked across the kitchen and opened the refrigerator.

"How was work?" her mother called out.

"Fine," Keisha said quickly. "Just busy, as usual."

"Your hair looks pretty," Lena said. She took another bite of baked chicken. "I see you decided to wear it down for once. It looks a little wild, but nice. Felt like changing things up today?"

Keisha's eyes widened. She quickly reached up to touch her head, suddenly realizing that she had forgotten to redo her characteristic chignon.

"Yeah," she said hesitantly. She retrieved her glass and filled it with ice water, her hands shaking slightly. She smoothed down her loose locks so they didn't look quite so tousled. "Just felt like trying something different," she murmured with an awkward smile as she walked to the kitchen table.

"Is your skirt on backwards?"

Keisha stopped and blinked. "Huh?"

"Is . . . your . . . skirt . . . on . . . backwards?" her mother repeated, enunciating each word.

Keisha stared down at her waist and realized in horror that her skirt was, indeed, on backwards. She must not have noticed in her rush to get dressed that the zipper, pleat, and split were now toward the front. Keisha grinned sheepishly as she sat down her glass on the kitchen table and returned her brown skirt to its proper position.

"How did *that* happen?" she muttered with a forced laugh, tucking her hair behind her ear. "God, I hope it hasn't been like that the whole day. Maybe I did it when I went to the bathroom. I wish someone had told me."

That someone being Will. The next time she saw him, she would give him an earful.

Keisha lowered herself into one of the chairs at the table. She raised the plate of food to her nose and inhaled its aroma. "Hmmm, smells good, Ma," she said, spreading a dinner napkin across her lap and grabbing a fork. "I'm sure any home-cooked meal by you is better than anything at a restaurant."

The two ate in silence for several minutes. Suddenly, Lena tilted her head and fixed Keisha with a piercing gaze. "Okay," she said with a loud sigh, "if you won't tell me, I guess I'll just have to ask."

"Ask what, Ma?" Keisha said, taking another bite.

"So what's his name and why haven't I met him?"

Keisha stopped mid-swallow, nearly choking on her chicken. She coughed loudly. "What?" she finally croaked. "What's whose name?"

Her mother rolled her eyes. "Don't play dumb, Keisha. You know what I'm talking about. The hair, the skirt, and you being late. He's the reason you stood me up tonight, isn't he?" Her mother cocked an eyebrow. "I know the signs. It's been a long time since I've had a man, but it hasn't been *that* long. Who is he?"

Keisha sat silently, shifting the food around her plate with her fork.

Her mother frowned. "He's not married, is he? He better not be! I didn't raise my daughter to steal some other woman's husband!"

Keisha quickly shook her head. "No, he isn't married," she blurted out. "You know I'd never date a married man, Ma! He's . . ." She stopped herself.

"Well, if he's not married, then why haven't I met him?" She pursed her lips. "Judging from your skirt, it looks like things have gotten pretty serious between you two."

Keisha sighed, now completely mortified. Her shoulders slumped. She felt like a teenager who had just got caught with her boyfriend in her bedroom. This was the second time that someone had sensed that she had a man in her life. Was she that obvious? "His name is Will Blake," Keisha said quietly.

Her mother's eyebrows furrowed as she lowered her fork. "Will Blake? Will Blake . . . it sounds familiar. Where have I heard that name before?"

"He works for Vincent Dupré."

"Oh." Lena's eyes widened. "Oh, *that* Will Blake." She frowned. "I thought you hated him."

"I didn't hate him. Hate is a strong word. I just . . . I just didn't trust him because he worked for Dupré."

"And now you do trust him?" Lena asked.

Keisha nodded. "Yes. He hasn't given me any reason not to." She paused. "I'm sorry I didn't tell you about him before, Ma. It's just . . . hard. Will and I can't be out in the open with this, at least before the election is over, because we work for different camps. Things could get really complicated if people knew we were together. We could even . . . lose our jobs in the worst-case scenario."

"I see," Lena said, slowly nodding her head. "Forbidden love," she murmured, her eyes suddenly glazing over. "I knew another couple like that. They really loved each other and wanted to be together but . . . life just got in the way. I guess it wasn't meant to be." She shook her head. "And now my baby's in love," she whispered in awe.

"Ma, please," Keisha said, fidgeting uneasily in her chair.

"And he loves you, too?"

Keisha frowned. Why was her mother asking her these questions? She didn't want to think about this stuff. She just knew that she was happy. All the sundry details about who loved whom wasn't important—at least for now. Keisha shrugged helplessly. "I don't know. I think . . . he might . . . love me . . . maybe. He seems to. We don't really talk about it. I've never asked him."

Lena reached across the table, placing her hand over her daughter's. She smiled warmly. "Well, don't you think you should?"

"No!" Keisha exclaimed. *What do you want me to do? Scare him away?*

Keisha pulled her hand away from Lena's and grabbed her fork again. She began to angrily shove food into her mouth. "We have enough stuff to deal with. I don't want to talk about that topic with him right now." And judging from the look on Will's face when she had accidentally told him she loved him, Will wasn't eager to talk about that topic, either. "We have chemistry and passion. That's all I need . . . for now. That's all that counts."

"Pardon? '*That's all that counts*'?" Lena slowly shook her head in disbelief. "You're sneaking around with this man and you don't even know if he loves you! You said yourself that both of you could lose your jobs if someone found out that you're together. That's a heavy price to pay, in my opinion!"

"Well, you're entitled to your opinion," Keisha said frostily.

Lena snorted. "I might take a risk like that for love, but I damn sure wouldn't do it just for some 'chemistry'!"

Keisha stared down at her plate. "Ma, can we change the subject, please?"

Lena defiantly crossed her arms over her chest. "No, we can't." She leaned forward and gazed at her daughter earnestly. "Keisha, honey, I've never lied to you. If I see you making a mistake, I tell you. And to me this sounds like a *big* mistake!"

"Look, the way Will and I are handling this works for us, Ma," Keisha said firmly, slamming down her knife and fork. "We don't need to muddy the waters talking about love or the future or expectations right now! I don't want to ask those questions. I just want to enjoy the here and now. I don't want to pin him into a corner."

Lena pursed her lips. "Sounds like the coward's way out to me."

"I am *not* a coward!" Keisha shouted. "Besides, why are you lecturing me? You're telling me to take a chance and ask him if he loves me so I can just scare him away. But you never take chances! Your last date was when? Almost five years ago! You want me to put myself out there, and yet you've never done it yourself!"

Lena quickly stood from the table and angrily glared down at her daughter. "Keisha Reynolds, don't you ever, *ever* tell me what I've done and what I haven't done! Okay? You don't know as much as you *think* you do! I've taken chances and I've sacrificed more than you could ever imagine! But I was willing to do it for love, not just for some rolling around between the sheets!"

Keisha stubbornly stared down at her dinner plate, feeling tears welling in her eyes. In her heart, she knew her mother was right. Keisha was taking a lot of risks for a man she wasn't even certain loved her. So eager to live in the moment, she had been up in the clouds for almost a month, refusing to ask herself the questions her mother was now asking. But Keisha knew eventually the thrill of their affair would wear off and one day she might come to the realization that for Will, the past few weeks had been little more than a hot and heavy fling. The very idea broke Keisha's heart.

Lena took a calming breath and sighed. "Keisha, look at me. Look at me, please."

Keisha raised her reddened eyes to gaze at her mother. Lena took Keisha's chin in her hands.

"Baby, I just don't want you to get hurt," she said softly. Her lids lowered. "I know what it's like to be hurt. It's hard to come back from it. I don't want the same thing to happen to you."

"Ma, I'm not going to get hurt," Keisha insisted quietly, though she knew there was no way to be sure. "I'm in this with my eyes wide open. I'm prepared for whatever way this turns out, good or bad," she said, despite the seeds of doubt being planted in her heart. Part of Keisha started to wonder if she had learned little in the twelve years since she had fallen for the point guard on the school's basketball team. Would she once again end up weeping in her pillow from a broken heart?

Lena smiled sadly as she gazed into her daughter's eyes. "I hope you mean that, baby," she said softly. "I really hope you do."

CHAPTER 23

Will rounded the corner, feeling sweat pour in rivulets down his back and stomach as he jogged another block. He had been running around his neighborhood for almost two hours straight now and the muscles in his legs were starting to feel as if they could give way at any moment. But he needed this. He needed the monotony of a long Sunday morning jog to clear his head and relieve his worries.

Even after he had jogged what felt like the equivalent of the distance from Annapolis to D.C. and back, the jog still wasn't helping to clear his thoughts. With each breath he took his thoughts returned to Keisha.

When they finally gave in to the sexual tension and became lovers, he had thought all this angst would disappear. But now he was even more confused and frustrated. Worse, his behavior was becoming more erratic. He could be caring and passionate one moment and jealous the next. It was almost as if . . . It was almost as if he had fallen . . .

"No," he told himself as his block finally came into view, "don't even think it."

She could get all dewy and say that she had fallen in love but he couldn't, he wouldn't. Even if Will felt it, he had to keep his emotions in check. One of them had to be the stronger one. There was no way he could let the relationship be anything more than sex right now. They barely knew each other and things were already intense between them. He could only imagine what would happen if love was thrown into the mix. *Where is this all going? Do we take a chance and tell people that we're together and hope they respond well? What do we do if they don't?*

He wanted her in his future but for now, it would all be just too much too soon.

Will was on the verge of exhaustion as he drew closer to his front lawn. When he saw his mailbox he lunged for it to steady himself. He removed the lid of his water bottle.

"Good God!" he heard a voice call out to him. "You look like you've just come in from the cotton fields. Did you have a slave driver running after you?"

Will downed the rest of his water and squinted against the harsh bright light of morning and the salty sweat that was now caking around his eyes. He blinked in surprise as Keisha smiled and slowly rose from his front steps.

"Keisha?" he murmured in confusion between deep breaths, holding his hand against the pain in his ribs. "What . . . what are you doing here?"

"I came over to make you breakfast and to say thank you for the cake since I had to rush off Thursday," she explained, wiping the back of her flared, knee-length red skirt and pointing to the bags of groceries that now sat on his steps. "I brought eggs, croissants, sausages, and blueberries, of course." She grinned.

She looked so beautiful in her skirt and white cashmere sweater with her hair flowing over her shoulders.

"I hadn't expected you to take this long to get back, though," she said, walking down the driveway toward him. "It's past breakfast, so I guess I'll have to make you brunch instead." Keisha's smile faded as she drew closer to Will. "Are you okay?"

"I'm . . . fine," he said as he slowly straightened. "Just . . . overdid it a little," he said dismissively with a wave of his hand as he was overwhelmed by a dizzy spell. Will suddenly fell to one knee on the cement sidewalk.

"Whoa!" she cried with widened eyes, rushing forward. "Wrap your arm around my shoulder."

Will gazed up at her. He didn't want to dirty her up, to cover her with his sweat. Will slowly shook his head. "I'm fine. I don't . . . I don't need help."

"Wrap your arm around my shoulder. I'm not gonna leave you here on the sidewalk!" When he didn't budge, she crossed her arms over her chest. "Look, either you let me help you inside or I'm dragging you up there. Make your choice!" she ordered indignantly.

Will cocked an eyebrow. Just who did she think she was? He would have fought her if he had the energy, but he didn't. He didn't have equilibrium, either. The world still seemed to be spinning beneath his feet. He gave in and wrapped his arm around her slender shoulder and she wrapped her arm around his waist.

"One, two, three!" she said as she helped hoist him to his feet. "Now lean on me. Come on, lean on me."

It took her a few seconds to steady herself under the burden of his weight, but she did.

"I'm sorry for . . . for being on top of you l-like this," he murmured as they began the slow, laborious walk up his driveway.

"It wouldn't be the first time," she said between gritted teeth, "you were on top."

At that, he chuckled

"Where are your keys?" Keisha asked when they finally reached his front door.

"Right . . . hip," Will said weakly. He felt her dig into the pockets of his shorts.

Minutes later, Will landed on the leather cushions of his living room sofa with a thud. Keisha stood over him, slowly shaking her head as her chest heaved up and down.

She fanned herself with her hands and sighed. "So tell me, Mr. Blake," she called over her shoulder as she walked into his kitchen. Will heard her turn on the sink faucet. Seconds later she returned with a glass of water and handed it to him. "What exactly did you think you were doing out there? If I hadn't have showed up you would have passed out on your lawn or worse, died of heat exhaustion!"

"It's September, Keisha," he replied as he sipped from his water glass. Will's nausea and dizzy spell had mercifully subsided in the cool light of his living room. He watched as she opened his front door again to retrieve her grocery bags. "It's too cold for heat exhaustion."

"Uh-huh," she murmured. She carried the two paper bags into his kitchen, kicked off her shoes, and sighed.

"Seriously, you couldn't tell that your body was worn out? Why did you keep running?"

To stop agonizing over you, Will thought, but he answered her with silence instead. Will slowly rose from the couch and stretched. "Thanks for all this, Keisha. I think . . . I'm going to take a shower now."

"Okay," she said as she began to open an egg carton. "Brunch should be done by the time you get back."

He paused to gaze at Keisha, watching as she opened his drawers and kitchen cabinets, searching for a bowl and a spatula. Funny, when Gretchen had done the same thing several months ago, it had grated on Will's nerves like nails on a chalkboard. But with Keisha, it felt natural. He liked having her there. Will's heart swelled as he watched her work.

When Will returned from the shower fifteen minutes later, it was to the smell of sausages.

"You're feeling better, I hope?" she called out to him as he walked into his kitchen.

Will tugged a clean T-shirt over his head, shoved his arms inside, and sighed. He also had switched from his soaking wet running shorts to a pair of faded jeans. "Much better."

"Good." Keisha smiled as she motioned for him to sit at the dinette table. "Give me a few minutes to finish up the eggs and brunch will be done."

He lowered himself into one of the wooden chairs and watched as she worked over one of the burners on his stainless steel stove. His "top of the line" appliance had been used less than ten times since he moved into his home. Will smiled, realizing that today was probably the first time he was finally getting his money's worth.

He watched as Keisha paused from her cooking to pull her hair up into a causal bun atop her head. A few loose tendrils still escaped around her ears, temples, and the nape of her neck. She had removed her cashmere sweater while he had been taking a shower. Now she wore only a white tank top that revealed her golden shoulders and back. He watched as she absently hummed an old R&B tune while scrambling his eggs. She seemed so at home standing there.

"You look comfortable," he murmured.

Keisha turned from the stove and stared at him in puzzlement. "Huh?"

He pointed at her bare feet.

She followed his gaze. "Oh, sorry," she murmured with a bashful smile as she turned off the gas burner. "I always cook with no shoes on. I like to feel the cold tile underneath my feet." She wiggled her toes on the ceramic tile. "That's how I cook at home. I hope you don't mind."

"Not at all," Will said with wry grin. "I like it. It's very . . . ," he paused, ". . . charming."

Keisha pursed her lips. "That's an interesting way to describe it." She chuckled as she removed the frying pan from the burner and scooped a mound of eggs and several link sausages onto a plate. Keisha fixed him with her warm, doe-like eyes as she walked across the kitchen and placed the plate in front of him.

He looked up at her and noticed she wasn't making a plate for herself. He frowned. "You're not eating?"

"Nope, I had a big breakfast already," she murmured as she lowered herself into a chair facing him. She silently watched him eat a few forkfuls before hesitantly opening her mouth and then closing it. "Actually, Will," she began, "I wanted to make you breakfast to make up for last week, but I do have an ulterior motive for coming here, too."

He leaned forward and continued to eat his eggs. "Is that so?" he asked as he glanced up at her. "And what would that be?"

She squirmed anxiously in her chair and sighed, making him frown. "It's hard for me to talk about this. In fact we *never* talk about it probably because it's so awkward to talk about," she rambled. "But I think . . . I think we've reached the point where . . . we . . . *have* to talk about it."

Will stopped eating. "Okay," he said. He lowered his fork to his plate and leaned back in his chair. "What do we need to talk about?"

"Will, I . . . we . . ." She paused as if trying to find the right words. "What are we going to do if . . . someone finds out about us?"

He gazed at her suspiciously. "Why? Are you worried?"

"No." She quickly shook her head. "I mean yes. I mean . . . I don't know. I mean . . . if they do . . ." She tucked her hair behind her ears. "What do we tell them? I kind of feel like there should be a game plan on . . . what to do, how to respond. I mean, if George found out about us, how would you explain *this* to him?" she asked as she pointed around the kitchen, as if evidence of their affair was everywhere, even on the walls.

Will's frown intensified. "I'm still trying to figure out why you think anyone would find out." He paused. "Have *you* told someone, Keisha?"

She blinked and quickly shook her head. "No! No, I-I haven't . . . told anyone," she said a little too loudly, making him suspicious. "I mean just . . . hypothetically. If Phil found out, what should I tell him?" She tilted her head. "What should I say?"

Will stared at her in confusion while she gazed at him intently. "I don't know," he muttered before wiping his mouth with a napkin and shrugging. "Tell him whatever you have to tell him to keep your job, I guess," he answered flippantly. "Hell, tell him it was a momentary fit of insanity. Say it was a mistake that will never happen again."

Her shoulders slumped. She actually looked hurt. "Is that *really* what you would say, Will?" she asked quietly as her gaze fell to the table.

He sighed gruffly with impatience. "Keisha, what is this about?"

She looked up at him. Her eyes were watery. "It's about *us*, Will! It's about what would happen if you were cornered and *forced* to say how you felt about . . ." Her voice faded. He watched as she suddenly rose from the dinette table. She reached for her sweater, which had been draped over the back of her chair, and quickly shoved her arms into each sleeve. "I have to go," she said abruptly.

"What?" he asked, frowning with confusion.

She walked across the kitchen and gathered her purse. "I still have my Sunday errands to finish."

"*Errands?* Wait. Dammit, Keisha, wait!" Will leapt up from the table as she rushed across the kitchen. He grabbed her arm just as she reached the entrance to the living room. He dragged her back toward him. "Don't act like this. Just tell me what's wrong!"

"*Everything*'s wrong, Will," she said irritably as she yanked her arm out of his grasp. She tried to walk out of the kitchen again but he extended his arm across the door frame, blocking her path. Will watched as she tightly pursed her lips.

"Will, get out of the way."

"I will when you *talk* to me," he said, making her sigh loudly. "You asked me a question and I answered it. Why are you angry?"

"I'm . . . I'm . . ." She furiously shook her head. She closed her eyes and sighed. "I'm risking so much to be here, Will. I'm taking such a huge risk, and I don't know why."

At that, he blinked. "What do you mean, you don't know why?"

"I just wonder if I should take the chances that I'm taking just for this, for a 'momentary fit of insanity'?" she said, spitting his words back at him. "I mean . . . is it really worth it?"

He gritted his teeth and lowered his arm, feeling the sting of her words. *Is it really worth it?* What she really meant was, "Are *you* really worth it, Will?"

He took a deep breath. "You tell me, Keisha," he said quietly, trying his best to mask his anger. He silently counted to ten, urging himself not to lose control again.

"I've been floating around without a tether," she said as she turned away from him and crossed her arms over her chest. "I realize that now. I've been avoiding facing the truth for way too long."

He cocked an eyebrow as she began to pace in front of him. "What truth?"

"That I'm too far gone!" she exclaimed, raising her arms helplessly. "I'm just dangling out there! I realized that this may just be some fling that—"

His eyes widened. "Some *fling*?" he repeated with disbelief. Did she realize how much she was insulting him?

"Don't look so shocked, Will," she insisted. "Two minutes ago you said as much yourself. This could be just some *fling* that could probably come back to bite me in the ass and make me look stupid! The sex is good but it's not *that* good! I can't just ignore reality!" she cried, making his nostrils flare as he fought to keep his emotions under control. "Can you promise me that I won't be disappointed? No. Can you promise me that I'm not going to lose my job if someone finds out? No. Can you promise—"

"Dammit, Keisha!" he shouted, unable to control his anger anymore. "No, I can't promise you anything! But nothing's been promised to me, either!"

She fell silent and blinked at him in surprise.

"You're not the only person who's risking anything around here!" he boomed. "What the hell do you think

I've been doing for the past *fifteen* years? This isn't my first campaign, you know! It took a long time for me to get where I am today, to build a reputation, and I'm not eager to blow it all to hell, either! Not to mention the fact that Dupré trusts me like a son," Will spat. "Do you think I like lying to the man, to everyone else? Do you think that makes me feel good?"

Keisha frowned and gazed up at him guiltily. She opened her mouth and closed it. She finally slowly shook her head. "No, I don't," she said quietly.

"So don't tell me about how much you're risking, all right?" he bellowed. "Because you're not the only one who can mess up your career with this, and you're not the only one who could get your heart broken for the sake of 'some fling' either! I'm dangling out there, too!"

The kitchen fell silent. Keisha stared at Will dumbfounded. *"Heart broken?"* she repeated with disbelief.

Will rolled his eyes. Why did he blurt that out? So much for keeping his emotions in check. He crossed his arms over his chest. "You heard me," he said stubbornly, refusing to repeat it again.

Keisha's eyes widened and her face went a shade of pink. "I wasn't sure . . . I mean, I didn't know that you . . . that you felt the same way," she said in a barely audible whisper. "When I . . . When I said Thursday that I . . ." She sighed. "You didn't say anything back. I thought . . . I thought you might not . . ." She fell silent.

"Yeah, well, now you know," he mumbled, refusing to meet her searching eyes. But Keisha wouldn't let him look away. She reached up and placed her hands on his cheeks and turned his face toward her so that their eyes locked. Her piercing gaze seemed to look right at his very core.

"What?" he asked indignantly, furrowing his brows and frowning down at her.

"You really do love me, don't you?" she whispered, slowly breaking into a smile. She was awed by the realization.

He stubbornly held fast, refusing to speak. Finally, he begrudgingly nodded. Keisha breathed in sharply and blinked rapidly, fighting back another onslaught of tears.

He sighed before finally giving her a smile. "Keisha, don't cry," he murmured before rubbing her shoulders.

Her eyelids lowered as she suddenly stood on the tips of her toes, wrapped her arms around his neck and raised her lips to his. The kisses she showered on his lips and cheeks were sweet and achingly tender. All the love that was poured into them was so palpable it hit him like a punch to the gut. Unable to resist, Will wrapped his arms around Keisha, pulling her closer to him. He closed his eyes and kissed her back with equal tenderness, wanting to say with action what he still did not feel comfortable saying with words. He let his kisses slide along her lips, the edges of her mouth, chin, and ears. He tugged her sweater off her shoulders and pulled down the straps of her tank top to place the same kisses along her neck and collarbone as she tilted back her head. He heard her moan and instinctively his mouth returned to hers. He brought one hand to her breast while the other quickly undid her bun. As her hair fell around her shoulders,

Keisha parted her lips to let their kiss deepen. Will felt himself harden as her hand lowered the zipper of his jeans.

Everything from that point happened in a flash. It took only seconds to get her on the dinette table. Their mouths never separated even as her panties slid to her ankles, and then off, and he lowered his hand to feel the slick wetness between her thighs. His heart pounded wildly in his chest. His breathing deepened. When he quickly parted her legs and entered her, Will couldn't help himself. Against her mouth, he began to babble, to say everything he couldn't say before. He told her that he loved her, that he needed her and that he would never hurt her. Everything after that faded into a blur.

CHAPTER 24

"Forty-four more days to D-Day," Will thought with relief as he climbed out of his Audi and quickly headed to the front door of campaign headquarters. The steady clap of his shoes ricocheted off the cement sidewalk. He glanced down at his watch, squinted against the dim light from the overhead street lamp, and sighed. "Make that forty-three days and 7 hours."

Will had been counting down the days, hours, and minutes to the election for the past two weeks, waiting for it to finally arrive. For the first time in his career, he wasn't relishing the highs and lows of the campaign. He zoned out during conference calls and sleepwalked his way through meet and greets with constituents and campaign contributors. He was finding it harder and harder to put up the pretense of interest. He suspected that some of his fellow campaign staffers were starting to notice, but he didn't care. His focus was locked solely on Keisha and the treasured hours they managed to sneak in with one another despite their packed schedules. In fact, he had just canceled one of those cherished evenings to head back to the office to finish some last minute work.

He had lots of plans for the future now, and only a few included politics. He could see himself slowing down and settling down with Keisha . . . if she would have him.

He'd give it a few months before he asked her how much it would cost to get out of her apartment lease. No need to overwhelm her by asking too quickly. Once she got out of the lease, she could move in with him into the two-story Tudor that his real estate agent had advised was too large for a single man. Keisha could decorate his place any way she wanted, add her womanly touches as she chose, and make it a home. He'd give her a few more months to get comfortable—and then he would ask her if she was ready to take their relationship to the next level.

So soon, a voice in his head asked. *You've barely known her a year.*

Will gave a wry smile. It was true. He was moving forward pretty quickly but he had given up trying to hold back his desires and his emotions. His heart was telling him not to wait. It had been telling him that for a long time. Why keep trying to convince himself differently?

He said hi to the guard at the front desk, glanced at his watch again, and boarded one of the elevators. When he stepped off on his floor, he could see that the offices were deserted, everyone having left for the day. Will flicked on one of the switches in the carpeted receiving area, filling the room with a blaze of light. He quickly made his way to his office, whistling as he swung the bag of Chinese takeout he had bought for that evening. He abruptly paused, thinking he heard the distant sound of a woman screaming. Will frowned and squinted. Had he been mistaken? But there was the scream again, this time coming from one of the offices down the hall. "Hey!"

Will said as his walk quickly morphed into a run. "Hey! Are you all right?"

The woman continued to shriek, this time letting out a scream that made Will's blood run cold. He ran over to the door to the room from which the yells seemed to be coming and turned the brass knob, only to find that the door was locked. "Ma'am, are you okay in there?" Will shouted. "Whoever the hell is in there . . . I'm going to call the cops!" There was no reply, only a thud and more yelps that further raised his alarm.

He wondered what he should do. Call the cops? Tell the guard downstairs that the door was locked and a woman inside seemed to be in distress? She shrieked again and Will couldn't take it anymore. He shoved at the door with his shoulder, using his body as a makeshift battering ram. After a second try, Will finally knocked the door open and tumbled into the office. He landed on his knees but quickly jumped to his feet, prepared to do battle with whoever was making the woman scream. But as he faced his foe, Will's mouth fell open and his balled fists dropped to his sides. "What the hell . . ." he murmured.

"Oh, Will!" George shouted with surprise as he bent down and hastily tried to pull up his plaid boxers and khaki pants. Red-faced and perspiring, he glanced from Will to Gretchen and back again. "I didn't know . . . We didn't . . . what are you doing here?"

Will turned away to avoid the further sight of George's hairy, pale backside. But in the corner of his eye, he could see Gretchen quickly climb off the office desk, close her blouse over her bare breasts, and shove down her skirt.

"I had to catch up on some work," Will muttered as the two continued to dress. "I heard the screams and I thought . . . I . . . well, I'll leave you two to do . . . whatever."

He quickly backed out into the hallway and slammed the door behind him. Will shook his head in disgust. *So George's wife* does *have a reason to worry*, he thought, wondering how long the affair between George and Gretchen had been going on.

∾◦∾

An hour later, Will was slumped in his leather desk chair and staring at his computer screen, having decided to forget about the scene he had come upon earlier. He held a carryout box in one hand and chopsticks in the other, finishing the last of his noodles and bean sprouts. When he heard a knock at his door, he looked up from the screen. Will swiveled his chair around and frowned as he watched Gretchen push his door open.

"Got a minute?" she asked perkily.

His eyebrows furrowed and his jaw tightened. "I guess," he muttered.

"Sorry about all the noise," she said with a chuckle. "But George likes a performance."

She's not even embarrassed, he thought as she slowly walked over to his cherry wood desk and sat on the edge. It was like what had happened an hour ago hadn't happened.

Gretchen crossed her legs, tossed her red hair over her shoulder, and tilted her head.

She actually seems to be relishing it!

"You're a busy bee tonight," Gretchen said lazily, glancing at one of the open file folders on his desk.

"Hadn't expected to see you here this late, either. Where's George?" Will asked casually.

"He left a few minutes ago. Had to head back home."

"I'm sure his wife is wondering where he is," Will said sarcastically as he chucked his empty carton into the nearby trash can. "Seems like he's been pulling a lot of late nights lately. Now we know why."

Gretchen noticed the sarcasm. Her smile disappeared.

"The day I let you look down on me for who I sleep with, Will Blake, will be the day hell freezes over," she said coldly. Then she blinked, and, in one second, her glistening, PR-worthy smile returned. "Now to get back to what I wanted to talk to you about. I guess you've seen the latest poll numbers."

Will sighed. "Yes, I get the same email stats that you do." He shrugged. "What about it?"

"What do you mean, 'What about it?' " she asked, throwing up her hands. "We're getting stomped! *Stomped*, Will! Look, I didn't join this campaign to watch it fail. I've put a lot of time and work into this!"

"We *all* have, Gretchen," he said. "And we all want Vincent to win. We're trying our best. What—"

She quickly shook her head. "No, we're not; not in the least. We need to get serious about this, Will. I'm tired of talking about it. I want us to *do* it!"

He tilted his head and crossed his arms over his chest, deciding to humor her. Maybe then she would leave. Just looking at her was making his stomach turn. George had had his twenty-third wedding anniversary about two months ago. He and his wife had three kids, with one in college. How could Gretchen not feel ashamed about what they were doing?

"So what do you suggest?" he asked.

She leaned forward as her smile widened. "Well, I was talking to George about it a few weeks ago. I wanted to make sure that we crossed all our t's and dotted all our i's when it came to researching Parker. So George told me that he has a friend who knows a friend who knows a guy who's a private investigator. He used to work for the CIA." She shrugged her shoulders. "Anyway, he was able to do a little more digging into Parker's background and something interesting came up."

Will narrowed his eyes. "Okay, go on."

She tossed her hair again. "Well, it seems our friend Parker had some dealings with the law when he was younger. He served some time as a juvenile for . . . guess what?"

Will shrugged. "I have no clue, Gretchen."

"*Trespassing and burglary.* Several counts," she said, letting out a low chuckle. "He spent about two and a half years in juvie."

Will didn't say anything in response, but instead continued to glare up at her.

Gretchen's smile faded. She slowly scanned Will's face. "You don't look surprised."

"I thought juvenile records were sealed," he said flatly, changing the subject.

"They are," she said. With a sigh, she hopped off his desk. "But I told you. The guy was in the CIA. I guess he has connections and ways of getting stuff that most people can't."

Will gritted his teeth. "So now you want to blast this information all over the airwaves to discredit Parker. Plant it with some reporter at one of the big metros, I guess?"

"Sure. Why not?" Gretchen said with a shrug. "It could definitely edge us up in the polls."

"Maybe it could, but then again, maybe it couldn't," Will argued as pushed his chair away from his desk and rose to his feet. "It's not worth the chance." He paused. "Look, this campaign has been clean since the primaries, Gretchen. We don't want to start down this road. If we can dig up stuff on Parker that should have remained hidden, I can only imagine what they could find out about Vincent if they dig deep enough. Dig deep enough into any saint's past and you're bound to find a few sins." Will quickly shook his head. "No, we won't do it, and I won't support it! If you or George go to Vincent with this, I'll shut you down. I can promise you that."

She slowly gave a knowing smile and walked around Will's desk. "George thought you would say that."

Will nodded. "Well, George knows me well."

"I bet not as well as he thinks," she said cryptically as she took several steps toward him. "Look, Will, you aren't going to say a damn thing when we tell Dupré its time to go for the jugular. No, in fact, you'll say it's a great idea, a *fabulous* one."

His jaw tightened. "And why the hell would I do that?"

Will watched as she reached up to adjust his tie, making him flinch. Gretchen smiled and fiddled with the loosened knot anyway, tightening it around his neck like a noose. "Because I'll let both Dupré and George know about your little extracurricular activities with Keisha Reynolds."

Will's mouth momentarily fell open in shock, but he clamped it shut and shoved Gretchen's hand away. He frowned. "What are you talking about?"

"Oh, please, Will," she said with a dismissive wave. "Don't play stupid with me. I know you and that little slut have been hooking up for months now. What you see in her, I do *not* know, but I've kept my secret for a while, waiting for just the right time." She slowly closed her eyes, tugged at his tie and dragged his mouth down to hers. "Just the right place."

She planted a moist kiss on Will's lips and he jumped back as if a viper had bitten him, making Gretchen laugh.

"Oh, Will, you're so silly," she said with a giggle, tossing her hair over her shoulder. She turned and walked toward his office door. "Tomorrow George and I will pitch this idea to Dupré. I expect that you will be on board. Or I'll tell them about you and Keisha. I'll tell them you knew this information about Parker all along and didn't tell us. Then we'll see if you still have a job." She turned around and smiled. "No one will ever trust you again, Will. Your career in politics will be over. *Finito!* Unless . . . you cooperate with me. From now on, *I'm* making the big decisions for this campaign," she said. "Understood?"

Will remained silent, glaring at her as she laughed again.

"I'll take that as a 'yes,' " she said over her shoulder as she walked out of his office.

Will swallowed loudly. He took a deep breath. God, if this news came out he was going to lose Keisha. He had never felt so desperate in his life.

CHAPTER 25

"Why do I feel like singing?" Keisha asked playfully as she swung Will's hand. She then leaned her head on his broad shoulder.

He gave a wry smile. "I don't know. Why do you feel like singing?"

Keisha grinned. "Because this is the first night in a week that I've had off," she proclaimed. "Because I'm walking with the man I love to get hot chocolate—the greatest drink in the world. And because you look so cute in your hat," she said. Playfully, she tugged the bill of his navy blue baseball cap.

They continued to stroll down the promenade, glancing in store windows as they made their way to the coffee shop at the end of the block. Keisha's breath sent gusts of clouds into the cold air. She shoved her free hand into her pocket and then snuggled closer to Will for warmth.

"I wonder if it's going to snow this weekend. It's a little early in the year, but it's been so frigid lately."

"Don't know," Will murmured.

"Were you here in town for the big snowstorm last year? We got eight inches, which is a rarity. I was so excited. It reminded me of the snow back in Philly. I ran outside and fell on my back and made snow angels." She sighed. "I'd love for one of those snowstorms to come again. Can you imagine us on the couch, under a blanket, drinking red wine and watching a movie with the snow falling outside your bay window?"

He stared blankly into a furniture store window. "Yeah, I guess," he muttered distractedly.

Keisha frowned. "Are you all right, Will?"

He blinked, turned, and looked down at her. "I'm fine," he said a little too quickly. "Why wouldn't I be?"

Her frown intensified. Will was really preoccupied lately, almost forlorn. *Twenty bucks says it's something to do with the election*, she thought. But they had made a rule not to talk about work, or politics in general, at least until the election ended. It just made things easier for them and reduced the possibility of an argument. But she knew things were getting harder for him. The polls were showing that Parker was in the lead, and that undoubtedly put pressure on Dupré's campaign staff. Their headquarters probably wasn't the jolliest of places right now.

"It's almost over," she said softly as she gazed up at him. She figured he knew instantly what she meant. "That's what I keep telling myself anyway. 'It's almost over.' "

He slowly nodded and wrapped an arm around her shoulder, giving her a squeeze. He then leaned down and kissed her lovingly.

Minutes later the two sat in the coffee shop, gazing out the window into the dark night outside. Crackling logs burned in a fireplace along the far wall, adding a glow and warmth to the room. Keisha closed her eyes and took a sip of hot chocolate, savoring the smell and the taste.

"Mmmm, that's some really good cocoa," she murmured. "How's your latté?"

Keisha opened her eyes to find that Will hadn't touched his drink. Instead, he was anxiously licking his lips. She watched as he suddenly reached across the small bistro table, grabbed her hand, and squeezed it. He stared at her intently with a sense of urgency that made her nervous.

"How many more months do you have on your apartment lease?" he asked.

Keisha squinted, confused by the abrupt subject change. She lowered her cocoa mug and shrugged. "I don't know. Three or four, I think. Why?"

"Don't renew it," he said suddenly. "Move in with me."

Her eyes widened in shock. "What?" *Move in with him?* She leaned back in her chair and slowly shook her head. "Will, where is all this coming from?"

"I'm just . . ." He sighed impatiently. "I'm just tired of waiting. It's like a game of chess. We're strategizing one step and then the next step and then the next. We're wasting time, and for what?" He quickly shook his head. "Besides, things don't always turn out the way we intend, right? Even with the best of plans. Life throws you curve balls, right?" He let go of her hand and shoved up the sleeves of his sweater. He fidgeted, bouncing his knees as he leaned forward in his chair. "Well, from now on, I'm just going to run with it, Keisha. I'm not going to fight it anymore. After this campaign is over, I want you to move in with me. I promise you, I won't do another campaign. I'll just stick to consulting or work at a think tank. Our time will be ours. No one will come between us again."

Will was acting manic. He had been so quiet earlier, and now he was babbling words that were making her head spin. *Quitting campaigning? Moving in together?* When he started to talk about going to the paint store to get swatches, she had to hold up her hands to quiet him.

"Wait. Wait!" Keisha almost shouted. "Slow down! Now let's talk about this," she said slowly, tucking a lock of hair behind her ear. "First of all, what do you mean, you won't do another campaign? You *love* politics, Will! You said this is what you want to do, what you've *always* wanted to do since you were a teenager. Why the sudden change? And living together . . ." She sighed and shook her head. "Will, for most of my life I've either lived with my mother or with roommates. I like finally having my independence. Besides, the only man I plan to live with is the one I intend to marry. I'm not a big fan of playing house. I never have been."

He furrowed his brows and frowned. "So you're saying you'd need an engagement ring on your finger before you'd move in with me?"

Keisha rolled her eyes with annoyance. "Not necessarily," she began. "It's just—"

"Because that could be arranged."

"—more important that we establish that we're really compatible. We . . . wait, what?" She blinked. Had she heard him correctly? *"What?"*

He shrugged. "A long engagement would probably be better. We should live together for a year or two before we get married, but I have no problem popping the question before you move in. If that's what you need, I'm fine with it. You'd probably want to go to the jeweler with me, though. I'd want you to pick out something you really liked." He tilted his head and cocked an eyebrow. "Does mid-November work for you?"

Keisha stared at him blankly. "Huh? Does mid-November work for me to do what?"

He smiled. "To pick out a ring." She watched as he finally took a sip from his latté and grimaced. "Hell, I let it sit for too long. It's gotten cold."

Keisha raised her hands to her temples, feeling them throb against her fingertips. *What the hell is going on?* Had he just proposed? And why was he treating the proposal like a contract negotiation? He was jumping from subject to subject like a crazed bumblebee from flower to flower. Where was the logical, thoughtful Will she knew and loved? This guy was definitely freaking her out.

She slowly shook her head, as if awakening from a daze. "Will, I really think that we need to slow down. You're not making any sense."

"Keisha," he began earnestly, reaching across the table and grabbing both of her hands. "I love you and I want to spend my life with you. If that means getting engaged before we live together, fine. If it means not getting engaged, I don't care. Whatever steps you feel need to be taken, we'll take them."

"But why now all of sudden?" she asked with disbelief. "Why the—"

He quickly leaned across the table and kissed her. She felt that old familiar knot of need in her stomach and all the words she had planned to say suddenly floated away. When Will pulled back seconds later, he ran a finger along her cheek and jaw line and her eyes slowly fluttered open.

"Look, I just want you. I know it all sounds sudden, but don't say no just yet, okay? Just . . . just think about it," he whispered against her lips. "Do that for me." He grinned. "I'm going to get a refill. Do you need anything?"

"No, I'm fine," she answered, still in a daze. Keisha watched Will rise from the table and walk back toward the front counter. When his back was turned, she dropped her head into her hands, feeling as if she were going to faint. *God, this is moving so fast,* she thought desperately. But was Will right? Why wait if they were both in love? Why wait if deep down it was what she secretly wanted too—to spend her life with him? But it was such a huge risk.

The ringing of her BlackBerry tore Keisha from her thoughts. She looked down at the glass screen and frowned. It was Phil, and, more importantly, he was calling her during one of her coveted, rare evenings off. She sighed and rolled her eyes.

"Hey Phil," she answered. "What's up?"

"Are you alone?" he asked abruptly.

Keisha blinked and frowned. "Uh . . . yeah. Wait." She glanced at the counter and saw that Will was still standing in line. She quickly rose from the bistro table and walked out the coffee shop's front door. A bell tinkled overhead with her exit. She stood under an awning as a light snow began to fall. Keisha looked around and noticed that the outdoor shopping center was almost deserted. She was indeed alone. "Okay, now I am," she said into her phone. "What's wrong?"

"Keisha, did you tell anyone, *anyone* about Sydney's prison record?" Phil asked. "I need you to be honest with me."

Keisha's mouth fell open. Her palms began to sweat under her wool mittens and the hairs on her neck stood on end. She loudly cleared her throat. "Uh, no," she lied. "Why . . . why would I do that, Phil? What's wrong? Just tell me what happened."

Phil sighed heavily on the other end of the line and then fell silent for what felt like an eternity before speaking again. "Sydney got a call about an hour ago from a reporter at the *Post* asking about the time he served when he was fifteen years old. He was completely ambushed, Keisha. They knew about the charges, where the burglaries took place. They knew everything! He refused to answer any questions, but, at this point, his silence just makes him look guilty. The story's going to appear on the front page tomorrow."

Keisha glared at the ground in shock. "Oh, God. Oh, God, Phil, I . . ." She brought her hand to her chest, feeling her heart pound rapidly against her rib cage. "Do you want to meet back at the office? We can go over how to handle this. I can—"

"Parker and I already discussed how to handle it," he interrupted. "Kelly is drawing up a statement right now. She and I have already talked about the wording. We're going to grant an interview with one of the local TV stations. We haven't decided which one yet. I suggested the reporter over at Channel 7. She'll probably be sympathetic to Parker since she did that glowing segment on him earlier this year."

Keisha quickly nodded. "That sounds good. Is there anything you need me to do? Maybe I could—"

"We've got it covered, Keisha," he said firmly, cutting her off again. "Look, I didn't call for additional help. I just called to make sure that no other surprises are in store, if you know what I mean."

Keisha fell silent. She frowned. "No, Phil, I . . . I don't know you mean."

"Nothing else is going to come out of the woodwork, is it, Keisha?" he asked impatiently. "If it is, I need to know right now."

Her eyes started to sting. He really believed that she was the cause of all this. Worst of all, she couldn't vouch for sure that she wasn't.

"Phil, I didn't tell the reporter at the *Post*!"

He sighed heavily again. "Keisha," he began with eerie calm, "I know about you and Will Blake."

Her breath caught in her throat.

"I let it slide and didn't confront you about it because I believed, perhaps stupidly, that no matter what you did in your personal life, you wouldn't compromise the integrity of this campaign. I thought I knew how much this means to you," he continued. "But if I find out that you screwed us over, you're done. You understand me?"

She then heard a loud click that made her flinch. The line went dead. Keisha's hands shook as she tucked her phone into her coat pocket. She was absolutely shell-shocked. How could this have happened? How had the *Post* found out? The only person she had told was Will, and he wouldn't have told anyone else. *Would he?*

"What are you doing out here?" Will asked. "You should get back inside. It's cold out here."

She turned to find him standing in the doorway, gazing at her. Just the sight of him piqued her anger. Will instantly frowned. "What's wrong?" he whispered. He rushed forward.

"You were the only person I told," she said angrily, stepping away from him. "It's not enough that you would let them drag a man like Parker through the dirt, but you had to betray me like this *too*? You were the only person I told and you swore . . . you *swore* to me that you wouldn't tell anyone else!"

His frown intensified. "What the hell are you talking about?"

"What do you mean, what the hell am I talking about? Phil just called me!" she yelled hysterically. "He told me that the *Post* tried to interview Parker about the time he served when he was a teenager! How did they find out about that if you didn't tell them?"

Will froze. He suddenly closed his eyes and shook his head. "Shit," he muttered.

Her eyes widened. "So you *did* tell them?"

"No. No!" He quickly shook his head. "It's just . . . I'm just shocked." He raised his hands helplessly. "I didn't . . . I didn't expect Gretchen to work that fast. I thought . . . I thought I had more time."

Keisha gazed at him in disbelief. "Gretchen? So *that's* who you told?"

"I didn't tell her, Keisha!"

She wasn't hurt anymore; she was furious. Will had actually betrayed her to a woman he used to sleep with. *Who says he used to*, a voice in her head prodded. *What makes you think he isn't still sleeping with her?*

Keisha could feel her blood boil as she imagined Will in bed with Gretchen, sharing Keisha's precious secrets. They had probably shared quite a few laughs at her expense. She had been so gullible, so trusting. *Isn't that what Tanya told you in the beginning? 'You're playing with the big boys. Wear a cup.' Remember?*

Will gritted his teeth. "Keisha, I didn't tell her anything. I swear. Gretchen and George had some guy dig this up on his own. I swear to you—"

"Don't swear anything to me, Will!" she yelled as tears streamed down her face. "Don't swear another damn thing to me! You lied! You lied right to my face!" She then turned on her heel and walked away, letting the flakes of snow melt on her hot cheeks.

"Keisha!" Will called as he followed closely at her heels. "Keisha, wait!" But she ignored him and continued her angry strides, wiping at the angry tears streaming down her face. She stopped only when she felt his vise-like grip around her arm.

"Take your hands off me," she bellowed, trying to yank her arm away. "Let go of me!"

"No!" he barked. "Not until you listen, dammit!" Will closed his eyes and took a deep breath. "Keisha, I know this is hard. I understand that you're upset," he began as he finally let go of her.

"What gave you that idea, Will?" she asked sarcastically.

"Look, going after Parker like that was below the belt," he continued. "I know that. But that doesn't give you the right to call me a liar," he said, making her eyes widen.

"*Doesn't give me the right?*" she repeated, her voice tinged with outrage. "Are you kidding me?"

"Keisha, I'm not lying to you. I never have. I swear—" He stopped himself and sighed. "Everything I told you, everything that I've ever told you, is the truth. I *do* love you and you *can* trust me. Dammit, I just asked you to move in with me! I said I wanted to spend my life with you! Do you think I was lying about that, too?"

"Okay, fine. Fine, Will!" Keisha said, raising her hands in surrender. "I'll play along. You didn't tell Gretchen. You're not lying to me. You're completely innocent." She then glared up at him. "So if that's the case, why didn't you warn me? Why didn't you tell me this was going to happen? I would have told you. I wouldn't have let you get blindsided like this!"

At that, Will's shoulders fell. He didn't say anything in response. Instead, he gazed at her with a pained expression.

"Is this why you want to get out of politics?" she asked resentfully. "Because you know what you've done?

Because you see what you've become?" Keisha gave a caustic laugh and shrugged. "Or maybe you were like this all along. Maybe Tanya was right after all."

At that, his eyebrows furrowed. A tick formed along his jaw line as he glared down at her.

"Keisha," he began quietly, "I love you, but if after all this time and after all the things I've told you, you could say something like that to me . . ." He slowly shook his head. "Maybe I was wrong about us. Maybe we should go our separate ways."

She stood silently in the falling snow, gazing up at him. Then, finally, Keisha slowly nodded.

"Well, maybe you're right." She shoved her hands into her pockets and turned. "Goodbye, Will," she said, refusing to look back at him.

CHAPTER 26

The trick is to keep busy, Keisha thought two weeks later as she pulled her Ford Focus into a parking space in front of her mother's home. The cherry blossom trees she loved so dearly now had bare branches, and a cold wind swept fall leaves along the sidewalk.

You don't have time to think about heartache when your schedule is full.

For the past week, Keisha had been jumping from meeting to meeting like the Energizer Bunny with springs to outrun her misery. A few of the staffers had even remarked about how fervent Keisha seemed lately, how tireless she had become. She had explained it away, claiming the Dupré campaign's dirty tricks brought out the fight in her, but there were other reasons.

First of all, Phil was now watching her like a hawk. She was starting back at square one with him and had to prove to him again that, above all else, she wanted Dr. Parker to win and she was willing to do anything necessary to make that happen.

Another reason, *the most important reason* Keisha was working so hard, was because she wanted to outrun the sadness she felt now that her romance with Will had ended. The two hadn't seen or spoken to one another since that night at the coffee shop, and she had no intention of ever seeing him again. But Keisha hadn't felt a pain like this in her life. It was like her heart had been ripped out of her chest and crushed underfoot. In her weaker moments, she would just start crying, even sobbing. But those moments were becoming farther and farther between. Keisha was slowly figuring out how to cope, how to take a deep breath and shift her concentration to something else. Today she would shift her focus to her mother, who was now stuck at home with a bad cold.

Keisha quickly climbed the steps to her mother's brownstone with shopping bags in hand and painted a smile on her face that she hoped would fool the woman who always managed to see right through her. She unlocked and opened the front door and found her mother lying on the living room couch, watching television with a wool blanket over her legs.

"KeKe," Lena croaked hoarsely with a smile. The older woman wiped her nose with a tissue and opened her arms to her daughter. "Thank you for coming by, baby. You didn't have to, though," she said as Keisha leaned down and kissed her cheek. Lena stared at the grocery bags and frowned. "What do you have there?"

Keisha grinned as she patted one of the bags. "Lots of cough syrup, OJ, and the ingredients for a fresh batch of chicken soup," she proclaimed.

"Chicken soup?" Her mother slowly rose from the couch, but paused to release a phlegm-filled cough that made Keisha cringe. "I have plenty of cans of chicken soup, KeKe."

"Not that processed stuff, Ma," Keisha said over her shoulder as she walked into the kitchen, shrugged out of her wool coat, and set her grocery bags on the counter. "I'm talking about *real* chicken soup. You know, like the kind you used to make me when I was little."

"Well, thank you, honey," Lena murmured as she slowly lowered herself into one of the chairs at the table on the other side of the kitchen. She loudly blew her nose again and sighed. "But you didn't have to. I'm sick and I appreciate seeing you, but I could just as easily heat up a bowl of soup myself."

Keisha quickly shook her head as she pulled off the shrink wrap from a chicken breast. She had already tossed carrots and celery into a strainer that was sitting under running water in the stainless steel sink. "Ma, of course I have to," she insisted. "You aren't feeling well. What else should I be doing?"

Lena chuckled. "You could be at home snuggled up with that man of yours, for one." Lena adjusted her robe belt and tilted her head. "When do I finally get to meet him, anyway? I've heard so much about him. I'm interested in seeing this Will Blake in person. Why don't you invite him over for one of our Thursday dinners?"

The blade that Keisha had been using to methodically slice the chicken breast stopped. She could feel the tears welling in her eyes again. She took a deep breath, blinked, and then forced the smile before returning to cutting the chicken into strips. "I don't think that's possible," she said, clearing her throat. "Will and I . . . well, we decided to go our separate ways."

Lena's mouth fell open. "*Separate ways?* But I . . . I thought you two were in love." Lena rose from the table and walked over to Keisha. She placed a warm hand on her daughter's shoulder. "I'm so sorry, honey," she murmured. "I'm so . . . What . . . what happened?"

Keisha shrugged. "Oh, you know how it goes," she replied, trying to sound casual. "Boy meets girl. They're hot and heavy one moment and arguing the next. Then they step back and realize that it just isn't going to work. Boy loses girl. The end." She shrugged again, refusing to meet her mother's eyes. "We both agreed it was for the best. No hard feelings," Keisha lied as she bent down to retrieve a sauce pan and lid from one of the floor cabinets. She filled the pan with water. "Do you want some orange juice, Ma? It may help your throat."

"Keisha, look at me," her mother ordered.

"Huh?" Keisha asked distractedly. She turned off the faucet.

"Look at me, baby."

Keisha turned and met Lena's warm dark eyes. *She's going to see everything*, Keisha thought with dread.

The older woman stared up at her, slowly scanning her features, reading them like a book. Lena then closed her eyes and sighed. "This isn't what you wanted," she said with a slow shake of the head.

"Yes, it *is*," Keisha insisted. "It's what we agreed to."

Lena slowly walked back to the kitchen table and slumped into one of the wooden chairs. "It may be what you agreed to, KeKe, but your heart wasn't in it. It's written all over your face." She frowned. "I don't know what happened, but I hope he didn't hurt you. Because if he did," she said fiercely, "I'll hunt him down and hurt *him*."

Keisha gave a wry smile. Her mother was sweet and protective, Keisha's five-foot, one-inch defender. But she couldn't go around beating up all the men that broke Keisha's heart. She couldn't make them love her back.

"Don't worry about me, Ma," she said softly as she began to fill a glass with orange juice. "I'm a big girl who can take care of herself . . . and I can heal quicker than you think," she said as she placed the glass in front of Lena. "I'm already starting to get better."

Lena gave a heavy sigh as she pushed her dreads over her shoulder. "Yeah, I thought I was a quick healer, too, KeKe, a *long* time ago. But you figure out that the wounds just become calloused over. You're never going to be the same again. They will always be there and—"

"Ma," Keisha said impatiently, holding up her hands. "Can we . . . can we change the subject, please? I'll talk about anything else you want, just . . . not this."

Lena grew silent and then slowly nodded her head. "Okay, baby. If that's what you want." The older woman peered around the kitchen, looking as if she were trying desperately to think of something less painful to talk about. "Well, I'm glad to have your company anyway, KeKe." She gave a soft laugh. "I think this is the first time in a long time that I'll see you twice in one week."

Keisha placed the strips of chicken into the sauce pan, placed the glass lid on top and frowned. "Actually, that's the other reason why I wanted to come over today,"

Keisha said as she adjusted the temperature for one of the burners to poach the chicken. She turned to face her mother, wiped her hands with a dish towel, and shrugged. "I'm afraid that I'll have to cancel our Thursday dinner this week."

"Oh, no," Lena said, looking crestfallen. "Work again?"

"Afraid so," Keisha said as she wiped the Formica countertop. "Phil wants us to meet some guy for drinks Thursday evening who says he knows a deep, dark secret about Dupré." She swung the towel over the edge of the sink and rolled her eyes. "Personally, I think the whole thing's stupid. Even if he does have some dirt on Dupré, I don't think this is the best tactic to take. But when Dupré's campaign started playing dirty first, it didn't leave us with many options." She shrugged. "Because of the revelation of Dr. Parker's juvenile record, the voters are starting to shift back over to Dupré again, according to poll numbers. Phil's sure that we have to move forward with this if we want to stop that trend."

Keisha turned to find Lena staring at her. The expression on the older woman's face was peculiar, as if she had just seen her daughter sprout another head. Keisha guessed the cold medicine was finally starting to take effect. "You all right, Ma?" she asked with concern. "You're looking a little weird."

"What dirty secret, Keisha?" Lena asked quietly.

Keisha frowned and shrugged again before starting to slice the vegetables for the chicken soup. "I have no idea. He said he'll tell us when we get there. He was pretty vague. Phil thinks he wants to maintain the element of surprise," she said sarcastically as she popped a slice of carrot into her mouth. "But personally, I think the guy's full of crap and we're wasting our time."

Lena vigorously shook her head. "Don't go."

Keisha glanced over her shoulder at her mother, only half listening. "What?" she asked distractedly as she started to chop the celery.

"Don't go!" Lena shouted hoarsely as she quickly rose from her dinette table. "I can't believe you would even *think* about going to do . . ." Lena stopped short and pointed angrily at Keisha. "This . . . *this* is why I didn't want you to give up your teaching job and get mixed up in this mess! I knew this would happen!"

Keisha gazed at her mother in confusion. The older woman was visibly trembling. "What would happen? What are you talking about?"

Lena furiously shook her head. "You can't do this! You *can't* do this!" her mother shouted, making Keisha flinch. She continued to stare at her mother in bewilderment. "Understand something, Keisha Jeanette Reynolds. You are going to lose with this one. Nothing good can come from it! Nothing good!"

"Ma, I have no choice. I have to do it." Her shoulders fell as she sighed. "Look, somehow Phil found out about Will and me before we broke up. He's paranoid that I'm some kind of double agent, working for the other side. If I tell him we shouldn't do this, I'm probably going to lose my job!" She closed her eyes. "Ma, I understand you don't like this sort of thing. I'm not crazy about it, either. But this is politics. This is how the game is played and—"

"That is crap, Keisha! And you know it!" Lena glared at her. Her little nostrils flared. "I can't . . . I can't even . . ." Her words trailed off as she began to walk out of the kitchen.

"Ma!" Keisha called. "Ma, where are you going? What about your soup?"

"I'm not hungry!" her mother shouted back. Keisha heard her mother's bedroom door slam shut seconds later.

She slowly shook her head. "What the hell was that about?"

CHAPTER 27

"So who should do most of the talking?" Jason asked as they quickly walked down the sidewalk two days later. He peered apprehensively at the steel façade of the swank art deco restaurant and frowned.

In five minutes, they were scheduled to meet Daniel Forester, Dupré's former life-long friend, for drinks. Phil had suddenly come down with a twenty-four-hour flu bug and couldn't attend the important meeting. He had sent Jason instead.

To keep an eye on me, I assume, Keisha thought tersely.

She had done her prep work before coming this evening. She knew Forester was a local real estate mogul who had come from old money, like Dupré. She knew the names of his three children and four ex-wives. She knew where he lived (Chantilly, Virginia) and even what his house looked like (a 5,800-square-foot colonial with an adjacent guesthouse). But she still felt uneasy, as if she wasn't prepared for what was about to happen today. Perhaps it was because Forester still had not given any hint of the big secret he would reveal, or maybe it was because she didn't know why he suddenly had an axe to grind when it came to Dupré.

No, that's not it, Keisha thought. She was uneasy because her mother was angry at her; even worse, she was "disappointed", as she had told Keisha on the phone the night before. She said she was disappointed that her daughter would play the dirty game of politics and purposely try to destroy someone else's reputation. She said she was disappointed that Keisha cared more about her job than the privacy of another human being. When Keisha tried to explain herself, her mother cut her off. "Just tell me, are you still going to that meeting tomorrow, Keisha?" her mother questioned. When Keisha said yes, her mother hung up on her, shocking her once again.

Lena's condemnation weighed heavy on her. So much so that—despite the fear of angering Phil—she had seriously contemplated not showing up at the restaurant today. She had even sat in her car for a good ten minutes, debating over whether she should just leave the restaurant's parking lot and go home. But in the end, her sense of duty outweighed her sense of guilt.

"I've never done anything like this before, Keisha," Jay now admitted as they paused by the restaurant's glass doors. "Maybe you should talk first."

"I'm a virgin at this, too, Jay," Keisha muttered, blowing warm air onto her gloved hands, which were numb either because of the biting cold or her frayed nerves. "I'd be just as awkward as you at this."

"I still say you talk first," he insisted.

Keisha glared at him in response.

"Well, rock, paper, scissors then?" he whined.

"Are you serious?" she asked.

Jason clinched his hands and sighed. "Okay, fine. Let's just go in then. I guess we'll just . . . play it by ear."

They both nodded and took a deep breath. Jason held the restaurant door open for her and they immediately walked over to the hostess who stood behind a marble counter.

"Seating for two?" she asked perkily.

Jay loudly cleared his throat. "Uh, no. Actually, we're meeting someone, thank you. I believe he's already here."

The brunette slowly nodded and extended her hand toward the tables. "Go right ahead."

They slowly made their way across the restaurant to the table where Forester now sat. He was portly, with a sprinkling of freckles along his nose that stood out against his wrinkled jowls. The hair along his temples was graying, and the hair on his forehead had long ago receded and left only a few stray strands clinging to his scalp. He wore a white starched shirt, gray slacks, and penny loafers and currently seemed to be nursing what looked like a scotch on the rocks.

Keisha pasted on an award-winning smile as they neared his table, deciding if she was going to do this, she would do it well.

She stepped forward first to Forester and extended her hand. "Mr. Forester?"

"Yes," he rumbled in a heavy baritone as he looked up absently.

"Keisha Reynolds, sir. It's pleasure to meet you."

His eyes widened. "Pleasure to meet you, too," he replied as he shook her hand firmly. The words were kind but there was no warmth in his voice.

"And this is Jason Wheeler, Phil Levine's assistant," she said as she turned to Jason.

Jason eagerly shook Forester's hand. "Unfortunately, Mr. Levine has fallen ill and won't be able to be here, Mr. Forester," Jason said. "But we are fully capable of handling this ourselves, sir."

Forester glanced up at Jason warily. "I should hope so," he said dryly. The older man leaned back in his chair as they lowered themselves into two of the three empty seats at the table.

"I half expected to find you guys wearing dark sunglasses, fedoras, and trench coats, considering all the intrigue," he said with a dry smile and a chuckle before tossing back his drink. "The fake name I gave to the hostess," he continued with another chuckle. "I feel like I'm in the CIA."

A waiter stepped forward and asked if Keisha or Jason would like to see a menu. She shook her head and ordered just a glass of white wine. Jason did the same.

Jason leaned forward. "Mr. Forester, all this 'intrigue' is simply for protection, sir. We didn't want to put you in a . . . a . . ." Jason looked up in the air, as if he was searching there for the right word. ". . . a compromising situation, shall we say. We understand you are very old friends and have a close relationship with Congressman Dupré."

"Not anymore," Forester proclaimed as he took a quick gulp from his glass. "Don't worry. When the axe falls, I want Vincent to know who did it to him," he said with an icy smile that sent a chill down Keisha's spine. "Plaster it on a *wall* for all I care."

Keisha frowned, biting back the question, "So revenge is your motivation for talking to us?"

"What Vincent did to me with that whole land deal was inexcusable, unforgivable!" he suddenly boomed. "Do you two know how much money I had invested in that deal?"

He paused as if they would answer, but in fact they had no idea what he was talking about.

"I needed his support on that congressional committee and he just left me swinging in the wind," he said, waving his hand for illustration. "He said he had to do it . . . but I don't buy that for one second. He's goddamned Congressman Vincent Dupré, for Chrissake! Minority Whip of the House! He can do anything he goddamn wants!" Forester spat. "He hurt my ambitions, now I plan to hurt his. He plans to become president one day, you know." He smiled. "Fat chance at that when *this* comes out!"

"When what comes out, Mr. Forester?" she asked, hoping to steer him back to the subject at hand. There was something about this guy that made her queasy. The less time she spent around him, the better.

Keisha watched as Forester leaned back in his chair again, staring at her across the table. He took another gulp from his glass, sucking an ice cube as he did so. "Oh, it's good," he said before loudly crunching on the cube of ice. "Believe me. But I warn you that you have to confirm what I'm saying first, before you take it to the press. I can tell you only what I know. You'll have to track her down if you want to find out for sure."

Jason frowned. "Track who down?"

"The mother of his child," Forester said impatiently, waving to the waiter to get him another drink.

Now both Keisha and Jason frowned.

"Not Sara Dupré," Forester elaborated. "The one before that. The one he didn't marry."

Jason slowly shook his head. "Dupré has *another* child?"

"Yes, illegitimate. Bastards are what they called them back in my day!" Forester boomed, making Keisha's and Jason's eyes widen in shock. "No one would guess it of Vincent Dupré. Not Mr. Family Values," he said sarcastically. "Look, I can say with 90 percent certainty that he has some other son or daughter running around out there, but, like I said," he murmured with a shrug, "you'll have to track her down to know for sure. I can't remember her name. The last time I saw her was many, many years ago. Back in the late '70s. I believe it was at a hotel in Philadelphia."

Keisha pursed her lips. The only clue he had was she was last seen walking around Philly more than thirty years ago? *Great*, Keisha thought flippantly. She had been right to be wary of the information Forester had to share. *This is like looking for a needle in a haystack*, she thought. They'd probably have a better chance of finding Jimmy Hoffa than they would of finding this woman.

Keisha and Jason exchanged a look: his was of disappointment, hers said, "I figured this would happen."

Ever the good employee, Jason pressed forward. "Well, can you . . . can you tell us anything *else* about her, Mr. Forester?" he persisted. "About their relationship? Maybe talking about it could help us or help jog your memory."

Forester gave a long sigh before closing his eyes. "She was short and black," he blurted out.

Keisha gazed at Forester in shock. *Black?* She leaned forward eagerly. This was definitely getting interesting.

"She had dark skin and she was a dancer...I think," he continued. "They lived in D.C. together for a year or two when he was younger, back when he had loose morals. But I could tell from early on that the relationship was doomed."

"Why?" Keisha asked.

"Well, besides the black thing, they didn't exactly run in the same circles, if you know what I mean," Forester said as the waiter placed wine glasses in front of Keisha and Jason. "Vincent comes from a family that's very wealthy and highly respected, and here was this . . . this . . . *nobody*," Forester said with a disgusted curl to his lips. "She was this little black girl, and I mean *girl.* She was barely eighteen years old. She had no money and no family to speak of. She barely graduated from high school," he remarked. "All she had going for her was a pretty face, and that will only carry you so far. She was severely in over her head," Forester declared.

"I asked him at the time, 'Vincent, what do you think you're doing with this girl? Have you *completely* lost your mind?' And he said, 'I can't help it, Bill. I love her.' He was always a hopeless romantic. Idiot," Forester spat. "I remember when he decided to bring her to one of his parents' dinner parties so he could introduce her to everyone. His parents were barely speaking to him by then. I warned him against it. You have to understand," he explained. "People didn't necessarily object to the relationship. Plenty of Southern men . . . gentlemen, if you will . . . keep young ladies like her on the side."

You mean like Strom Thurmond? Keisha thought with disgust.

"But you don't flaunt it! You don't throw it up in everyone's face!" Foster slowly shook his head. "But Vincent wouldn't listen. So he brings her to the dinner party and she shows up in this gigantic afro, these big platform shoes, and this cheap little sundress. She was so out of her element! I think it took her ten minutes to figure out which fork to use." He cruelly chuckled again.

Can we go easy with the insults, buddy? Keisha thought.

"Needless to say, Mrs. Jacqueline Dupré was not amused." He slowly shook his head. "And later she let her son and his new girlfriend know it. I would say that was the beginning of the end for them. But when that girl got pregnant, that was the finale."

"So Dupré's managed to keep his child a secret for all these years?" Jason said with awe. "I'm surprised no one's discovered it by now."

Keisha stared at Jason. He of all people should know how easy it was to keep secrets. Besides Keisha, only a few people in their campaign knew Jason was gay.

"Well, it wasn't exactly a secret," Forester replied. "I don't think he's trying to hide the child. I don't think Dupré even knows she *had* a baby. When he found out she was pregnant, he tried to do the noble thing. Like an idiot, he asked her to marry him. But she told him no, thank God. She was going to have an abortion instead. I wasn't surprised. Who knows how many abortions she may have had before," Forester quipped. He had more of his drink. "They had this big blow-up and went their separate ways. But I ran into her during a business trip in Philadelphia." He cocked an eyebrow. "Believe it or not, she was one of the maids cleaning at the hotel where I stayed. I wasn't sure at first if it was her because she was just so . . . so big," he said, motioning to his plump stomach. "She had always been a tiny thing, but this woman had to be about seven or eight months pregnant at the time. I second guessed myself because I remembered Vincent saying that she had gotten an abortion. But after looking at her for a bit I knew it was her walking down the hallway with that cleaning cart. I could tell it was her by the face and of course, she was still wearing the locket he had given her," he said casually.

Keisha narrowed her eyes. "A locket?"

"Yes, a silver locket with roses engraved on the front with a pearl embedded at the center. It was one of a kind—a family heirloom. His grandmother got it from her mother. The old gal had it made in Paris at the turn of the century, from what I was told. And it wasn't cheap. I was surprised his ex-girlfriend hadn't pawned it by then," he said derisively as he drank from his glass.

Keisha reached instinctively for the locket hidden beneath her suit jacket—a tarnished silver locket with roses engraved on the front with a pearl embedded at the center. Was that why Dupré had seemed so shocked all those months ago to see her wearing it? Was that why he had asked her where she had gotten it? Maybe he had mistaken her locket for the antique locket he had given his lover all those years ago.

Keisha frowned. She was starting to feel pity for Vincent Dupré, and that wasn't the emotion she wanted to have right now. Sure, letting the world know that he had lived with a woman—a *black* woman at that— before marriage and possibly had an out-of-wedlock child with her could destroy his Christian image and sink him with the right-wingers, but the story didn't seem as straightforward as all that. He had *tried* to marry her. He had fallen in love with her against his parents' and society's wishes. The sight of Keisha's locket had drawn an extreme reaction from him thirty years after the fact, showing that his emotions for this woman must still be strong—much like the emotions Keisha's mother still felt for her deceased father. *Maybe Dupré and my mother should set up a support group,* Keisha thought flippantly. Again she pressed her hand against the locket that she loved so much. She suddenly blinked, taken aback by a thought that had bubbled to the surface. Forester's words had started to create a pattern that she found disturbing.

She was short. She had dark skin and she was a dancer. I ran into her during a business trip in Philadelphia.

And now the locket; he had described the locket her mother had given her almost perfectly.

Keisha's eyes widened and her stomach plummeted as a wave of awareness suddenly swept over her. *No*, she thought with shock as she slowly shook her head. *No, don't even think about it. That is not possible. These are all just coincidences. Your father died a long time ago.* But she couldn't help thinking it. She couldn't help asking herself. Why did her mother have so much in common with the woman Forester described? Why had Keisha never been able to find out anything about her father? Why had her mother been so angry when she mentioned that Forester planned to reveal Dupré's secret?

There is no way in hell that Vincent Dupré is my father!

Are you sure about that, a nagging voice inside her head asked in return. *Are you really sure?*

"Jason," Keisha said quickly, "maybe you should pop out and let Phil know what we found out. Keep him updated."

Jason frowned. "You want me to do it now?"

"Why not?" she persisted. "I'm sure he's waiting for one of us to call. His Bluetooth probably hasn't left his ear for hours."

Jason gazed at her for several seconds before slowly nodding his head. "You're right," he said. "If you'll excuse me, Mr. Forester, I'll be right back."

Forester nodded as Jason rose from the table.

Keisha watched and waited until Jason was out of earshot before she turned back to face the older man. "Mr. Forester, I think we're going to need a little more help here," she said slowly, "if we're really going to track down the woman you were talking about."

He rolled his eyes in exasperation. "Young lady, I told you all that I know! I can't—"

"Her name," Keisha continued, cutting him off, "you really can't remember it?"

He thought for several seconds before slowly shaking his head. "I'm sorry, but like I told you before, I just cannot recall."

"Was her first name . . . Lena?"

She watched as he looked up in the air and squinted. She sat with bated breath, silently willing him to deny it. *Please say 'no', please*, she thought.

"Lena," he murmured. "Lena . . . Lena . . . actually, that does sound familiar. I believe that could be . . ." He pursed his lips. "Now that I think of it . . . ," he tilted his head, ". . . It was Lena and something with an R. Raymond . . . Reginald," he muttered. "It was something like that." He frowned. "How did you know her name was Lena?"

This is not possible, Keisha thought with panic. She closed her eyes, wanting to break down into tears, to drop her face into her hands and sob, but she couldn't. She needed to know the truth. She had to ask Forester one more question and Jason would probably return soon. She didn't have much time to ask it.

"Mr. Forester, I want to show you something," she said as she quickly opened the buttons of her jacket, making him raise his eyebrows in surprise. "I want you to have a look at this," she said as she pulled her locket out of her shirt, holding it toward him. "Does this at all look like the locket that Dupré gave to his girlfriend back then, before they broke up?"

Forester gazed at the silver piece and slowly reached out to touch it. "Where did you get that?" he whispered, transfixed.

She quickly shook her head. "Never mind that!" she almost shouted. "Just please, please tell me if it looks like the locket?" she pleaded. "Do you think it's the same one?"

Forester's frown intensified. He leaned back in his chair and studied her carefully. "Young lady, I believe I've said enough. You seem to know a lot more about the story than you're letting on. You knew her name and here you are with Vincent's locket. This is all very . . . very suspicious to me," he said. "It's very . . . disturbing."

"It's very disturbing to me, too, Mr. Forester," she said quietly, feeling as if the world was spinning around her. "You have no idea how much."

"Well, I'm back," Jason suddenly piped as he sat back in the chair beside her. "And you were right, Keisha, Phil was elated to hear the news. He wants to start tracking this woman down ASAP. He wants you to call him when you get the chance."

Keisha quickly shook her head. "I have to go, Jason," she said as she rose from the table and gathered her purse and her coat. "I can't . . . I can't stay here."

Jason frowned up at her while Forester gazed at her angrily. "Wh-what do you mean you can't stay?"

"Tell Phil that I'll talk to him tomorrow," she said hurriedly over her shoulder.

"Keisha! Keisha, where are you going?"

She ignored him as she made her way across the crowded restaurant, feeling her whole body tremble.

"You have a good afternoon, ma'am," the hostess said merrily as Keisha pushed open the glass door and nearly ran into a couple as she walked quickly toward the parking lot. She knew instantly where she needed to go—if only she could stop shaking long enough to get there.

CHAPTER 28

Hours later, Keisha slowly climbed the concrete steps to her mother's home, feeling as if lead weights were strapped around her ankles.

She hadn't called. She hadn't warned her mother that she was coming. She hadn't even bothered to ring the doorbell. She used her key to get inside.

"Ma," Keisha called out into the darkened foyer.

"Up here, Keisha," her mother answered from her bedroom upstairs.

She dragged herself up the steps and paused in the hallway outside her mother's cracked bedroom door. A guitar riff from an Earth, Wind and Fire tune was playing as she stood there. Keisha slowly shook her head. Not only would it be painful to have to ask her mother the question she planned to ask, but she wasn't sure if she really wanted to know the answer. *Did my father die in an accident like you said, Ma, or have you been lying to me for the past thirty years?*

The young woman took a long, shaky breath, resolving that no matter what, she had to confront her mother about this. She had to ask. There was too much at stake now. Keisha slowly pushed the bedroom door open only to find her mother quietly painting on a canvas in the corner of her room. She would usually be singing and dancing as she painted, but not today. Today something was different.

Lena Reynolds coughed softly before tossing her brush into a soup can filled with water. She then placed her palette on top of a nearby wooden stool and reached over to turn off the stereo before turning to face her daughter. "I thought you weren't coming today." She tilted her head. "Did you decide not to go to your meeting?" A slither of hope was in her voice and her eyes.

"No, I went," Keisha said flatly. "And I . . ." Keisha struggled to find her words. "Ma, I'm going to . . . I'm going to ask you a few questions. And I really need you to be honest with me." She hesitated. "Did you know Vincent Dupré back in the '70s?"

The older woman's gaze faltered as she licked her full lips and adjusted the straps of her overalls.

"Ma?" Keisha repeated.

"Yes," Lena finally said quietly and then nodded. "Yes, I knew him."

"How?" Keisha persisted. "How did you know him?"

Lena fidgeted impatiently. "We worked together back in '78 and '79 at a community center in D.C. We were instructors there. He coached baseball and did some tutoring with the kids. I taught dance."

Keisha took a deep breath. "Were you . . . friends?"

Keisha watched as Lena turned and slowly walked over to her dresser.

"I mean . . . were you ever . . . were you . . . did you become *more* than friends?" Keisha gritted her teeth as her mother continued to ignore her. "Ma! Ma, answer me!"

The older woman let out a loud sigh as she unclasped the lid to one of her jewelry boxes. "Why don't you just ask me what you really want to ask me, Keisha," she said as she began to rummage through a pile of costume jewelry. She shoved aside decades' worth of earrings, pendants, and brooches as she dug her way through the heap. "You're taking the long way around when you and I both know exactly where you want to go," Lena said, suddenly turning to face her daughter. She extended her brown hand towards Keisha.

Keisha's eyes narrowed as she looked at the folded handkerchief her mother held. She frowned. "What . . . What is it?"

"Open it," her mother commanded.

Keisha slowly opened the handkerchief and stared down at a well-worn, one-inch photo. It was a headshot of her mother in her late teens or early twenties and a smiling white guy with long hippie-like brown hair. *Who the hell is that?* Keisha wondered. She squinted at the picture. The face was much younger, but she could spot those green eyes anywhere. *That's not just some "smiling white guy,"* she suddenly thought. *That* was Vincent Dupré!

Keisha's hands began to tremble.

"I always told you I didn't have any pictures of your father," Lena slowly began, "but that wasn't true. I do have one—that one—and except for the lock of hair I clipped from you when you were a baby, this is the most precious thing I've ever owned." Lena took a deep breath. "The picture used to be inside your locket. That locket belonged to your father's grandmother, your great-grand-mother, and he gave it to me. We took the picture in the park one day . . . me and your father," Lena said forlornly.

"Even when Forester said it . . . even when he told me the story, I thought it couldn't be you because you told me he was dead. You said my father had . . . ," Keisha whispered with halting breaths. She stumbled across the room. "I need to . . . I need to sit down. I'm going to be sick." The photo fell from Keisha's hands as she grabbed the edge of her mother's four-poster bed to steady herself. A moment later, she slumped to the floor. The tears that had been brimming in her eyes suddenly welled over onto her cheeks.

Lena slowly shook her head as she gazed at her daughter mournfully. "Baby, I never wanted you to find out like this. I never wanted to lie to you."

"So why did you?" Keisha sobbed. "Why didn't you . . . Why didn't y-y-you tell me the truth?" she asked as she pounded her fists against her thighs. Yelling at her mother only made her feel worse. She fought to control her sobs and hiccups as she huddled on the floor in front of her mother's bed.

"How was I supposed to tell you?" her mother pleaded as she knelt at Keisha's side, wrapping her weeping daughter in her arms. She rested her cheek on Keisha's forehead. "I couldn't do it. Not after all this time. Baby, I had no idea you were ever gonna meet him!" She paused. "But you did, and I swear to God, Keisha, I didn't know what to do. That was the reason I didn't want

you to take this job! I *begged* you to go back to teaching!
I begged you! I told you not to go snooping around,
trying to find dirt on him for the campaign. I wasn't just
protecting him, Keisha. I was trying to protect you, too!
I figured this . . . this would be what you discovered. I
knew what you found out could hurt you just as much as
it could hurt him."

"You told me my father was dead!" Keisha shouted,
shoving her mother away. "*You* made up that story! And
you never warned me! You never said any differently!"

"I tried to tell you not to go snooping around,
Keisha," Lena repeated softly. "I tried, baby. I *swear* I did."

"You stuck to your lies and you left it to me to find
out the truth!" Keisha yelled. "You let me walk into that
. . . that . . . *trap* with no warning! I had to sit there and
listen to all those horrible things that bastard had to say
about you—about *us!*" Keisha shook her head. "Why?
Why didn't you tell me? Why would you do that? You
didn't think I had the right to know?"

"I'm so sorry, KeKe," her mother said mournfully as
she slowly shook her head.

"*Sorry?*" Keisha shouted in disbelief. "Don't tell me
sorry! I want to know how you could do this to me, to
your own daughter? How could you be so selfish?"

Lena stilled. "*Selfish?* You think I'm selfish?" She
quickly rose to her feet and glared. "Let me tell you
somethin'. When I had you I was nineteen, alone, and
scared! When I left Vincent, I was a wannabe dancer with
$40 in my pocket and no place to live. But I did what I
had to do. I swallowed my pride and took waitressing

jobs. Seven months pregnant and I was cleaning hotels! Mopping floors! On my hands and knees scrubbing toilets! I sacrificed and I saved to take care of *you!*" she shouted as she pointed down at Keisha. "So don't tell me I'm selfish! Don't act like I'm some horrible mother! Because I'm not! I've been bustin' my ass to keep you happy since the beginning!"

Lena's chest heaved up and down as she fought to rein in her anger. She slumped to the floor beside her daughter, lowered her head into her hands, and closed her eyes. The room filled with silence.

"I know you don't want to hear it, KeKe, but I need you to believe me when I say I'm sorry," she began softly several minutes later. "Because I am. And you're right. I shouldn't have let you walk into that. But I didn't know what to do to stop you. I couldn't tell you. If I told you the truth about Vincent it would just . . . cloud things up for you. And when you get so used to lying, KeKe, it's hard to just stop." She sighed. "I know it's my fault. I'm the one who made up the stories. But I . . . I knew I had to give you something to cling to. If I told you he was still alive and who he was, I thought you'd probably try to find him. What if you wanted to meet him one day?" She slowly shook her head. "I just . . . I just didn't want you to get hurt. That's all, baby."

Keisha frowned and gazed at her mother in bewilderment. "Why would I get hurt?" she asked. "Mom, Forester told us that Dupré wanted to *marry* you! Do you honestly believe that he would've rejected you or me if someone told him the truth?"

Lena furiously shook her head. "Vincent asked me to marry him because he thought he had to, not because he wanted to. I knew the truth! And deep down I knew if we got married, eventually he'd think the same thing about me that his family and friends had been thinking all along." She gritted her teeth. Keisha watched as several decades' worth of buried pain quickly rose to her mother's face, darkening her usually luminescent eyes. " 'This little black ghetto tramp wants to bring me down,' " she spat. " 'She finally got her hooks into me and she's going to take me for all I'm worth.' " She closed her eyes again, her long lashes dampening with tears.

" 'Colored gutter tramp' . . . that's what his mother called me the first time she met me. She was so disgusted that he would be with someone like me . . . that he would dare to bring me to her dining room table! 'Can't you see? Can't you see what she really wants from you, Vincent?' " Lena said, imitating the late Jacqueline Dupré's Southern drawl. "But I didn't want anything from him, not a dime. Hell, it wasn't like he had a dime to give. Without his parents' money, he was poor like I was. But I had grown up that way. Vincent hadn't," she said, choking up on her own words. "I knew it was hard on him. We could . . . we could barely take care of ourselves. How were we supposed to take care of a baby, too? I didn't want him to hate me for getting pregnant. I didn't want him to see me as a dead weight, the gutter girl." She sighed and closed her eyes. "So I told him we didn't have to get married. I told him, yes, I was pregnant, but I would take care of it. I would round up enough money from friends to . . . to get an abortion." She took a deep breath. "He hated me for saying that but he just . . . he didn't understand. We fought about it that night. He went to the center the next day and I didn't. While he was gone, I packed up what little I had. By the time he came home again . . . I was gone," she said quietly. "I said I would take care of it . . . so I took care of it . . . *my* way. He could go back to his people and law school. He could live his life and be happy. I would go somewhere else and take care of my baby." She sighed again. "What I did, Keisha, might sound wrong but it just . . . it just felt like . . . the right thing to do at the time."

Keisha gazed at her mother with reddened eyes. "Ma," Keisha whispered. She gently wrapped her arms around her mother's shoulders, enveloping her in an embrace. So she finally had the whole story. Dupré wasn't some misogynist, some careless jerk who had deserted his pregnant girlfriend. He had tried to do right by her mother. But her mother had undervalued her self-worth and dismissed his love.

Lena shrugged and quickly shook her head as she held her daughter. "It's okay, Keisha. It's okay. I'm sad that things happened the way they did, but in the end it was probably for the best. I knew Vincent was meant for great things." She pulled back from her daughter and gave a wistful smile. "And just look at him. He's a millionaire and a congressman! That was the path he was meant to take. And you, my dear," she said as she held her daughter's chin and gazed into the younger woman's eyes, "you didn't even know him and ended up going in the same direction. It's in your blood. But I always knew you were meant for greatness, too."

Keisha frowned. "But what about you, Ma? You keep talking about what everyone else was meant for. What about you?"

Her mother leaned her head back against the mattress. The older woman shrugged. "Life didn't turn out the way I planned. There was a lot of struggle in the beginning but . . . it got better. I'm happy. I have my art," Lena said as she glanced at her nearby canvas. "I have my beautiful daughter," she whispered as she smiled at Keisha. "I have my health and a few dear friends. I've lived a full life and hopefully I have many more years to come." She tilted her head and gazed at Keisha, scanning her face. "I know what you found out today was hard to hear, baby," she said as she pushed a lock of hair away from Keisha's temple. "I know it probably turned your world upside down. But you'll make it through. I know you will."

Keisha sighed. She hoped her mother was right.

CHAPTER 29

"Keisha. Keisha!" Phil called as he leaned out a doorway and she shrugged out of her coat and swiftly made her way down the corridor. "Could you come in here for a sec?"

Keisha paused. She had hoped to get to her office, shut the door and use a few precious minutes to get her bearings before she ran into Phil. Her head was still spinning from the night before. She was still trying to decide what on earth to do with her mother's revelation and was in no mood to talk, but Keisha knew she could not tell Phil that.

"Sure," she said quietly. She then followed him into the campaign headquarters' "war room."

The 10-by-10-foot space was filled with staffers. Some sat at the mahogany table in the center of the room, but most stood along the gray walls. Keisha frowned in confusion.

"Are we having a meeting?" she asked.

"Yes, sort of," he said before turning to the surrounding audience. "Ladies and gentlemen, yesterday Keisha and Jason did something very important, something that could change the course of this campaign. They discovered some fairly explosive information about our opponent and, as far as I'm concerned, it's fair game."

His eyebrows furrowed angrily. "The Dupré folks took their swing, but we're not down for the count. No," he insisted as he jabbed his fist into the air. "We're about to take our swing and we're about to knock them on their asses," he said, eliciting a shout of "Yeah!" from one of the campaign staffers. A few people laughed, but the room quieted again as Phil continued.

"I called all of you in here because I know you've been discouraged lately. For the first time in many months we're sliding in the polls. You're probably desperate to hear some good news, and we're here to give it to you today." He looked around the room again. "Everything said here needs to stay within these walls, people. We want maximum impact when we release it to the public." He tilted his head toward Keisha. "Now I'm going to hand the floor over to Keisha and let her do the talking." He extended his hand and nodded. "Come on, Keisha. Tell us what you found out yesterday."

Keisha stared at him blankly, caught completely off guard. She cleared her throat and looked around the room, desperately trying to think of what to say. She instinctively reached for the locket around her neck and held it. It now contained the photograph that had been removed all those years ago but had been returned to its rightful place. Holding the locket was like twisting on a light bulb in her head. Keisha instantly realized what she had to do.

"Go ahead, Keisha," Phil persisted as he gestured toward the front of the room. When she didn't budge, he laughed awkwardly. "Don't tell me you're nervous."

She could feel the heat of their expectant gazes. What she was about to do, she had to do privately. If she was about to step before the guillotine, she didn't want an audience.

"I need to talk to you," she said quickly, pointing towards the doorway.

His eyes widened in surprise. He stared at her, not saying a word for several seconds before slowly nodding. "Lead the way," he said.

The two walked into the hallway, leaving those behind in shocked silence. They entered Keisha's small office, which was at the end of the corridor. She sighed as she draped her coat over the back of her desk chair. She then turned back to face him. Phil closed her office door and crossed his arms over his chest.

"So what do you want to tell me?" he asked. His voice was tinged with suspicion.

"Phil," Keisha began. She paused and looked down at her feet, trying to find the right words. "Look, I know Jason told you what Forester said but . . . we can't run with it. We can't come out with the story like that about Dupré. We just can't."

"Why not?" he asked impatiently. "This is how it's done, Keisha. They slap you and you slap them back . . . *harder*!" He quickly shook his head. "Look, I didn't initiate this. I didn't put our campaign in jeopardy."

. . . *like you probably did.* It was the phrase that seemed to be hanging in a word bubble over his head.

Keisha knew that's what Phil wanted to say. She sighed again, closed her eyes and held up her hands. "Phil, just . . . just hear me out, please."

"This isn't a crisis of conscience, is it?" he suddenly asked. "I'd like to know where this crisis of conscience was when you were *slinking* into hotels with Will Blake!"

Her eyes flashed open. Keisha could feel anger and humiliation adding pink to her cheeks. He had meant for his words to sting her, but she wasn't going to back down. Keisha squared her shoulders, gritted her teeth and pressed on.

"What Will Blake and I did together is irrelevant to this conversation," she said icily, making Phil snort with contempt. "What we're talking about—"

"What we're talking about is your inability to do what needs to be done!" he yelled with outrage. He vigorously shook his head as his face reddened. "I knew it. I knew I shouldn't have left something this important up to you! Sydney still trusts you for *some* absurd reason even after I told him about you and Blake!" He pointed his finger at her. "But you did exactly what I thought you were going to do! You can't be trusted!"

Keisha gaped in astonishment for several seconds. "You told Dr. Parker about me and Will?" she finally asked, dumbfounded.

"Of course I did," Phil said as he adjusted his jacket. "I wanted Sydney to know what kind of woman he had hired, but he didn't believe me. He said there must be some other explanation." Phil's nostrils flared as he quickly changed the subject. "Look, Keisha, we don't need you to be on board with this. Jason was there and Forester also told him the woman's name! We'll feed it to the newspapers and let them track her down and she'll show Dupré for the bastard that he is!" Phil shouted. "So we'll carry on without you!" he said with a wicked curl to his lip. "We'll handle it from here!" She watched as Phil angrily swung open her office door.

"Jason may know her name but he didn't talk to her, Phil. *I did*," Keisha said quickly as she pointed at her chest. She hesitated when Phil stopped in his tracks. He turned to glare at her.

"And . . . and she won't talk," Keisha said, mustering up her courage again. She boldly stuck out her chin. "She told me she wouldn't."

He stood in the open doorway. "You found her *already*?" He then slowly shook his head. "I don't believe you. That's impossible."

"No, it isn't impossible because I *did* find her and she won't talk! No matter how many reporters beat down her door, she won't utter a word," Keisha said defiantly. "You guys can dig up as much dirt on him as you want. She's still not going to help you bury him."

Phil took several menacing steps toward Keisha. She met him halfway. They stood nearly nose to nose, glaring at one another, now engaged in a battle of wills. "What the hell did she tell you?" he roared.

"None of your damn business!" she shouted back, now past angry. She was completely furious.

"Hey! *Hey!*" Dr. Parker yelled. He looked questioningly from one campaign manager to the other. "What the hell is going on here?"

Keisha blinked. "Dr. Parker!" she exclaimed. Within a second her anger switched to embarrassment. "I . . . thought you were in . . . Annapolis."

"The meeting ended early," he said testily, looking at both of them with disgust. "But I probably could have heard the two of you yelling all the way in Annapolis."

Keisha gazed down at her feet.

"I will not have my staff behaving this way," Parker said in his teacher's voice.

"Dammit, Sydney, Keisha is working for the Dupré campaign!" Phil shouted as he jabbed his finger at her, his frantic accusation catching her by surprise. "I know it now! She talked to the woman who had Dupré's child and talked her out of saying anything against him! She's here to sabotage us, Sydney!"

Keisha's eyes widened. She sputtered, at a loss for words again. She had known Phil would be angry when she stood up to him, but she had no idea he could be this venomous, this cruel. She slowly shook her head.

"Need I remind you, Sydney, of her affair with Will Blake . . . to which she has admitted," Phil said. "Maybe that was her intent all along . . . to feed him information. I still think that's how the Dupré campaign found out about your record."

The longer Keisha stayed lost in shock, saying nothing, the more Phil spoke and continue to smile with victory.

"Is this true, Keisha?" Dr. Parker asked quietly.

By now Phil and Keisha's fight had drawn an audience. Several people lingered in the campaign headquarters' hallway, shamelessly leaning their heads so they could peer through the doorway and get a better view of the battle.

Keisha furiously shook her head, then nodded it, then shook it again. She *did* have an affair with Will but she *wasn't* some Mata Hari he had sent to spy on the opposition. She had leaked the information about Dr. Parker's juvenile record to Will, but that had been an accidental slip. There was no evil intent behind it.

Keisha grumbled in frustration. "Some of it's true," she finally said reluctantly, making Dr. Parker's eyes widen. A sharp intake of breath signaling surprise came from several of the lingerers in the hallway. "B-but it didn't happen the way Phil's making it sound," she rushed, hoping to explain. "Will and I were . . . have been . . . together but I would never betray you! I'm not working for them."

At that, Phil snorted. "More lies," he mumbled cynically.

"Look, I have no reason to hurt you, Dr. Parker! Please believe me. I've been busting my ass for this campaign!" She turned and glared at Phil. "When Phil wanted to give up, I stayed and I convinced him to stay, too! Why would I do that? Why would I do that if I was trying to sabotage everyone?" she asked desperately.

Parker shoved his hands in his pants pockets and gave a deep sigh. He looked from Keisha to Phil and back again. "Phil, will you excuse us, please?" he asked softly.

Phil's eyes widened with disbelief. "*What?* Don't tell me that you actually believe this . . . this *garbage*, Sydney?"

"I'm not saying anything," he said quietly. "I'm just asking to have some time alone with my deputy campaign manager. That's all."

Phil balled his fist before stomping to Keisha's office door. He turned and opened his mouth to speak again.

"Would you close the door behind you?" Parker asked quickly before Phil could say anything.

Phil scowled and paused before slamming the door shut.

Keisha watched as Parker slowly walked toward her, his eyes downcast. He had changed so much from the days when he was her professor. Gone was the man who wore wrinkled corduroy pants and hair badly in need of a comb. In his place was a politician who wore slick, tailored suits and went to the barber once a week. But Keisha believed that somewhere inside this new shell was the old Dr. Parker. She still believed in him and he still believed in her . . . *right?*

"Do you still trust me, Dr. Parker?" she asked, pain now painting every contour of her face. "You don't really think I was trying to hurt your chances of winning, do you?"

As he stood gazing at her silently, Keisha became more and more afraid of his answer. Parker finally shook his head. "No, Keisha, I don't."

She gave a sigh of relief.

"But why are you fighting this so much?" he asked quietly. "And tell me the truth. If we didn't find out about Dupré's child, someone else would have. That's the nature of politics. I know that now." He took a deep breath. "Skeletons in the closets are bound to fall out eventually. But what I can't understand is why you're fighting this tooth and nail. His side has already done it to us. I would imagine they're anticipating that we'll do something in return and they're preparing for it. They know the rules."

The room was silent save for the sound of her swallowing as she leaned back her head and gazed at the ceiling. Keisha could feel the tears welling in her eyes. They were on the verge of spilling over, despite her efforts to hold them back.

"Tell me what this is about. Are you trying to protect someone? Is all this about William Blake?"

She closed her eyes, letting the tears fall down her cheeks. She slowly shook her head again.

"Then what is it?"

"He's my father," she suddenly blurted out, unable to hold it in anymore. "Vincent Dupré is my father," she sobbed.

Dr. Parker gaped.

"I didn't know," she continued between hiccups. "Please believe me, Dr. Parker! I didn't know about it until yesterday!" She wiped her nose on the sleeve of her blouse as she cried. "My mother told me all my life that my father was dead! I didn't find out the truth until I talked to Forester. And he remembered her . . . after all these years, he remembered her."

Keisha fell into her office chair and dropped her face into her hands. She slowly shook her head. "I've daydreamed about my father for so many years, Dr. Parker.

Out of all the people in the world, why did it turn out to be Dupré? I don't understand it." She reached for a box of tissues on her desk, removed a Kleenex and loudly blew her nose. "I want you to win, sir. I really do! But I can't do this. Not to my own father. Not to my mother. She's tried so hard to put all this behind her. It wouldn't just humiliate him." She sobbed. "It would hurt her, too."

Dr. Parker sat on the edge of Keisha's desk, gazing down at her. "Did he abandon your mother?" he asked softly.

Keisha quickly shook her head. "No, sh-sh-she left him," she stuttered.

"Did he ever make any attempt to contact you, to find you, Keisha?" he persisted.

She sat back in her chair, contemplated for several seconds and shrugged. "I don't know. I don't think so. But then again . . . according to Forester, Dupré doesn't even know I exist."

Keisha watched as Dr. Parker slowly nodded his head. "That may be the case but still . . . it's out of our hands now."

Keisha lowered the tissue from her nose as she narrowed her swollen, reddened eyes. "What do you mean 'it's out of our hands'? I told you the *truth!*" she insisted. "I explained to you why we can't do this! Just tell Phil to call it off! He'll listen to you!"

Parker slowly shook his head. "No, Keisha you explained to me why we *shouldn't* do this. There's a fundamental difference between that and *can't.*" He sighed.

"Look, I understand that you're worried about embarrassing your family," he muttered as he stood and adjusted his jacket. "But I can assure you that we'll handle this as delicately as possible. I'll ask Kelly to sit in on all interviews with you and your mother. If any reporter asks a question that's out of line or any question that makes you uncomfortable, then the interview ends instantly."

Keisha blinked rapidly, trying to comprehend what Parker was saying. *"Interviews?"* she repeated. "Why would we do interviews? Interviews about what? About Dupré?"

Parker frowned and shrugged. "Why not? I'm sure the newspapers will want your perspectives. They'll want to talk to the mother and daughter who were left to fend for themselves while Dupré went on to power and riches. I would imagine that's how the storyline will go."

"But that's *not* the storyline," she choked with frustration. "That's *not* what happened!"

"Add to that the fact Dupré's daughter is black *and* is working for the opposing candidate," Dr. Parker continued as he slowly paced the room, as if he hadn't heard her protests. "It's almost Shakespearean. The reporters won't be able to resist the story."

Keisha stared at Dr. Parker, both staggered and heartbroken. Even after she had told him *everything*, even after she had poured her heart out to him, he still wanted to go ahead with this smear campaign in hope of winning the election. It seemed that he had changed both inside and out. Or maybe he had been this power hungry all along and she hadn't seen it.

Keisha slowly shook her head. "I'm not going to talk to reporters, Dr. Parker. I told you that I can't do it!"

Dr. Parker stared at her. "Can't or won't? Once again, Keisha, there is a fundamental difference between the two," he said calmly as he paced back in forth in front of her. "You could do this, but you're choosing not to. Even though you know it's three weeks before the election and we're behind in the polls. Even though your loyalty has been called into question and you admit that part of the accusations are true." He sighed. "This all puts me in a very awkward position, Keisha. There are so many people here who have worked hard for this campaign, who've worked hard for us to win. And here it seems I have our deputy campaign manager undermining that effort in almost every way. You tell me. What should I do, Keisha? What would you do if you were in my shoes?"

Keisha gritted her teeth as she stood. She suddenly thought of Will. He had once remarked that she would find out the truth about the ugliness of politics one day. *"You've got a lot to learn, Miss Reynolds,"* he once said. *". . . You think you know a person you respect and then suddenly they just . . . change."*

Dr. Parker had changed and the disappointment of that reality crushed her.

"Well, I'm not in your shoes, Dr. Parker," she finally began, "so I can't say what you should do. But I know now what I'm going to do. I probably should have done it a while ago," she said quietly as she gathered her coat and purse. She walked around him and headed to her door. "I'll email you my formal letter of resignation by the end of the day," she said over her shoulder before swinging open the door.

Several startled faces greeted her. They stared at her eagerly, looking for some sign of whether Dr. Parker had fired her. Keisha looked around the crowd, noticing a few all too familiar faces.

Jay stood in the hallway with his eyes downcast, refusing to meet her gaze. Tanya stood rigidly with her arms crossed over her chest. "I told you," she mouthed before closing her eyes and angrily shaking her head.

Keisha took a steadying breath before pushing back her shoulders. "I'm not going to cry again," she told herself as she walked past the throng of staffers. "I'm not going to cry."

And she didn't. She held back her tears until she walked out the front door of the campaign headquarters and only cried silently when she reached her car.

CHAPTER 30

Will slowly shook his head at the television screen in his kitchen as he flipped channels. His shoulders fell further with each station he landed on. He scraped his uneaten plate of toast and eggs into the sink, now that he was officially sick to his stomach, and turned on the garbage disposal. Its loud grinding momentarily drowned out the drone of the television. He leaned back against the counter.

"Dupré's 30-Year-Old Secret!" a red banner read as it zoomed across the screen. Suddenly, Dupré's and Keisha's pictures appeared side-by-side, making Will cringe.

The titillating story of the powerful Vincent Dupré's "long-lost daughter" had hit the newspapers and twenty-four-hour news channels like a hurricane three days ago, and it seemed that the hurricane still had not weakened. *The Washington Post, The New York Times*, CNN, Fox News . . . they were all covering it ad nauseum.

"Must be a slow news week," Will muttered as the watched the newscast.

The news outlets and political bloggers hadn't been able to resist the inherent drama of the story: self-proclaimed staunch white conservative congressman gets a poor black teenaged-girl pregnant thirty years ago while he's slumming and on vacation from law school. He then deserts her and her baby to move on to greatness. Throw in the twist that his child grows up and gets involved in politics, only to seek revenge on her father by working for the man who wants to rob him of his congressional seat. Now there you had the stuff of soap operas!

But Will sensed the story wasn't true. Not all of it, anyway. There were a lot of assumptions being made, mainly because neither Keisha nor Dupré were granting interviews and sharing their sides of the story. Dupré had even banned Gretchen from issuing any press statements on his behalf. The whole topic was strictly "No comment." The talking heads were left with nothing to do but speculate and the story was getting bigger and bigger, wilder and wilder with each passing day.

One blogger speculated that Keisha had really been in cahoots with her father and had been sent to work for Parker to destroy his campaign. One pundit argued that Dupré should lose his congressional seat since he probably owed years of back child support. The *National Enquirer* ran a story online that another woman had come forward saying that she was *also* Dupré's daughter. And so on and so on and so on.

Once he got past the initial shock of the story, Will instantly thought of Keisha. What was she going through right now? He had heard through the grapevine that she had quit the Parker campaign. No one had seen her since the news broke. He imagined she was pretty torn up—to see your personal life dissected on television had to be horrendous.

Dupré wasn't doing much better. He hadn't been to the headquarters in days and hadn't returned anyone's phone calls. George said yesterday he had finally gotten an email from the old guy. It was filled with three simple words: "SUSPEND THE CAMPAIGN."

"He's given up, Will," George had said over the phone earlier that morning. "He's just . . . given up. I don't think the election matters to him anymore."

Will knew the feeling. He sighed before pushing himself away from the counter. He needed to do some talking and needed a few questions answered.

No more phone calls. It was time to pay Vincent Dupré a visit.

∞∞∞

Will took a deep breath before he raised his hand to knock on one of the maroon-colored French doors of the tawny D.C. townhouse. He watched as Sara Dupré hesitantly pulled back the muslin curtains. Blonde curls fell about her face. She gave Will a weary smile before dropping the curtains and undoing the lock.

"Come in, Will," she said quietly, cracking the door only wide enough for him to creep inside. "I'm so glad it's you. I was hoping it wasn't one of those reporters."

Will slowly shook his head. "No, they're all hovering across the street." He looked around the foyer and then the family room. Kendall was perched at the end of the sofa, talking loudly on her cell phone. Paul sat on one of the love seats, silently flipping channels on the widescreen TV. The young man, who was the spitting image of his father, lowered the remote long enough to turn and look at Will. He nodded his head and gave a weak smile in greeting. Will waved in return.

"How is he?" Will asked Sara quietly.

"Kendall," Sara said tightly, "can you keep it down, please?" She then shook her head as she shut the door and locked it behind him. "Not too good. He just started accepting a few phone calls today. One from George, another from his cousin Jeffery. No visitors, though. But it isn't like we've had to turn anyone away besides reporters. None of our neighbors have come by. None of our friends." She sighed forlornly. "I guess it doesn't matter, though. When times get tough, you find out who your *real* friends are. Perhaps we had more acquaintances than friends after all."

He reached out and touched her shoulder. "I'm sorry, Sara."

She shrugged. "Oh, it's okay, Will. Even if he . . ." She cleared her throat and wiped away a tear from her eye. "Even if he loses the election, I'm fine with it and so is he—deep down. There are worse things. I just hate for it to happen this way. He doesn't deserve this, Will. He's a good man and it's so heartbreaking to see what he's going through right now." She sniffed as she peered down at her feet. She then glanced at Kendall who laughed loudly on the phone. "Vincent hasn't left the house in five days, Will," Sara whispered. "*Five* days."

Will didn't say anything in reply. If Sara thought Dupré was suffering, he could only imagine what Keisha was feeling right now. Did Sara, or anyone else in this house, give any thought to that?

Will had come today to help Dupré if he could, but also to ask a few important questions. Had Dupré really deserted Keisha's mother all those years ago when she needed him the most? If so, all sense of loyalty toward Dupré would end. Will needed to know the truth and hoped that Dupré would tell it.

"Where is he?" Will asked, looking around the room again.

"He's holed up in his study," Sara muttered, tilting her head toward the back of the house. "You can see him. He's probably in need of a visitor, someone who can distract him from his melancholy."

Will nodded and quietly walked down one hallway and then another before arriving at Dupré's private study. The door was ajar but Will knocked anyway.

"Yes?" Dupré asked softly.

Will pushed the door open and breathed in audibly, taken aback by what he saw.

Dupré sat at his desk. His face was partially illuminated by the orange glow of a Tiffany lamp and small shafts of light coming through the drawn shades of his plantation blinds.

He looks horrible, Will thought.

The fifty-eight-year-old man looked at least fifteen years older. His normally handsome face now seemed haggard with wrinkles that had miraculously developed overnight. His once luminescent green eyes were dull and watery and he looked as if he hadn't shaved in days. He was wearing a terrycloth robe, T-shirt, wrinkled pajama pants, and slippers. Newspapers and magazines were splayed on his desk. All the pages were opened to pictures of him and Keisha. Will watched as Dupré tore his attention away from them, slowly looked up, and smiled.

"Hello, Will," he said, gradually rising from his leather chair. "How you doin', son?"

"I'm okay, Vincent," he said as he shook the older man's hand. "How about you?" he asked quietly.

Dupré chuckled. "I've . . . been better," he said. "Have a seat, Will." He motioned to the chair on the other side of the desk.

Will lowered himself into it and faced the older man. "You haven't been returning phone calls, Vincent," Will began quietly.

"No desire to," Dupré said succinctly as he sat back in his chair and shuffled one of the newspapers on his desk. "Mostly reporters on the phone anyway. Those who aren't reporters are usually trying to talk about campaign strategy and spin, which I couldn't give a fig about."

"Where's your fighting spirit?"

Dupré sighed and continued to stare at the pages in front of him. "It didn't get out of bed this morning."

Will tilted his head, watching as Dupré scanned a few lines of text. "So you're just giving up, then?"

The older man suddenly looked up at Will. His gaze hardened. "Look, Will, I love you like a son, but if you're here to give me a pep talk, you might as well leave now.

I have no interest in hearing it from you or anybody else. Understood?"

Will paused and then slowly nodded. He watched as Dupré tapped Keisha's photograph with his index finger.

"You know, I knew it . . . deep down. The minute she told me her name, I knew it," he muttered. "I said maybe the last name, Reynolds, was just a coincidence. And that locket. I tried to talk myself out that, too. I kept telling myself its one that's just like my grandmother's, Mama Jeanette's." He slowly shook his head in bewilderment. "I thought she might be Lena's daughter but I never . . . I never imagined in a million years that she was mine. After all these years, all this time," he murmured. He gave a soft chuckle. "I thought Lena went to New York to try her hand at Broadway. I didn't know . . . I didn't know . . ." His voice faded.

"She was the dancer?" Will asked quietly. "The one with the amazing body?"

Dupré barely nodded his head, still engrossed with Keisha's picture.

"Is the baby what made things so . . . complicated?" Will asked, making Dupré's eyes leap up from the broadsheet's pages again. "She wanted the baby and you didn't?"

Dupré gritted his teeth. "Well, that's what the newspapers are saying, isn't it?" he spat. "I deserted her when she was pregnant because I didn't want to be a father. I was ashamed of my little half-black baby! That's what they're saying. So it must be true! I was coldhearted and power hungry back then! And I'm an old racist hypocrite and liar now! "

Will closed his eyes. "Vincent, I'm just—"

"No!" Dupré bellowed. "No, that's not what happened!" He shoved the newspapers and magazines aside and stood from his desk. "But what does it matter anyway? Who cares?" he said as he grabbed one of the papers and walked across the room to his study windows. He opened the shades, glared at the stone terrace in his backyard and then stared at the broadsheet again.

"People are going to think what they want to think, Will. That doesn't hurt me. What hurts me is that I can't understand why Lena did this. Why did she walk away? I mean . . . does she remember it happening this way?" he asked as he jabbed at one of the articles. "Because I sure as hell don't. She told me she wasn't going to have the baby. That's not what I wanted. I *begged* her to keep it! But it wasn't what she wanted! Or at least . . . at least . . . that's what I thought. But that was so long ago," he said quietly. Dupré cringed. "Keisha must hate me so much. Maybe that's why she went to work for Parker." He shook his head ruefully. "Revenge against the old man who deserted her."

"That isn't why she worked for Parker," Will said as he quickly rose from his chair. "She's not like that. She wasn't trying to get back at you. She didn't even know you were her father, Vincent. Her mother told her that her father was dead. She said that you . . . you died in a car crash before she was even born."

Dupré frowned. *"A car crash?"* he mumbled as if in a daze. He suddenly turned to Will. "Wait, how do you know all this? How do you know what her mother said?"

Will cleared his throat. "Because . . . because she told me."

"She told you?" Dupré's tossed his newspaper aside. His frown intensified. "Well, what else did she tell you?"

Will sighed. "That she missed you. She missed never having a father around and always wondered what you were like, what you looked like. She wished she knew more about you."

Dupré tilted his head as he searched Will's face. "You seem to have gotten to know her very well."

"Yes." Will cleared his throat again. He figured he might as well share his own secret. "Yes, we became . . . friends," he mumbled.

"Friends?" Dupré repeated, his stare now unwavering. "Rather close friends, I should say, if she told you all that."

Will lowered his eyes. He shoved his hands into his pockets. "Yes, we were."

"*Were?* You mean you aren't anymore?"

"No," Will said tersely as he turned his back toward Dupré, hoping that Dupré would change the subject. Wasn't it obvious that talking about his relationship with Keisha made him uncomfortable? Couldn't Dupré see the hurt on his face? Because Will felt it. The hurt weighed on him like a leaden shroud.

"Why not?" Dupré persisted. "What happened? If you two were such close friends—"

"Vincent, just like there are things that are painful for you to talk about, I have things that are painful for me to talk about, too, okay?" he said loudly, his nostrils flaring.

"So can we just drop it? I'm telling you that she's not angry at you. She's not trying to get back at you. So let's just leave it at that!"

Dupré's eyes widened as he gazed at Will in surprise. Even Will was taken aback. He had never raised his voice to Dupré before, nor could he have ever imagined a circumstance when he would do so. But here he was, glaring down the older man, yelling at him to back off.

"Well, well," Dupré remarked as a smile slowly crept to his face. "I guess my daughter must be one extraordinary woman." Dupré slowly walked over to Will and rested his hand on the younger man's shoulder. "She'd have to be for you to fall in love with her."

Will frowned.

The older man shook his head as his smile widened. "You had me worried for a second there with that whole 'friends' baloney." Dupré snorted and rolled his eyes. "I may be old but I'm not in a coma. I know what that means. I've always known that you've had your share of *friends*, Will, being the ladies' man that you are. But I'm glad to know that my daughter wasn't one of them. It sounds like she meant a lot more to you."

Will didn't respond.

"So you really don't want to tell me what happened?"

Will gritted his teeth and shrugged. "It's an election and we're playing for different teams so . . . things got complicated."

"And you both decided to go your separate ways?"

"Yes," Will said succinctly.

"Sounds familiar," Dupré said with a grimace as he crossed his arms over his chest. "It also sounds like Keisha inherited a lot more from her mother than good looks."

Will slowly nodded his head, giving a forlorn smile. "Your daughter is a very stubborn, very argumentative, and very *proud* young woman, Vincent. Once she gets fixated on something, it's hard to convince her any differently."

"But you love her, don't you?"

"Yes, I did."

"You did . . . but not anymore?"

Will gritted his teeth. "I don't know. I think . . . I might . . . still love her."

"There's no think, son," Dupré said flatly. "Either you do or you don't."

Will contemplated for several seconds before slowly nodding his head. "I do."

Dupré frowned. "So *why* let history repeat itself?" he exclaimed. "So what if she's stubborn? Shout her down if you have to! You don't want to be like me, son," Dupré urged, furrowing his brows. "An old man left always wondering what could have been. What could have happened if I'd fought Lena harder that night? What could have happened if I hadn't left her alone in the apartment the next day? I should have stayed. I should have stayed and talked to her, but I was so angry and disappointed and . . ." He closed his eyes. "Look, don't get me wrong. I love my wife. I love my children, Will. But I will always regret the way I handled that day. I will always regret that Keisha had to grow up without a father. Don't let regret plague you for the rest of your life, son," he said quietly. "It will make you bitter and old before your time."

"Well, what am I supposed to do, Vincent? Knock her over the head with a rock and kidnap her? Tie her up and *make* her listen to me?" he asked, raising his hands helplessly. "She is set in her ways!"

"Just go to her," Dupré said softly. "Not call her or email her. Just *go* to her and . . . I'll go with you."

This time, Will frowned in confusion. "You'll go with me?" he repeated, wondering if he had heard Dupré correctly. "You're serious?"

"Yes, I am," Dupré said firmly, vehemently nodding his head. "Why wouldn't I be? I didn't get to meet her properly the first time we spoke and I don't have another thirty years to waste hoping that the opportunity will come again."

The two stood in silence for several seconds as Will considered the older man. "Well, if I *am* going to take you over to her apartment, you're going to need to change your look a bit."

Dupré's hands instantly reached for his face. "Yes," he said, running his hands over his stubbly, unshaven chin and then glancing down at his T-shirt and pajama pants. He gave a sheepish smile. "I don't look very presentable, do I? It's been a hard week. I will need to shave and change clothes, I suppose."

"Not just that," Will muttered with a slow shake of the head as he gave him the once-over again. "Do you have a hoodie and sunglasses?"

"A hoodie and sunglasses?" Dupré asked, a little confused.

"Don't worry," Will assured. "I'm sure Paul will have them if you don't."

Dupré frowned. "Wait, why am I—"

"You'll need them if you're going to see her, Vincent. You want your reunion with her to be private, don't you? If that's the case, you can't show up at her apartment door in a suit and tie. All those reporters and photographers hanging around there will know instantly who you are. Why give the media more fodder to gossip about?"

Dupré slowly smiled. "You're right, Will. I knew I hired you for a reason," he said. "I should go to her in some type of disguise. I'm sure I have suitable sunglasses, but I'll have to ask Paul about the hoodie." He snapped his fingers as his eyes widened. The dullness of each iris had disappeared and the familiar bright gleam of Dupré's green eyes was coming back. "You know, Will, I think I still have the fake pirate mustache from the Halloween costume party Sara and I went to last year. It'll be perfect!"

Will cocked an eyebrow, fighting back a smile. "A fake . . . pirate . . . *mustache?*"

CHAPTER 31

"Do you want mayonnaise on your sandwich, honey?" Lena asked from the kitchen.

Keisha peered up tiredly. She sat on the couch Indian-style in a pink bathrobe and flannel pajamas, reading a book. Her thick hair was pulled into a haphazard pony-tail atop her head.

"What did you say, Ma?" she murmured. She then glanced irritably at the ringing phone.

It had been ringing almost constantly for the past three days. She had unplugged it at least eleven times already, when she couldn't take the steady electronic bleating anymore. Each time she would wait a few hours before plugging it in again, hoping that whoever was trying to call had finally given up. But that was never the case. The annoying bleating would resume and she would ignore it until it finally got to her. She was growing weary of repeating this routine.

"I said, 'do you want mayonnaise on your sandwich'?" her mother shouted over the ringing.

"Mayonnaise is fine," Keisha muttered. She then returned to the yellow-tinted pages of the book sitting in her lap.

"You plan to put on some clothes soon, KeKe?" her mother asked, peeping around the edge of the kitchen entryway.

Keisha glanced down at her pajamas and frowned. "I *do* have on clothes."

Lena sighed heavily, tossed aside a dish towel, and crossed her arms over her small chest. She leaned against the door frame, cocked an eyebrow, and pursed her lips. "I mean clothes that *aren't* pink and shoes that don't have bunny rabbits on them, baby."

"What difference does it make?" Keisha muttered. She flipped another page in her book. "I'm not going outside anyway."

The two women had decided to hang out at Keisha's place, determining that there was more strength in numbers. They had been hounded by reporters for days and neither one wanted to be cornered alone by a pack of photographers. They felt like prisoners, nay, cellmates, in Keisha's third floor apartment but they refused to venture outside—at least, not until the media storm calmed down.

Her mother rolled her eyes. "Keisha, you can't keep doing this."

"Doing what?"

"You've been acting depressed *all week*," Lena exclaimed, flapping her arms helplessly. "You've been walking around your apartment in those pajamas for days! Have you even washed your face? Brushed your hair?"

Keisha lay back against the sofa cushion and closed her eyes. "Ma, this has by far been the worst month in my entire life. How would you expect me to behave? Should I throw on a sequined dress and high heels and go clubbing?"

"Keisha, that's not—"

She stopped when the doorbell rang.

They both looked at one another, exchanging the same expression of panic. The bell rang again, now joining the persistent bleat of the house phone. Lena stirred uneasily in the kitchen doorway.

"Who do you think it is?" Lena asked anxiously.

"Oh, Ma, you know who it is! Who else could it be but one of those reporters," the younger woman spat, tossing aside her book in frustration as the doorbell rang yet again, this time in quick succession as if someone were holding their index finger on the button and refusing to let go. "I'm getting so *tired* of this," she said through clinched teeth. She balled her fists at her sides.

"Keisha, just ignore it, baby," her mother pleaded as Keisha stomped toward the front door. "Don't answer it, please!"

"No, Ma! I am fed up to here with this!" Keisha shouted over her shoulder. Her mouth twisted with frustration. "The phone is ringing off the hook every day. Now I have people ringing my doorbell. I may be miserable but I refuse . . . I *refuse* to let them drive me crazy, too," she yelled before turning back to face the door again. "Get away from my door!" she bellowed. When the ringing continued, Keisha's nostrils flared. "Get away from the door or I will call the police!"

And abruptly, the ringing stopped. For several seconds the living room was filled with nothing but the sound of Keisha's panting breath. After some time, she finally relaxed her stance. She took a deep breath and looked over her shoulder at her mother.

"Maybe you scared them off," Lena whispered hesitantly.

"Maybe," Keisha said. She began to walk back toward the couch but stopped when the doorbell rang again. Her eyes widened.

"That's it," she muttered. "That is it! Ma, get the phone!" Keisha quickly unlocked her front door, preparing to curse whoever stood on the other side. She angrily swung it open. Her lips were curled and her teeth were bared. A hand rested on her hip. "I warned you!" she yelled. "I told you that if you didn't get away from my door I would—"

Keisha paused when she saw Will's sad, dark eyes gazing down at her. Her heart seemed to skid to a halt and she gaped openly.

"Will," she murmured breathlessly.

"Hi, Keisha." He gave an awkward smile that looked more like a grimace. "How are you?"

Keisha quickly slammed the door shut.

Her mother frowned in confusion. "Why did you do that?" Lena asked. "Was it a reporter?"

"It's Will. It was Will!" Keisha exclaimed. Panicked, Keisha instantly reached for the scrunchy atop her head and ripped it off. She lowered her hair and quickly tried to finger-comb her matted locks, but to no avail. She knew she probably looked horrible. She gazed down at her pajamas and bunny slippers, wishing that she had heeded her mother's advice and changed her clothes.

Keisha closed her eyes and took a deep breath before quickly opening the door again, just as Will turned to walk back down the hallway toward the elevator.

"Wait!" she shouted, grabbing the sleeve of his jacket. "Please don't go! Don't go!"

He frowned. "But you shut the door. I thought—"

"I'm sorry," she pled. "I didn't mean to. I mean . . . I didn't mean to slam the door. I . . . I . . ." She sighed. "I'm so sorry."

In so many ways, she thought helplessly. *You have no idea how sorry I am, Will.*

He quickly shook his head. "No, I'm sorry for laying on your doorbell like that," he said quietly as he shoved his hands into his pockets. "I didn't know if you would answer if I didn't."

"It's okay. I, uh, I-I-I . . . I didn't . . . I didn't know it was you." She fought to regain her words but couldn't.

Might have considered looking through the peephole, she thought to herself.

Part of Keisha was happy to see him, but the other part of her wanted to burst into tears. So much had happened since the last time they had spoken. She had dreamed of one day finding the courage to go to Will and tell him that she was sorry. "Will, you were right," she had wanted to say and ask for his forgiveness. He had been right about Parker. He had been right about politics. He had been right about everything. And now he was standing at her door, finding her in ratty pajamas with bags under eyes, and she couldn't formulate a comprehensible sentence because she was so confused, so tongue-tied.

"I've brought someone to see you," he said, glancing over his shoulder.

"To see *me*?" she asked, surprised. Who else could be out there? Keisha blinked and stared into her apartment hallway in bewilderment.

A man then stepped forward. She could barely see his face under the navy blue hood of a Georgetown sweatshirt and the large aviator sunglasses that were perched on his thin nose. He grinned sheepishly behind a thick, black mustache that looked rather odd on his face, as if it were a little bit too big for his head.

"Hello," he said softly.

Keisha squinted. The voice sounded vaguely familiar.

"I-I apologize for . . . my appearance," he said as he pushed the hood off, revealing salt and pepper hair. "I-I . . . just wanted . . . to see you," he said as he removed his sunglasses and then peeled off the strange-looking mustache. "Will and I thought this would be . . . the best way . . . to do it," he said hesitantly.

Keisha's breath caught in her throat as Dupré's smile widened. Her stomach clinched.

She was being assaulted with so many bombshells today that they were leaving her staggered and bemused. She swallowed loudly and licked her lips, desperately thinking of something appropriate to say to him. "C-c-congressman Dupré," she stuttered awkwardly, extending her hand toward him for a shake, "g-g-good to see you again, sir. Would you please come in?"

Always the politician, Dupré's face remained firm, but she could tell from the look in his eyes that this was not the greeting he had expected. He stared down at her hand for several seconds before taking it within his own. He then patted it gently. His green eyes seemed to glaze over with tears.

"Good to see you again, too, Keisha," he said quietly as he stepped through the door. "I am . . . truly . . . glad to . . ." He stopped, then abruptly dragged her into his arms. Keisha's head landed hard against his shoulder as her eyes widened in shock. She watched as Will gave them a warm smile from the doorway.

"Congressman Dupré?" Keisha whispered.

She listened to Dupré weep softly as he buried his face in her hair, and she instinctively began to rub his back to comfort him. "It's okay," she whispered, closing her eyes as she felt them dampen with tears. "It's okay, really."

They stood in silence for several minutes, just holding one another. Keisha was amazed. For decades, she had imagined doing this, feeling her father's arms around her. But, believing that her father was dead, she had assumed that any hope of one day being in his embrace was just a fantasy. But here he was in her living room and she could feel his warmth, smell his aftershave. It was definitely a dream come true.

After some time he finally stood back and cupped her face in his hands. "Such a beautiful girl," he murmured softly, scanning her features as his thumbs absently rubbed her cheeks.

She smiled bashfully before wiping away an errant tear. Was he kidding? *I have to look a total mess*, she thought.

Keisha watched as Dupré slowly shook his head. "I know what you're thinking, but you are," he said. "You are beautiful. You know that? And when you smile like that, you look just like my mother when she was your age. I swear you do," he insisted as he squinted his eyes. "I wish I had a picture of her with me," he said. "It's just . . . uncanny how much you look like her."

"I always thought so, too," her mother interjected quietly from the other side of the room.

Dupré blinked. He slowly pulled his hands away from Keisha's face and swallowed loudly as he looked at Lena. He must not have realized that he and Keisha were not alone in the living room. Keisha watched as his face went ashen as he stared at her mother, as if looking at a ghost.

Lena gave a warm smile as she tentatively stepped toward them. "I always thought that she looked a lot like your mother, too. You see it when she frowns, when she gets that little wrinkle between her eyes," Lena said, pointing to the juncture between her brows. "I think it all the time. 'There goes Mrs. Jacqueline Dupré all over again,' " she said, laughing slightly, though no one laughed with her. She tilted her head. "Hello, Vincent. It's good to see you."

Dupré didn't respond and only continued to gaze at her.

Keisha stood back, not knowing what to expect. She searched Dupré's eyes, seeing hurt and anger welling up in them. Her heart went out to both him and her mother. She knew this had to be hard. She couldn't imagine being in their shoes, seeing a former lover after so many years, after so much had happened.

"I'm glad you came," Lena continued gently despite his cold silence. Her dark eyes glazed over with tears. "I'm so glad that . . . that Keisha finally has gotten the chance to meet you as her . . . her father." She clasped her hands in front of her before bringing them to her chin, as if she was praying. "That makes me so glad."

Dupré frowned and cocked an eyebrow. "It . . . *does?*" He sounded surprised.

Lena quickly nodded. "Yes, of course it does, Vincent. And I'm . . ." She sniffed. "I'm sorry for making you two wait so long to do this. I hope . . . I hope you can forgive me."

"You really mean that? This . . . this isn't an act?" he suddenly blurted out.

Keisha's mother frowned, looking hurt by his words. She slowly shook her head. "No, Vincent, it's not an act. I mean every word I say."

"Is that right?" Dupré narrowed his eyes. "Then can you explain to me why you *did* decide to make us wait so long?" he rumbled. "Why didn't you tell me I had a daughter? Why did you just run off without a word? I didn't know where you were, what had happened to you!" he said, raising his voice. "You left me wondering for *all* those years, Lena!" he shouted. Dupré angrily pointed a finger at his chest. "I want you to tell me what I did to deserve that, to be treated that way! Was I cruel to you? Did you think I'd make a bad father?"

"No! No, Vincent, it wasn't anything like that!" Lena sighed. "All of this happened when I was very young," she explained softly. "*We* were young. I thought . . . I thought it was the best thing to do at the time. It was a mistake. I know that now."

Keisha watched as Dupré gritted his teeth. "All this time, all these years, Lena," he kept muttering. "Do you realize what you did that day? You didn't just pack up a bag and walk out on me! It wasn't as simple as that."

"I *know*, Vincent," she pled. "I never meant to hurt you. I just—"

"You changed me, Lena!"

Keisha felt that they were being propelled back in time, that she was witnessing the continuation of an argument that had started in her parents' small apartment in Southeast, D.C., back in 1979. The bitterness and hurt between them was probably as strong today as it was thirty years ago.

"But you got to finish law school," Lena argued quietly, her voice faltering. "You went on to bigger and better things." She looked as if she wanted to weep. "Like I knew you would. Like I *always* knew you would, Vincent. I didn't want to drag you down. I just wanted the best for you. That's all."

"*You* got to decide what was best! But you never asked *me!* I had no choice but to move on!" he yelled, the veins bulging in his throat as his face reddened. "It was either that or sitting around feeling sorry for myself! I had to focus on something! I was ambitious, Lena, not because I wanted to be. I was ambitious because I was cold and empty and you made me that way!" he yelled, pointing his finger at her.

"Vincent, I can't—"

"If it wasn't for Sara I never would have opened myself up to anyone ever again," he continued, cutting Lena off, "*especially* any woman!" He took a deep breath. "You crushed me, Lena. Do you realize that? It's time that you realize what you did!"

Lena opened her mouth and then closed it. She looked down at the floor with a pained expression, accepting her long-delayed reproach for the decisions she had made all those years ago.

He took another deep breath. "Oh, that felt good," he murmured, placing a hand to his chest. "It felt good to finally say it. You have no idea how long I've wanted to yell at you, Lena."

She gave a sad, wry smile. "I'm guessin' thirty years," she muttered in return. "It looks like it felt good to get it off your chest."

"And you!" Dupré said, suddenly turning to face Keisha.

Keisha blinked and frowned. "Me?" *What on earth did I do?*

"Yes, you!" Dupré replied, nodding his head firmly. "I hear that you're just as obstinate, just as hell-bent on calling your own shots regardless of reason or how the other person feels."

Keisha's frown intensified. What was he talking about?

"I know," her father said. "I know about you and Will, Keisha."

Her eyes widened in surprise. She hadn't imagined Will would tell Dupré what had gone on between them. And judging from the glare and the angry expression on her father's face, it seemed that Will had told him a lot. She crossed her arms over her chest, refusing to meet Dupré's gaze. Instead, she stared at her bunny slippers.

"I also know what happens when you choose to go the route you've chosen: silence and stubbornness," he said. "You believe you know what you're doing, I presume? You don't have to answer for your actions to anyone? Well, is feeling that you're right going to keep you warm on those nights when you realize that *you're* the reason why you're alone?"

Keisha opened her mouth and then closed it, not knowing how to defend herself. She suddenly turned to her mother, hoping the older woman would come to her defense, but Lena helplessly threw up her hands as she fell back onto the sofa.

"Don't look at me, baby," Lena said with exasperation. "According to your father, I don't have too much room to talk."

Keisha resisted the urge to pout. Suddenly, having a father wasn't quite so enjoyable anymore. They had officially reunited only five minutes ago and he was already lecturing her. Keisha had already come to these conclusions on her own. She didn't need Dupré telling her all this.

"I know what you're thinking," he said.

"Really? What am I thinking?" she asked, mimicking his deep baritone. *What was he, an all-knowing genie?*

Dupré gave a smug smile. "That you're ready to apologize to him for the way you treated him. Unfortunately, it's too late. He's no longer here."

Keisha's eyes instantly darted to the door of her apartment. Her father was right. Will was no longer standing in the doorway. She frowned.

"Where'd he go?" she exclaimed, making Dupré shrug in return.

"I would guess he's probably heading back home," he said nonchalantly. "He has to start packing soon if he's going to make his flight."

Her frown intensified. "*Flight?* W-w-what flight?" she stuttered. "Where is he going?"

Dupré shrugged his shoulders again. "I'm not sure exactly. Somewhere in Texas. Houston, I believe. He has an opportunity for a big consultancy job down there. It should last quite a few months. He plans to leave immediately after the election. He told me about it before we came here and . . ." Dupré sighed, ". . . I gave him my blessing. The opportunity was too good to pass up."

Keisha quickly shook her head. "*Leave?* He can't leave for Texas!"

Dupré cocked an eyebrow. "Why not? The campaign's done for. Parker's going to win. Why shouldn't Will seek opportunities elsewhere, especially when . . ." Dupré's voice trailed off and his green eyes lowered.

"When *what?*" Keisha watched as her father crossed his arms over his chest.

"When there's nothing to keep him here," he finally replied.

That hit Keisha like a wallop to the stomach. "But what . . . what about me?"

Dupré raised his eyebrows in surprise. "I was under the impression that you didn't want to see him again. Or at least . . . that was what he told me," Dupré said with a tilt of the head. "But maybe he was mistaken. Maybe you could . . . let him know that."

Keisha quickly nodded and ran to the other side of her living room to grab her phone. "Okay," she said as she began to dial his cell phone number, "I'll call him and tell him. I'll ask him to come back so that I can explain everything and—"

"It won't work," Dupré suddenly interjected, vehemently shaking his head.

Keisha paused from dialing. She frowned over her shoulder at her father. "Why . . . why won't it work?"

"His phone's turned off. He was getting tired of the press calls. You won't catch him that way."

Keisha sighed, now feeling defeated. "Well, should I wait until he gets home? I wanted to tell him face to face. I wanted to—"

"It's not too late to catch him, Keisha," her father said. "He just left a few minutes ago. Maybe you can get him before he drives off."

It took only a second of hesitation for Keisha to quickly weigh the pro of running downstairs to find Will and throwing herself in front of his car, if necessary, to stop him from leaving for Texas, and the con of being seen by everyone, including the press, in her pajamas and bunny slippers with no makeup and her hair all over her head. She quickly decided it was worth the embarrassment. Keisha bolted toward her front door and down the apartment hallway to the elevators, pressing the glowing "down" arrow button.

"Come on," she barked as she waited impatiently for the metal doors to open. Keisha angrily pressed the button again, pacing back and forth. She finally gave up and ran toward the stairwell. Her heart was thudding in her chest by the time she finished racing down the three flights of stairs to the crowded lobby on the first floor. Keisha quickly realized that most of the throng was composed of reporters and photographers. She glanced around hesitantly and bit her lower lip.

Don't be afraid, she told herself. Keisha took a deep breath and bolted toward the glass-paneled front door. Most of reporters did double takes as she ran by them.

"Miss . . . Miss Reynolds?" one blonde man with a note pad in his hand asked, blinking in surprise at her ensemble.

"Not now, guys," she yelled over her shoulder. She almost fell through the entrance as she ran to the parking lot.

"Will!" Keisha shouted. "Will!"

Keisha looked around her desperately, gasping as she searched for Will's car. Her breath misted in the cold air. Her sense of panic increased with each second she didn't spot him.

Did I miss him? Tears started to well in her eyes. She'd jump in her car and head to his house in Annapolis if she could, but she left her keys sitting on the coffee table upstairs.

"Keisha?" a male voice called to her from across the parking lot.

Keisha squinted against the darkness. The instant she saw Will standing next to his Audi, her eyes widened and she smiled from ear to ear. "Will!" she exclaimed, running toward him.

Will shut his car door and frowned. "Keisha, what the hell . . . What are you doing out here in your pajamas?"

"I-I wanted to . . . I w-w-wanted to c-c-catch you before you l-left," she said as she fell against his chest, her teeth chattering from the cold.

"What?" he asked, squinting at her in confusion. He shrugged out of his coat and wrapped the garment around her shoulders. "Do you realize that it's almost 30 degrees out here?"

She pulled insistently at his shirt. "Yes, but—"

"So you *do* realize it?" he continued, gazing at her. "And for some reason you thought it was okay to go outside in this flimsy cotton," he said as he plucked the lapels of her pajama shirt and looked down at her feet, "and fuzzy animal slippers."

The conversation was definitely going off track. Keisha had to tell him how she felt and she had to do it before he left. There was no way she was going to wait six to eight months to profess her love. Who knew what could happen or worse, who he could meet in the interim?

She closed her eyes and took a deep breath. "Will, I just wanted to—"

"Did those reporters see you in this?" He rubbed her shoulders, trying to warm her up. "Good God, Keisha, are you trying to end up on the evening news?"

"Would you just let me finish?" she shouted, making him stare at her in shock. Keisha sighed impatiently. "Look, Will, I just wanted to tell you . . ." She closed her eyes again. "I just wanted to tell you that I was . . . sorry . . . for everything that happened, for everything I said. It wasn't fair to you and I-I just wanted you to know that before you left."

She opened her eyes to find him gazing at her somberly. He licked his lips and leaned back against the car door. "Why the sudden change of heart?" he asked.

She slowly shook her head. "It wasn't sudden, Will. I've been thinking about this for a few days now. It's just when I found out you were leaving for Houston, it was the kick in the butt I needed to finally tell you."

Will suddenly frowned. "*Houston?* What are you talking about?"

Keisha tilted her head. "The big consultant job. Dupré . . . I mean, my father," she corrected herself, "told me. He was fuzzy on the details. Maybe he got the wrong city. But please, Will, Texas is so far away," she whimpered. "I know it's a good opportunity and I understand why you'd want to leave, but before you do this please think about . . ."

She stopped talking when Will began to chuckle. She could feel his chest rumbling beneath her hands and within seconds he broke into full out laughter. This time, Keisha frowned. "What's so funny?" She glared up at him angrily. "What's so damn funny, Will?" she repeated, slapping his chest.

"That sneaky old bastard," Will muttered, slowly shaking his head. "Keisha, I'm not leaving for Texas and there is no big consultant job."

She blinked. "There . . . there isn't?"

"No, there isn't," Will said with a smile. "Is that why you came running down here in your pajamas? Because you wanted catch me before I 'left for Texas.' "

Keisha gritted her teeth. Dupré had fooled her. He had fooled her good. "Yes," she said sullenly.

"So why didn't you just call me? You didn't have to come running down here. I would have answered," he said as he pulled his BlackBerry out of his pocket.

"Because he said your . . . ." She closed her eyes. "He said your cell phone wasn't on." Keisha dropped her head into her hands as Will chuckled again and continued to rub her shoulders. Now she was officially humiliated. "Oh, I feel so stupid," she murmured. "I could kill him. I really could kill him, Will. Are he and my mother *incapable* of telling me the truth?" she exclaimed with exasperation.

"Only when they think they know what's best for you," Will replied. "Look, I wouldn't be too mad at him. He had good intentions."

She stared at her feet. "Which were *what?*" Keisha spat. "To prove yet again how gullible I am?"

"Of course not," Will said as he placed a finger beneath her chin and raised it so that she would look into his eyes. "To bring you to me." He then lowered his mouth to hers and kissed her so tenderly that all her anxiety and anger melted away. Keisha closed her eyes, leaned into him and sighed, so grateful to feel his lips again. When he pulled his mouth away, she opened her eyes and smiled.

"I missed you," they said simultaneously and laughed, though Keisha quickly became somber.

"There are so many things, Will," she said quietly as she stared at his chest, "that I wish I could take back, that I wish I could do over again."

He slowly shook his head. "Keisha, don't—"

"No, Will," she insisted as she raised a hand to his lips. "Let me finish, please." She bit her lower lip and then frowned. "I shouldn't have walked out on you that night. You didn't lie to me. I know that now."

"No, I did not," he said softly. "But I knew it was coming. I should have warned you. You were right about that. But I was scared that it would frighten you away."

"I shouldn't have put so much trust in Dr. Parker either," she continued. She then ruefully shook her head. "He didn't deserve that trust. He's changed, Will. And *I've* change. I see things . . . so differently now. I wish I could go back and change everything." She sighed and shook her head. "But I can't."

"No, you can't," he said quietly. "But you can try to make it better. You can learn from the mistakes you've made, Keisha. I should know," he said with a wry smile. "I've made many that I've had to come back from."

"But even with us," she said. "I don't know how—"

"Anything and everything that was said or done, I forgive you, Keisha," he said earnestly. "And I hope you can forgive me. Does *that* make you feel any better?"

She slowly smiled. "Yes, it does." But then she looked down again and frowned. "Though I wonder if my father will be just as forgiving. Thirty years ago Ma broke his heart and now I've ruined his career. I set out from the beginning to make sure that he didn't win this election." Keisha took a deep breath. "And now it looks like I'm going to get my wish."

Will and Keisha stood silently for several seconds. He tilted his head. "Not necessarily."

She cocked an eyebrow. "How do you figure that?"

"Step into my office, m' lady," he said as he slowly opened a car door for her. "It's cold out here and I have something I want to share with you."

It was now her turn to give a wry smile. "What do you have up your sleeve, Will Blake?"

He grinned. The old, methodical Will who could always find the right maneuver had returned and, yes, he did have something up his sleeve.

EPILOGUE

Keisha stood in a daze in the observation gallery of the House chamber with Will on one side and her mother on the other. She was nervous. She was excited. She gripped Will's hand tighter to steady herself. He glanced down at her and gave a reassuring smile.

She didn't know why she was so anxious. It wasn't *her* big day, but for some reason she felt that it was.

Am I really *here?* A year ago, she never would have imagined that she would be an honored guest at the Capitol, of all places, but here she was in the reserved seating area for the families of representatives who would soon be sworn in for the 112th Congress.

She adjusted the sleeve of her fitted navy blue dress and leaned back to look around Will's shoulder at her stepmother, Sara. The blonde woman looked trim and refined in her black Chanel suit and pearls—the perfect congressman's wife. Beside her stood Keisha's towering half-brother, Paul, in a blue jacket and khakis. He gazed earnestly at the busy house floor where Vincent Dupré would soon take the oath of office for the tenth time. At Paul's side stood her half-sister, Kendall, who, despite the importance of the moment, looked bored, as usual. The young woman glanced down at her French manicured nails before staring at the ceiling.

This is my family? Keisha thought with bemusement. *What a world.*

Life could always surprise you. Not only had Keisha discovered that she had a living, breathing father, a brother, and a sister, but she also had stumbled onto the love of her life when she least expected it. Keisha smiled as she gazed down at the engagement ring on her finger. It was the ring she had refused to pick out for herself. "Surprise me," she had told Will, trusting that she would love whatever he chose. And she did. The ring was beautiful with an antique design and amethysts—her favorite stone—encircling an emerald-cut diamond at the center. Will had made the perfect choice and she loved it even more because he had come up with it all by himself.

A tug of her hand brought Keisha's thoughts back to the present.

"It's starting," Will said.

She returned her gaze to the House floor where her father and the rest of the Maryland delegation walked toward the front of the huge room where the Speaker of the House stood behind an elevated podium.

Dupré looked confident as he raised his hand to take his oath, but she knew he hadn't always believed that he would make it there. A lot went into giving him his last-minute election win, and most of the heavy work had been done by Will.

It had been Will's idea to call one of the networks and finally grant an interview. Dupré had originally balked at the idea. "I'm not giving any more blood to those parasites!" he had exclaimed. But when Will explained that they would grant the interview only if they set the parameters first, Dupré started to listen to Will's plan. Keisha had initially panicked when she realized that Will wanted her to participate in the interview, too, but once he worked his calming magic, she, too, capitulated.

"I want you two to finally take control of this," Will had said vehemently in her apartment that day. "We're not letting everyone else tell the story for us anymore."

Will had stood on the sidelines beside the cameraman as Keisha and Dupré did their interviews. He was a reassuring presence as they poured their hearts out. Keisha knew she could not have done it without him.

When the two-part interview appeared on television a week later, Keisha didn't know what to expect. Would her words be twisted around? Would her father be embarrassed further? But it turned out better than she had expected. The segment was beautiful, sweet, and emotional. Dupré revealed a side of himself that most voters had never seen before, and, in her heart, Keisha knew it wasn't an act. Dupré really was a thoughtful man. Of course, politically he was more conservative than she liked, but she was quickly learning that people aren't always as simple as they seem. Her father was allowed to have some complexity, and she was, too.

Though Keisha had not talked to him since the day she walked out of campaign headquarters, she wondered what Dr. Parker was doing right now. He had called her father the morning after the nail-biting election night to offer his congratulations on Dupré's victory, but she had not received a similar call from her old mentor. She had gotten an email from Jay, though, and Tanya had sent the text message, "Congrats on the win and the engagement. I wish U the best." That text had surprised her. Keisha hoped an arctic thaw would end the frigid relationship she had developed with her old friends. After hearing from those two, she realized there was some chance they could be friends again.

"This is *so* weird," Keisha whispered in bewilderment.

Will smiled down at her. "Actually this is pretty run of the mill. After Vincent finishes his oath, they have a few bills coming up for vote on the floor." He chuckled as he leaned toward her. "I think one is about cows."

"No, *all* of this," Keisha said as she swept her hand around her, finally giving words to what she had been thinking all afternoon. "My father down there." She smiled up at him. "My mom on one side. You on the other. It's so . . . surreal. I never would have dreamed it." She laughed. "You're not going to dissolve into thin air, are you?"

He smiled and kissed her cheek. "Not anytime soon. I'll always be here, Keisha. Always."

"If any other man said that, I'd tell him he was full of it." She smirked. "But you made a believer out of me."

"You made a believer out of me, too," he said, winking and giving her hand a reassuring squeeze.

ABOUT THE AUTHOR

L.S. Childers is a native of the Washington, D.C. area and, since early childhood, she has always known she wanted to be a writer. She attended the University of Maryland, College Park, where she studied journalism, starting out as a crime reporter for a small local newspaper. She is currently an editor at a trade journal in Virginia.

She enjoys painting, watching comedies, and will read virtually anything written by Stephen King or Dean Koontz.

She currently resides in Maryland with her husband.

Her work has appeared in two short story collections: *All That and Then Some* and *Trippin' Over Love*. This is her first novel.

2011 Mass Market Titles

January

From This Moment
Sean Young
ISBN-13: 978-1-58571-383-7
ISBN-10: 1-58571-383-X
$6.99

Nihon Nights
Trisha/Monica Haddad
ISBN-13: 978-1-58571-382-0
ISBN-10: 1-58571-382-1
$6.99

February

The Davis Years
Nicole Green
ISBN-13: 978-1-58571-390-5
ISBN-10: 1-58571-390-2
$6.99

Allegro
Adora Bennett
ISBN-13: 978-158571-391-2
ISBN-10: 1-58571-391-0
$6.99

March

Lies in Disguise
Bernice Layton
ISBN-13: 978-1-58571-392-9
ISBN-10: 1-58571-392-9
$6.99

Steady
Ruthie Robinson
ISBN-13: 978-1-58571-393-6
ISBN-10: 1-58571-393-7
$6.99

April

The Right Maneuver
LaShell Stratton-Childers
ISBN-13: 978-1-58571-394-3
ISBN-10: 1-58571-394-5
$6.99

Riding the Corporate Ladder
Keith Walker
ISBN-13: 978-1-58571-395-0
ISBN-10: 1-58571-395-3
$6.99

May

Separate Dreams
Joan Early
ISBN-13: 978-1-58571-434-6
ISBN-10: 1-58571-434-8
$6.99

I Take This Woman
Chamein Canton
ISBN-13: 978-1-58571-435-3
ISBN-10: 1-58571-435-6
$6.99

June

Inside Out
Grayson Cole
ISBN-13: 978-1-58571-437-7
ISBN-10: 1-58571-437-2
$6.99

2011 Mass Market Titles (continued)

July

The Other Side of the
  Mountain
Janice Angelique
ISBN-13: 978-1-58571-442-1
ISBN-10: 1-58571-442-9
$6.99

Holding Her Breath
Nicole Green
ISBN-13: 978-1-58571-439-1
ISBN-10: 1-58571-439-9
$6.99

August

The Sea of Aaron
Kymberly Hunt
ISBN-13: 978-1-58571-440-7
ISBN-10: 1-58571-440-2
$6.99

The Finley Sisters' Oath of
  Romance
Keith Thomas Walker
ISBN-13: 978-1-58571-441-4
ISBN-10: 1-58571-441-0
$6.99

September

Except on Sunday
Regena Bryant
ISBN-13: 978-1-58571-443-8
ISBN-10: 1-58571-443-7
$6.99

Light's Out
Ruthie Robinson
ISBN-13: 978-1-58571-445-2
ISBN 10: 1-58571-445-3
$6.99

October

The Heart Knows
Renee Wynn
ISBN-13: 978-1-58571-444-5
ISBN-10: 1-58571-444-5
$6.99

Best Friends, Better Lovers
Ceyla Bowers
ISBN-13: 978-1-58571-455-1
ISBN-10: 1-58571-455-0
$6.99

November

Caress
Grayson Cole
ISBN-13: 978-1-58571-454-4
ISBN-10: 1-58571-454-2
$6.99

A Love Built to Last
L. S. Childers
ISBN-13: 978-1-58571-448-3
ISBN-10: 1-58571-448-8
$6.99

December

Fractured
Wendy Byrne
ISBN-13: 978-1-58571-449-0
ISBN-10: 1-58571-449-6
$6.99

Everything in Between
Crystal Hubbard
ISBN-13: 978-1-58571-396-7
ISBN-10: 1-58571-396-1
$6.99

Other Genesis Press, Inc. Titles

Other Genesis Press, Inc. Titles (continued)

Other Genesis Press, Inc. Titles (continued)

Do Over	Celya Bowers	$9.95
Dream Keeper	Gail McFarland	$6.99
Dream Runner	Gail McFarland	$6.99
Dreamtective	Liz Swados	$5.95
Ebony Angel	Deatri King-Bey	$9.95
Ebony Butterfly II	Delilah Dawson	$14.95
Echoes of Yesterday	Beverly Clark	$9.95
Eden's Garden	Elizabeth Rose	$8.95
Eve's Prescription	Edwina Martin Arnold	$8.95
Everlastin' Love	Gay G. Gunn	$8.95
Everlasting Moments	Dorothy Elizabeth Love	$8.95
Everything and More	Sinclair Lebeau	$8.95
Everything but Love	Natalie Dunbar	$8.95
Falling	Natalie Dunbar	$9.95
Fate	Pamela Leigh Starr	$8.95
Finding Isabella	A.J. Garrotto	$8.95
Fireflies	Joan Early	$6.99
Fixin' Tyrone	Keith Walker	$6.99
Forbidden Quest	Dar Tomlinson	$10.95
Forever Love	Wanda Y. Thomas	$8.95
Friends in Need	Joan Early	$6.99
From the Ashes	Kathleen Suzanne	$8.95
	Jeanne Sumerix	
Frost on My Window	Angela Weaver	$6.99
Gentle Yearning	Rochelle Alers	$10.95
Glory of Love	Sinclair LeBeau	$10.95
Go Gentle Into That Good Night	Malcom Boyd	$12.95
Goldengroove	Mary Beth Craft	$16.95
Groove, Bang, and Jive	Steve Cannon	$8.99
Hand in Glove	Andrea Jackson	$9.95
Hard to Love	Kimberley White	$9.95
Hart & Soul	Angie Daniels	$8.95
Heart of the Phoenix	A.C. Arthur	$9.95
Heartbeat	Stephanie Bedwell-Grime	$8.95
Hearts Remember	M. Loui Quezada	$8.95
Hidden Memories	Robin Allen	$10.95
Higher Ground	Leah Latimer	$19.95
Hitler, the War, and the Pope	Ronald Rychiak	$26.95
How to Kill Your Husband	Keith Walker	$6.99

Other Genesis Press, Inc. Titles (continued)

How to Write a Romance	Kathryn Falk	$18.95
I Married a Reclining Chair	Lisa M. Fuhs	$8.95
I'll Be Your Shelter	Giselle Carmichael	$8.95
I'll Paint a Sun	A.J. Garrotto	$9.95
Icie	Pamela Leigh Starr	$8.95
If I Were Your Woman	LaConnie Taylor-Jones	$6.99
Illusions	Pamela Leigh Starr	$8.95
Indigo After Dark Vol. I	Nia Dixon/Angelique	$10.95
Indigo After Dark Vol. II	Dolores Bundy/ Cole Riley	$10.95
Indigo After Dark Vol. III	Montana Blue/ Coco Morena	$10.95
Indigo After Dark Vol. IV	Cassandra Colt/	$14.95
Indigo After Dark Vol. V	Delilah Dawson	$14.95
Indiscretions	Donna Hill	$8.95
Intentional Mistakes	Michele Sudler	$9.95
Interlude	Donna Hill	$8.95
Intimate Intentions	Angie Daniels	$8.95
It's in the Rhythm	Sammie Ward	$6.99
It's Not Over Yet	J.J. Michael	$9.95
Jolie's Surrender	Edwina Martin-Arnold	$8.95
Kiss or Keep	Debra Phillips	$8.95
Lace	Giselle Carmichael	$9.95
Lady Preacher	K.T. Richey	$6.99
Last Train to Memphis	Elsa Cook	$12.95
Lasting Valor	Ken Olsen	$24.95
Let Us Prey	Hunter Lundy	$25.95
Let's Get It On	Dyanne Davis	$6.99
Lies Too Long	Pamela Ridley	$13.95
Life Is Never As It Seems	J.J. Michael	$12.95
Lighter Shade of Brown	Vicki Andrews	$8.95
Look Both Ways	Joan Early	$6.99
Looking for Lily	Africa Fine	$6.99
Love Always	Mildred E. Riley	$10.95
Love Doesn't Come Easy	Charlyne Dickerson	$8.95
Love Out of Order	Nicole Green	$6.99
Love Unveiled	Gloria Greene	$10.95
Love's Deception	Charlene Berry	$10.95
Love's Destiny	M. Loui Quezada	$8.95
Love's Secrets	Yolanda McVey	$6.99

Other Genesis Press, Inc. Titles (continued)

Other Genesis Press, Inc. Titles (continued)

Path of Thorns	Annetta P. Lee	$9.95
Peace Be Still	Colette Haywood	$12.95
Picture Perfect	Reon Carter	$8.95
Playing for Keeps	Stephanie Salinas	$8.95
Pride & Joi	Gay G. Gunn	$8.95
Promises Made	Bernice Layton	$6.99
Promises of Forever	Celya Bowers	$6.99
Promises to Keep	Alicia Wiggins	$8.95
Quiet Storm	Donna Hill	$10.95
Reckless Surrender	Rochelle Alers	$6.95
Red Polka Dot in a World Full of Plaid	Varian Johnson	$12.95
Red Sky	Renee Alexis	$6.99
Reluctant Captive	Joyce Jackson	$8.95
Rendezvous With Fate	Jeanne Sumerix	$8.95
Revelations	Cheris F. Hodges	$8.95
Reye's Gold	Ruthie Robinson	$6.99
Rivers of the Soul	Leslie Esdaile	$8.95
Rocky Mountain Romance	Kathleen Suzanne	$8.95
Rooms of the Heart	Donna Hill	$8.95
Rough on Rats and Tough on Cats	Chris Parker	$12.95
Save Me	Africa Fine	$6.99
Secret Library Vol. 1	Nina Sheridan	$18.95
Secret Library Vol. 2	Cassandra Colt	$8.95
Secret Thunder	Annetta P. Lee	$9.95
Shades of Brown	Denise Becker	$8.95
Shades of Desire	Monica White	$8.95
Shadows in the Moonlight	Jeanne Sumerix	$8.95
Show Me the Sun	Miriam Shumba	$6.99
Sin	Crystal Rhodes	$8.95
Singing a Song…	Crystal Rhodes	$6.99
Six O'Clock	Katrina Spencer	$6.99
Small Sensations	Crystal V. Rhodes	$6.99
Small Whispers	Annetta P. Lee	$6.99
So Amazing	Sinclair LeBeau	$8.95
Somebody's Someone	Sinclair LeBeau	$8.95
Someone to Love	Alicia Wiggins	$8.95
Song in the Park	Martin Brant	$15.95
Soul Eyes	Wayne L. Wilson	$12.95

Other Genesis Press, Inc. Titles (continued)

Soul to Soul	Donna Hill	$8.95
Southern Comfort	J.M. Jeffries	$8.95
Southern Fried Standards	S.R. Maddox	$6.99
Still the Storm	Sharon Robinson	$8.95
Still Waters Run Deep	Leslie Esdaile	$8.95
Still Waters...	Crystal V. Rhodes	$6.99
Stolen Jewels	Michele Sudler	$6.99
Stolen Memories	Michele Sudler	$6.99
Stories to Excite You	Anna Forrest/Divine	$14.95
Storm	Pamela Leigh Starr	$6.99
Subtle Secrets	Wanda Y. Thomas	$8.95
Suddenly You	Crystal Hubbard	$9.95
Swan	Africa Fine	$6.99
Sweet Repercussions	Kimberley White	$9.95
Sweet Sensations	Gwyneth Bolton	$9.95
Sweet Tomorrows	Kimberly White	$8.95
Taken by You	Dorothy Elizabeth Love	$9.95
Tattooed Tears	T. T. Henderson	$8.95
Tempting Faith	Crystal Hubbard	$6.99
That Which Has Horns	Miriam Shumba	$6.99
The Business of Love	Cheris F. Hodges	$6.99
The Color Line	Lizzette Grayson Carter	$9.95
The Color of Trouble	Dyanne Davis	$8.95
The Disappearance of Allison Jones	Kayla Perrin	$5.95
The Doctor's Wife	Mildred Riley	$6.99
The Fires Within	Beverly Clark	$9.95
The Foursome	Celya Bowers	$6.99
The Honey Dipper's Legacy	Myra Pannell-Allen	$14.95
The Joker's Love Tune	Sidney Rickman	$15.95
The Little Pretender	Barbara Cartland	$10.95
The Love We Had	Natalie Dunbar	$8.95
The Man Who Could Fly	Bob & Milana Beamon	$18.95
The Missing Link	Charlyne Dickerson	$8.95
The Mission	Pamela Leigh Starr	$6.99
The More Things Change	Chamein Canton	$6.99
The Perfect Frame	Beverly Clark	$9.95
The Price of Love	Sinclair LeBeau	$8.95
The Smoking Life	Ilene Barth	$29.95
The Words of the Pitcher	Kei Swanson	$8.95

Other Genesis Press, Inc. Titles (continued)

Order Form

Mail to: Genesis Press, Inc.
P.O. Box 101
Columbus, MS 39703

Name _____
Address _____
City/State _____ Zip _____
Telephone _____

Ship to (if different from above)
Name _____
Address _____
City/State _____ Zip _____
Telephone _____

Credit Card Information
Credit Card # _____ ☐ Visa   ☐ Mastercard
Expiration Date (mm/yy) _____ ☐ AmEx   ☐ Discover

Qty.	Author	Title	Price	Total

Use this order form, or call 1-888-INDIGO-1	
Total for books	
Shipping and handling: $5 first two books, $1 each additional book	
Total S & H	
Total amount enclosed	

Mississippi residents add 7% sales tax